Death Off Stage

DEATH
OFF STAGE

Richard Grayson

St. Martin's Press
New York

M
C.2

Library of Congress Cataloging-in-Publication Data

Grayson, Richard.
    Death off stage / Richard Grayson.
        p.   cm.
    ISBN 0-312-06951-0
    I. Title.
    PR6057.R55D4125   1992
    823'.914—dc20   91-41084
                                                                      CIP

First published in Great Britain by Macmillan London Limited

First U.S. Edition: April 1992
10 9 8 7 6 5 4 3 2 1

Death Off Stage

1

As he lay on his back, Gautier looked up at the ceiling of the bedroom. The ceiling itself was a pastel shade of blue with a gilded frieze below it and from the corners of the room golden cherubs, each holding a golden cornucopia full of flowers and fruit, looked down benignly on the bed. Even if he had not been aware that it was Sunday, the silence when he awoke would have told him so; the silence in the bedroom on which neither the ticking of the ormolu clock nor the breathing of the young woman lying beside him could make any impression, the silence in the hotel corridors and in Rue du Faubourg St Honoré, the silence of a still sleepy Paris.

Glancing at Sophia, he could not restrain a smile. He remembered other Sundays which stretched back, milestones in his memory. When his wife Suzanne had been alive and they were still sharing his modest apartment in the 7th arrondissement, they would go to Mass on Sunday morning and then lunch en famille with Suzanne's parents, her sister and her sister's husband, usually in a restaurant chosen by old Monsieur Duclos. His memories of those Sundays were redolent of bourgeois impressions and simple bourgeois pleasures, the smell of incense and the intoning of priests, the flavour of a good gigot and the bouquet of a fine red Burgundy. After Suzanne had left him to live with another man, there had been bachelor Sundays when he had found ways of filling his time or, more rarely, which he shared with some girl of casual and usually short acquaintance.

This was a Sunday morning with a difference, for he had awoken with a sleeping princess beside him. It was true that Sophia was not a princess by birth and had acquired the title only by a brief marriage to a Russian prince now dead, but she was even so recognised as a princess in Paris as well as in St Petersburg.

He glanced at her again. She lay there sleeping with her back towards him, covered only by a sheet which did not conceal the contours of her naked body. At the recollection of their lovemaking in the night, desire stirred again and he was tempted to wake her gently by stroking her shoulders, her back and her hips. Then, because he knew she must be worn out after the stress and excitement of the last few days, he withdrew his hand and climbed out of bed as noiselessly as he could.

He shaved in the bathroom, a rare luxury, for few houses or apartments in Paris had a bathroom and even in the Hôtel Cheltenham they had as yet been installed only in the suites. Guests in the ordinary rooms would wash and shave in hot water brought up to them by maids from the kitchens in the basement. Seeing his reflection in the mirror, he wondered, not for the first time, whether he should not grow a beard. He was the only senior inspector in the Sûreté who did not have one and, while this might have been excused because he was also easily the youngest, the excuse was scarcely tenable now that he had been promoted to Chief Inspector.

He left the hotel, using the stairs to reach the lobby rather than the cumbersome iron lift with its clanging doors. The concierge, whom he knew from the past, had not yet come on duty and a sleepy night porter opened the doors to let him out into Rue du Faubourg St Honoré. The streets were empty except for a priest who hurried by to prepare for the first Mass of the day and a solitary fiacre, which passed him slowly, the coachman sitting on his box asleep, the horse making its own way home as it often did at dawn. Fiacres did a good trade in the early hours of Sunday, taking debauched gentlemen from the *maisons closes* or high-class brothels in Rue de Richelieu to their houses in Faubourg St Germain on the Left Bank.

As he was walking through the Jardins des Tuileries, heading for the Seine, he paused to admire the splendid view, looking across Place de la Concorde up the full length of Avenue des Champs-Elysées to the Arc de Triomphe, golden in the early morning sunshine. Halfway along the avenue an automobile was crawling like a hideous black beetle. Even at that distance he could hear the splutter of its engine, fouling the silence. He frowned. The twentieth century was scarcely half a dozen years old and some American had already taken to the air. Automobiles were being followed by flying machines and who knew what other mechanical contraptions would come next. Gautier was not against progress;

he welcomed it, but he still had an uneasy feeling that these modern inventions might take more away from life and leisure and tranquillity than they could give.

A church bell began to ring as he walked along Quai du Louvre. He remembered then that it had been on a Sunday too when Princess Sophia and he had first made love. Had he not been on duty today, they might have gone out of Paris as they did then, to lunch in a *guinguette* on the banks of the Seine at Asnières. He smiled at the memory of how they had eaten and danced, enjoying the gaiety of the place and the company of other couples, working people from Paris spending their Sunday in the country. In the evening they had gone boating on the river and when Sophia had fallen into the water, he had taken her to a nearby hotel so that she could change her clothes. He did not linger now on the memory of the events that had followed, because they were pale and distant, overshadowed by the intensity of the passion they had shared only a few hours ago. She had gone to Russia soon after that night in Asnières and now she had returned as she had promised that she would. Gautier was uncertain of what lay ahead for the two of them, but he had already resolved that he would not think of that, not for the time being at least.

At the Sûreté the work that waited for him was the tidying up of the aftermath of a typical Saturday night's violence; clumsy attempts at burglary, pickpockets who had believed they were more adroit than they were, one pimp stabbing another in Pigalle. Usually it involved little more than paperwork, taking statements and preparing the dossier which the examining magistrate would require on Monday morning. Surat, his principal assistant, had already started on the work by the time Gautier arrived in his office.

'Anything unusual?' Gautier asked him, looking at the small sheaf of papers on the table which served him as a desk.

'Nothing that will tax our ability, patron.'

'No crime of the century?'

Surat laughed, recognising the allusion to a particularly sensational headline which a Paris newspaper had printed over the story of a triple murder case which Gautier had investigated some months previously.

'The only affair which interests me among all those' – Surat nodded in the direction of the sheaf of papers – 'is one which you may well think unimportant.'

'What is it?'

'A murder; infanticide to be precise. A Mongol baby of a couple living in the twentieth arrondissement was found dead. Apparently it had been thrown out of a window of their apartment on the fifth floor.'

'Do we know who threw it?'

'That's what I find strange. The father admits that he did but the mother says he is lying. She claims that it was she who killed the child.'

'Are there no witnesses?'

Surat pointed at the pile of papers once again. 'I've put it all down in my report there.'

'At what time did this happen?'

'Yesterday afternoon. The police from the twentieth commissariat brought the man and woman in. You had gone off duty so I dealt with it.'

'How late were you here last evening?'

'Not very late, patron.'

Gautier shook his head. Surat was older than he was, well into middle age and he had been passed by for promotion, so now in all probability he would never be given it. He was a good policeman, honest, brave and unswervingly loyal especially to Gautier. His fault, if it could be called one, was that he was over-conscientious.

'Your wife and children see too little of you,' he told Surat. 'The report could have waited until this morning.'

He read the report. The couple whose baby was dead were a Jacques and Marie-Louise Lebrun and the baby, their only child, had been almost eighteen months old. Shortly before midday on Saturday a woman living in a top floor apartment nearby, glancing out of her window, had seen what she thought at first was a bundle of clothes being thrown from a window of the Lebruns' apartment. She had watched it fall to the ground in a courtyard below and had only then realised that it was not a bundle but a small child in baby clothes. Hurrying down to the courtyard, she had found that the child was dead, its head crushed by the impact of the fall. The police from the local commissariat had been called and had gone to the apartment where Lebrun lived and found him asleep in bed. Madame Lebrun had not been there but had returned soon after the police had arrived. She had evidently been out shopping for food.

'So the neighbour cannot say who threw the child from the window?' Gautier asked Surat.

'No. She did not actually see it being thrown. She just saw it as it fell through the air.'

'Are you saying that both the husband and the wife have confessed to killing the child?'

'Yes, and each of them denies that the other was responsible.'

'But the wife wasn't in the building.'

'Not when the police arrived, no. Her story is that when she realised what she had done she was distraught and rushed out of the apartment, leaving her husband asleep.'

'I see that the concierge of the building has made a statement.'

'Yes, she says she saw the woman leaving the building; nothing more. You'll find her statement and the one made by the police officer from the twentieth attached to mine.'

Gautier decided that he would not read either document. In cases of this type he had found that reading the statements of other people was liable to influence one's own judgement, clouding it with the views and sometimes the prejudices of other people.

'Where are this couple now?'

'She is in the St Lazare prison for women, he in La Roquette. Expecting that you would wish to interview them I gave instructions that they should be brought to Sûreté headquarters in police wagons,' Surat replied and then he added, 'separate wagons of course.'

Gautier resisted the temptation to smile. Having the accused couple brought to Sûreté headquarters separately, even though both of them were admitting killing the child and accusing the other of lying, was typical of Surat. Everything he did was carefully planned to observe police regulations meticulously.

'They should be here within the hour.'

'So early? The poor creatures will get no breakfast.'

'That might be merciful, knowing the breakfasts which are served in our prisons.'

After Surat had left his office to wait downstairs for the arrival of the prisoners, Gautier read the other reports on his desk. As always they were depressing. Some crimes he could understand even if he could not condone them; theft by people living on the edge of starvation, a stab with a kitchen knife by a woman whose man had cynically exploited, terrorised and finally betrayed her, even the underpaid and bullied clerk who sought a kind of justice for himself by defrauding his employers. The crimes which depressed and angered him were those committed for greed or vanity or the pleasures of violence to which the Comte de Sade had given his name.

As he worked he found himself thinking of the contrast between what he was doing now and how he had spent the previous evening. The papers in front of him were a reminder of all that was sordid and depressing in man's nature, while at the Théâtre du Châtelet the previous evening he had watched the expression of what was most to be admired – imagination, creative invention, beauty and grace.

He had gone to the Châtelet with Princess Sophia Dashkova to watch a performance of the ballet company which she had been instrumental in bringing to Paris. She had hoped when she came to France the previous season to bring an opera company with her, but its tour had been cancelled when one of the leading singers had reneged on his contract. Now she had returned with the Dashkova Ballet Company which had just completed the first week of its engagement.

Until then, in France at least, ballet had been little more than an appendage to opera, providing a harmless diversion between acts. Audiences watching ballet would expect to see young women, chosen more for their charms than for any skill in their art, go through a routine of stilted classical steps wearing conventional classical costumes. Now suddenly they were dazzled by Sophia's Russians; athletic male dancers who leapt gracefully to incredible heights, ballerinas of astonishing virtuosity who had abandoned their tutus for bright, modern costumes, all dancing to strange, noisy and sometimes discordant music against stage sets of extravagant splendour.

Gautier had gone to watch them expecting to be no more than mildly entertained, perhaps even bored. Instead even now the impact of the evening, of the colour and gaiety and movement and, at the end of the performance, of the frenzied applause, still lingered in his senses. He put the memory on one side and read the sheaf of papers in front of him, initialling some to mark his approval, writing instructions for future action on others.

He had almost finished working his way through the documents, when Surat came into the office to tell him that the Lebrun couple had arrived at the Sûreté.

'Bring them up here,' he said and then added, 'together.'

A few minutes later when the couple came into the room, he recognised Lebrun at once. The man was a *bouquiniste*, one of those who sold second-hand books from stalls on the side of the Seine, and his stall was no more than five minutes' walk from Sûreté headquarters. Gautier had often passed it, stopping on occasions to glance at the titles of the books on display and he could recall buying at least one.

Madame Lebrun was a good deal younger than her husband, not a pretty woman but with pleasant features and long, well-brushed brown hair. For someone who had spent the night in St Lazare prison, sharing a cell no doubt with a dozen others, thieves and street-walkers and drunken old crones, she was surprisingly neat and tidy in her appearance, but she was clearly upset and badly frightened. From time to time she glanced at her husband, looking for comfort, imploring him silently to find an escape from the nightmare they were sharing.

Moved by a sudden sympathy, Gautier got up and helped her to a chair. Lebrun inclined his head to acknowledge the courtesy. 'Thank you, Inspector.'

Gautier could see that the man was not well; his eyes were watering, his face flushed and his shoulders had a hunched look, as though he were constantly fighting against a bout of shivering.

'Chief Inspector,' Surat corrected him.

'Inspector will do,' Gautier said smiling. 'We've met before have we not, monsieur? I have purchased books from you.'

'Only one book, Chief Inspector,' Lebrun replied, but without any reproach. 'A novel by Pierre Mounet. Did it help you in your investigation?'

'How did you know that I bought it for that purpose?'

'It was not the sort of book you would read for entertainment. Besides, soon afterwards Mounet was arrested for murder.'

'Yes, and guillotined.'

'Mother of God!' Madame Lebrun could not stifle a little cry of horror.

Gautier looked at her. He had made the remark deliberately. One or both of the two people facing him was confessing falsely to murder and they had to realise what their lying could mean.

'I need to know how your child died. Tell me in your own words,' Gautier said and then added, 'You first, Monsieur Lebrun.'

'I was at home in bed,' Lebrun began.

'On a Saturday? That must be one of the best days in your business.'

'He has had a grippe, Inspector,' Marie-Louise Lebrun said, 'for two days now.'

'I was trying to sleep, but little Anna was crying and would not stop. It got on my nerves. I think I may have fallen asleep for a time, for I remember a horrible dream, a nightmare. When I awoke I was in a frenzy. The baby was still crying. Suddenly I could not stand it any more. I lost control. The window was open and—'

Lebrun broke off in mid-sentence and looked at his wife. Her eyes were shut, her face twisted in anguish. Suddenly he was aware of the effect that his words were having on her.

'What my husband says is not true.' Regaining her self-control took an immense effort for Madame Lebrun, but she succeeded. She did not look at her husband as she continued, 'Our baby Anna was not normal and we knew she would never be able to do anything for herself. She was sickly too, always falling ill. I kept asking myself what kind of life the poor creature would have. What would happen to her after my husband and I were dead? Yesterday she was lying in her cot by the open window, for the day was hot and sunny. On a sudden impulse I decided to end her life. It seemed the kindest thing to do. I thought people would think that she had somehow wriggled out of the cot and fallen through the window. It never struck me that my husband would be accused of killing her. When I realised what I had done I was horrified and rushed out of the apartment in a panic.'

She had been speaking as her husband had, without emotion, carefully reciting the sentences in the way that a schoolchild recites a poem, indifferent to their meaning. Gautier realised that both of them had separately rehearsed what they would say to him. He could visualise them, each in a crowded prison cell, sleeplessly through the night choosing the words that would make the confession sound plausible to the police.

'Pay no attention to what my wife is saying!' Lebrun protested. 'She loved Anna, was devoted to her and was determined with her love and her help she would one day be able to live a normal life.'

Gautier glanced at Surat who had been listening impassively to what the couple had been saying. He wondered what Surat was thinking, what he should decide or what, for that matter, Solomon

14

would have decided in the same circumstances. A decision was required and he, Gautier, would have to make it.

'You two will appreciate,' he said to Lebrun and his wife, 'that I cannot believe both of your stories. To be candid, I am not sure which of you I should believe.'

'Monsieur l'Inspecteur,' Lebrun began, but Gautier held up one hand to silence him.

'Tomorrow an examining magistrate will be appointed to deal with this matter and you will both be required to appear before him. If you continue to give him conflicting explanations of what happened to your child, he will question you mercilessly and give you no respite until he is satisfied that he knows the truth. My advice to you is this. Go home and talk about what happened. Settle your differences. Come back tomorrow and be prepared to tell the truth.'

Lebrun looked at him in astonishment. 'Are you saying that we may go home?'

'Yes. I can see no reason for keeping you in prison – as yet.'

Lebrun went over to his wife and helped her from her chair. Unexpectedly, perhaps with relief, knowing now that she would be spared the horror of another night in prison, she began to cry, quietly stifling her sobs. The noise she made reminded Gautier incongruously of snowflakes driven by a wind bursting against a window pane. On their way out of the office, Lebrun stopped to face Gautier.

'Thank you, Inspector, for your consideration,' he said simply and with dignity.

When they were alone Surat looked at Gautier. He seemed puzzled and uneasy. 'Was it wise to let them go home, patron? How can we be sure that they will return?'

'They will not abscond. I trust them,' Gautier said. 'Besides, where could they go?'

'One of them is lying.'

'I have a feeling that they both are.'

15

2

That day Gautier lunched at a small café in Place Dauphine, not far from the Palais de Justice. The café held memories for him, as at one time it had been owned by a mother and her unmarried daughter from Normandy. Janine, the daughter, had been his mistress for a time in the days after his wife Suzanne had left him and in retrospect he was grateful for the distraction – he did not like to think of it as consolation – she brought him. Now she was back in Normandy, married to a farmer he had heard, and the memory of her was growing dim.

Before coming out to lunch, he had dealt with all the matters that had been awaiting his attention when he arrived at the Sûreté that morning. Now he believed he could look forward to a leisurely afternoon, for even the most obdurate criminals seemed to want a rest from their villainy on Sunday afternoons. That would give him a chance to catch up with his paperwork which, as always, had slipped into arrears and still allow him to leave the Sûreté early so that he could go home and change before meeting Sophia for dinner. They planned to dine tête-à-tête that evening and he was glad. Since her return to Paris Sophia had been doing all she could to ensure the success of her ballet and she and Gautier had spent their evenings mainly at soirées or dinners in the homes of fashionable hostesses, where she could meet people who might be willing to take boxes at the theatre for the whole season, give parties in honour of the leading dancers or support the ballet in other ways. As a result almost the only time they had been able to spend alone together had been when they were in bed. He was enjoying his lunch and had almost finished it when Surat came into the café and he could see from his manner that he had some kind of trouble to report.

'Sit down, Surat,' he told him, 'have a cup of coffee and a marc before you ruin my afternoon.'

'I apologise for disturbing you, patron.'

'I know you would not do so without good reason, but nothing can be so urgent that you cannot join me in a marc.' Gautier called out to the owner of the café who was just coming out of the kitchen at the back and placed his order. 'Well, what kind of trouble is it?'

'A fracas in a hotel on the Left Bank.'

'A fracas?'

'A stabbing to be precise.'

'Was anyone killed?'

'Not as far as I know.'

'Then it can be no more than assault. Surely the police from the local commissariat should be dealing with the affair?'

'In the normal way they would be, but a judge is involved and he is insisting that the Sûreté should be informed.'

'Which judge?'

'Judge Prudhomme. Apparently it is he who has been stabbed by a member of that Russian ballet troupe.'

'Is he seriously hurt?'

'It seems not, but he is complaining very strongly.'

'In that case you and I had better go and comfort him, but not before we finish our eau de vie.'

The two of them drove in a fiacre to the Hôtel Bayonne which was in a narrow street off Boulevard St Michel and which was where, as Gautier already knew, the Ballets Dashkova were living while they were in Paris. He was not surprised that they should have been called to deal with an incident involving members of the ballet. The company had been in Paris less than four weeks, the first two of which they had spent rehearsing, and in that short time they had already earned notoriety for their behaviour. The proprietor of the first hotel in which they had stayed had asked them to find other lodgings and there had been complaints from cafés and restaurants of their drunkenness, fighting and sometimes of their refusal to pay bills.

A policeman from the local commissariat was standing at the entrance to the Hôtel Bayonne and Gautier stopped to have a word with the man. He learnt that there was another policeman inside the hotel as well as a doctor who had been called to treat Judge Prudhomme's wounds.

'The judge refuses to be taken to a hospital,' the policeman added, 'until a senior officer from the Sûreté arrives. He is ranting

17

and cursing, demanding that his attacker should be charged with attempted murder. He has been badly frightened I should say, more frightened than hurt.'

'Do you know what provoked the attack?'

The policeman laughed cynically. 'One might call it an affair of the heart. The judge was found in the bed of one of the ballet dancers.'

'And stabbed by her jealous lover, I suppose?'

'His lover, you mean. The dancer was a man.'

Gautier sighed. He had come into contact with Judge Prudhomme not more than half a dozen times, but he knew that the judge had the reputation of being a difficult man, fastidious, ungenerous in spirit and stubborn. People said he was a pederast, but Gautier had been inclined to dismiss the suggestion. Homosexuality was a charge often made without any evidence against middle-aged men who had remained unmarried and never flaunted a mistress. He sensed that this stabbing would turn out to be a tiresome business and one that might easily develop into a scandal.

Inside the hotel lobby they found some thirty or forty men and women, whom he took to be members of the ballet company, standing around or sitting at tables in groups. Some were simply chatting, others drinking and one group at a table were playing a card game which seemed to provoke a great deal of shouting and swearing. Gautier could detect no signs of the nervous excitement which one might have expected after a man had been violently attacked and the police called. No one appeared in any way concerned or even interested when he and Surat passed through the lobby.

Judge Prudhomme, stripped to the waist, was being treated by a doctor in the hotel manager's office. The manager, recognisable by his frock coat and obsequious manner, was standing by attentively and a second policeman was standing near the door. Prudhomme was a large man, flaccid and with unhealthy, colourless skin and pale eyes. The doctor had finished bandaging his left forearm and was helping him into a clean shirt which the hotel had found for him. His own shirt, ripped at one sleeve and bloodstained, lay over the back of a chair. Gautier could see no sign of a knife or other weapon.

'So, Inspector,' Judge Prudhomme said when he saw Gautier. 'Finally you have arrived.'

18

'We have only now heard of the attack on you, Monsieur le Juge,' Gautier replied.

'By this time I might have bled to death had the doctor not been more prompt than the Sûreté.'

The doctor had finished his work and was standing behind Judge Prudhomme. He evidently had a sense of humour, for he raised his eyebrows, miming Prudhomme's pompousness and grinned at Gautier.

'Where is the person who attacked you, Monsieur?'

'He is playing cards with the others in the lobby,' the second policeman said.

'Would you go and ask the gentleman to join us?' Gautier said to Surat.

'Join us!' Judge Prudhomme exclaimed indignantly. 'What do you think this is, Gautier? A drawing-room conversation? The man should be in handcuffs. And make sure he isn't armed. He's mad enough to attack me again.'

Surat and the policeman from the local commissariat left the room and returned presently with Boris Ranevsky, the director of the Dashkova Ballet Company. Gautier knew who he was, for he had seen him at the Théâtre du Châtelet the previous evening when the director had joined the dancers on the stage at the end of the performance to acknowledge the applause of the audience. Ranevsky was a short, stout man with a large head which reminded Gautier of a bust of Beethoven that his former wife Suzanne had bought and kept on a mantelpiece in their living-room. At the theatre, in evening dress and flanked by ballet dancers no taller than himself, he had seemed an impressive figure. Now, at close range, he looked gross and sensual and, for one who directed a troupe of dancers, curiously clumsy. Looking at him, Gautier was reminded of an overweight and ageing frog. In one hand he was carrying a broad-brimmed felt hat, of the type popular at that time among artists, and in the other a cane.

'Monsieur Ranevsky,' Gautier said sternly. 'I understand that you made a criminal assault on the judge here.'

'Criminal assault! He tried to kill me!' Prudhomme exclaimed.

Ranevsky laughed contemptuously. 'If I had meant to kill you, my good man, you would be dead.' He spoke excellent French with scarcely a trace of an accent.

'With what weapon did you attack the judge?'

'This.'

Holding up the cane he was carrying, Ranevsky twisted its silver knob and drew out a sword blade fully a metre long. For a sword-stick it was unusually slender and as elegant as any of the canes carried by fashionable young gentlemen in Paris. Gautier noticed that if there had been any blood on the point of the blade, it had been wiped clean.

'My father and grandfather died serving in the armies of the Tsar,' Ranevsky said proudly. 'Swordsmanship is a tradition in our family.'

'That may be so, monsieur, but it does not entitle you to use your skill to attack other people, not in Paris anyway.'

'This creature deserves to be assaulted.' Ranevsky nodded in the direction of Judge Prudhomme. 'He was molesting one of my dancers.'

'That is a lie! I did no such thing!'

'Then what were you doing in Leon's bedroom?'

'The young man kindly invited me there to show me his scrapbook.'

'His scrapbook?'

'Yes. A book filled with mementoes, reviews of his performances, theatre programmes, picture postcards of the cities in which he has danced. You know the kind of thing, Inspector.'

'Then why, pray, had you taken off your coat and cravat? You were even taking off your spats when I came into the bedroom.'

Gautier forced himself not to look at the doctor. The scene in the dancer's bedroom with the judge caught in flagrante delicto and Ranevsky, stout as he was, standing with sword drawn ready to perpetuate the traditions of his ancestors must have been droll enough to be ludicrous, but Judge Prudhomme would not take kindly to laughter.

'Even if what you say is true,' he told Ranevsky, 'it does not justify attacking the judge with your sword.'

'Not a word of what he is saying is true!' Prudhomme protested.

'What is the name of the man in whose bedroom this attack took place?'

'Leon Bourkin, but everyone knows him simply as Bourkin,' Ranevsky replied and then he added, 'He is the greatest ballet dancer in the world, in all probability the greatest dancer the world has ever known.'

'Where is he now?'

20

'In his bedroom, sobbing. He feels humiliated. This black-guard insulted him.' Ranevsky pointed his sword blade at Judge Prudhomme, took up a fencer's position and made a lunge at him, though more in show than in earnest. Gautier stepped forward quickly, grabbed his arm and took away the sword-stick.

'We will have no more of that, monsieur.' Gautier turned to Surat. 'Let us bring this Leon Bourkin here and see what he has to say.'

'Perhaps I should fetch him,' the doctor suggested. 'The young man was hysterical so I gave him something to calm his nerves.'

As soon as the doctor had left the room, Judge Prudhomme began putting on the morning coat which the hotel manager had been holding for him. Intuition told Gautier that the judge had no wish to face the man whom he was accused of molesting.

'I must leave now, Inspector.'

'Surely you wish to hear what this man Bourkin has to say?'

'Not now. My godson celebrated his first communion today and we are having a dinner party to celebrate the occasion. We shall see what Leon has to say when this scoundrel Ranevsky appears before a *juge d'instruction.*'

The judge left the room with as much of a show of dignity as his anxiety to be gone would allow. Gautier watched him leave, convinced now that this business could only end badly. In his view it should have been easily and quickly settled. He did not believe that Ranevsky had intended to do any more than frighten Prudhomme. The man was too soft and effeminate to have an appetite for real violence and his play with the sword-stick had been no more than theatrical bravado. He might have been persuaded or bullied into apologising to the judge and buying him a new shirt, which could have been an end to the matter. Alternatively, if the judge believed that his honour had been insulted, he might have challenged Ranevsky to a duel. Even though duels were supposed to be against the law, squabbles between gentlemen were often settled by a meeting at dawn, with pistols or swords in the Bois de Boulogne, when neither party was ever hurt beyond perhaps a scratch and mutual honour restored over a good breakfast. As it was, the judge's insistence that Ranevsky should be brought before an examining magistrate made a simple and discreet solution to the affair impossible.

When Leon Bourkin arrived, accompanied by the doctor, Gautier recognised him, but far less readily than he had Ranevsky.

On stage, with the benefit of make-up and lighting, Bourkin had seemed to possess almost classical good looks and a virility enhanced by the agility and force of his dancing. Now, in shirt, braces and crumpled trousers and with his hair tousled, he was a forlorn figure. His face was that of a not very skilfully designed doll and his head was too small for his body, to the point of seeming grotesque. Ranevsky went over to him protectively and made a remark in Russian, to which Bourkin shook his head.

'Are you Leon Bourkin?' Gautier asked and when the dancer nodded he went on, 'I am here from the Paris Sûreté to investigate an incident in which you are said to have been involved; an assault on a judge.'

'It was nothing, monsieur,' Bourkin replied.

'Then tell me what happened?'

'Tell him how that dreadful man tried to molest you,' Ranevsky said.

'Kindly do not interrupt,' Gautier told Ranevsky. 'The gentleman must answer for himself.'

'I repeat, Inspector, the incident was of no consequence,' Bourkin said. His French was also good but not as fluent as that of Ranevsky.

'If that is the case why was Judge Prudhomme attacked?' Bourkin shrugged so Gautier asked him another question. 'Is it true that you invited the judge to your room?'

'He asked me if he might come there and I agreed. It was innocent enough.'

'Innocent!' Ranevsky exclaimed. 'You were on the bed and he was undressing.'

'I would never have allowed him to take any liberties.'

Ranevsky shouted at him in Russian what sounded like an obscenity. Bourkin flushed and began stammering some kind of excuse or explanation. The two of them started arguing, Ranevsky violently and passionately, Bourkin making what could only have been denials and seemingly on the verge of tears.

'Gentlemen!' the doctor protested. 'Restrain yourselves! Temper your anger! Continue like this and one of you will be struck with apoplexy.'

Gautier decided that to continue questioning the two Russians would be futile. This was a lovers' quarrel, one supposed, and all the more intense because the lovers were both men. The best course would be to allow Ranevsky's jealous anger to cool. There was always the possibility, too, that given time to reflect Judge Prudhomme might decide to withdraw any charges against the Russian.

'As the judge has been obliged to leave us,' he told Ranevsky, 'we cannot resolve this matter today.'

'So what happens?'

'Both of you will report to me at Sûreté headquarters tomorrow at three o'clock in the afternoon.'

'That is a most inconvenient time,' Ranevsky protested. 'Tomorrow we need the whole day to rehearse a new ballet.'

'That may be so, but you will do as I say,' Gautier replied. Then he added, 'And in the meantime I must insist that both of you surrender your passports to me.'

3

That evening Gautier dined with Princess Sophia in a small, unpretentious restaurant not far from Les Halles. He had chosen that restaurant because he was confident that Sophia would like it, for its ambience as well as for its cuisine. Since her return to Paris they had either dined in the homes of the *gratin* or upper crust of society, or gone in parties to have supper after the ballet in exclusive restaurants – the Ritz, Lucas or Maxim's. He knew from experience, though, that Sophia really preferred bourgeois restaurants in which one could find the ordinary people of Paris.

Her remark as they studied the carte du jour confirmed that he had chosen well. 'I'm really going to enjoy this meal,' she said. 'Almost every dish they are offering is one of my favourites.'

'In that case, how will you choose one?'

'That's easy. You shall choose for me.'

'I'm not adventurous,' Gautier warned her. 'Like most men I tend to stick to the same few dishes.'

'There's nothing wrong with that, as long as they are good ones.'

'In my case they are usually the dishes we were given at home.' He smiled. 'And I was a country boy, remember.'

'And I a children's nurse.'

From time to time they both claimed that they came of peasant stock, but it was only a kind of game and in neither case true. Gautier's father had been a tax collector in a small market town, while Sophia's father had sold leather goods and saddles and harness. When his business had collapsed, she had fled from Turkey to avoid an arranged marriage to a man she found repugnant, crossed to Greece and found employment there as a children's nurse.

Gautier ordered cassoulet for both of them, reminding her, 'My mother came from Languedoc.'

While they were waiting for the cassoulet, they drank from a bottle of robust, red *vin du pays* which the proprietor of the restaurant had brought them with his compliments. Gautier had dined there before and, as he explained to Sophia, he had once been able to help the proprietor when he had been having difficulties over a minor legal matter. On most evenings the restaurant would have been crowded with porters from the nearby markets, but on a Sunday it was patronised mainly by family parties.

Looking around her, Sophia said, 'I feel really at home in this place.'

Gautier knew she meant what she had said and that it was not part of their game, but he could not resist asking her, 'More so than at the imperial court banquets in St Petersburg?'

In Greece, while she was still a girl, Sophia had met and married a widower, a wealthy merchant who had died when she was only twenty-four, leaving her a substantial fortune. With no ties in Greece and not wishing to return home to Turkey, she had amused herself by travelling in Europe and it had been in Baden-Baden that she had met a young, impecunious and sickly Russian prince. Their marriage which followed had been a happy one but short; in less than three years the prince had died of consumption, leaving her a widow for a second time.

'When I first came to Paris last year, the newspapers told the world I had escaped from a Turkish harem,' Sophia complained. 'Now I cannot escape from being labelled as a princess.'

'There is one thing I meant to ask you,' Gautier said. 'You clearly loved your father and he must have been a kind man. Why did he wish you to marry a man you did not love?'

'There were two reasons really. He had been defrauded of a great deal of money and we were very poor. On top of that my younger sister was very much in love and wished to marry, but in our country the younger daughters cannot marry before the eldest.'

Gautier did not tell her that he found Turkish customs curiously old-fashioned. One of the qualities which he admired most in Sophia was her frankness; another was her independence, and that he supposed was the result of her having to leave home at such an early age. These qualities, he felt sure, were the reason why the visit to Paris of her ballet company was proving so successful.

'How did you spend your time today?' he asked her.

25

'I lunched with the Comtesse de Meslée at Auteuil.'

'And did you enjoy it?'

'Very much. Everyone told me I was mad even to contemplate going all the way to Auteuil for lunch. From what they were saying one would imagine it was as distant as Siberia but it's only by the Bois de Boulogne.'

Gautier laughed. 'The *gratin* in Paris don't mind going to Auteuil for the races but they cannot believe that anyone would actually live there.'

The Comtesse de Meslée had once been a great beauty in Paris society and reputedly a great wit. Invitations to her salons had been more highly prized than those of other well-known hostesses like Madame Lydie Aubernon and Madame Armand de Caillavet. Her many secret lovers were supposed to have included the greatest poets in the Académie Française and they may have thought it an equal honour to be cuckolding her husband who came from one of the noblest families in France and one of the few to have survived the Revolution. Then, without warning, after the Comte died she had moved from their apartment in the Plaine Monceau to a house in Auteuil, largely so that she could exercise her dogs in the Bois de Boulogne. Her friends had warned her that she would be cutting herself off from Paris society. Anyone with such a malicious wit, they had said, should not live so far out of Paris.

'Did all the other guests she had invited come to the lunch?' Gautier asked Sophia.

'They did, though most of them were grumbling all the time for having to come so far. I'm glad I went, because one of the other guests was a man I particularly wished to meet.'

'Who was that?'

'Monsieur Labat, the industrialist.'

'Emile Labat? He owns flour mills, does he not?'

'Many of them. He told me that one-third of all the bread baked in Paris every day is made with his flour. Missia who came with me to the luncheon introduced us. She knows him well.'

The reason why Sophia had wished to meet Emile Labat, she told Gautier, was that he was a patron of the arts. In addition to owning a fine collection of early Italian paintings, he had financed concerts by young musicians and helped struggling poets to have their verses published.

'I told him about my Russian ballet company,' Sophia concluded, 'and he has promised us financial backing.'

'I understood that the funds you need to finance your company's visit to Paris had all been subscribed.'

'We thought they had,' Sophia replied, 'but only yesterday we learnt that the grant which the Russian Government had promised us has been withdrawn.'

'Why is that?'

'The excuse we were given is that the funds available in the Privy Purse for subsidising opera and ballet are all spent. The real reason is that Boris Ranevsky has offended the Tsar in some way. Boris has a genius for provoking quarrels. Anyway we have no reason to worry now. Monsieur Labat has promised to make up the deficit.'

Gautier was surprised to hear that the Dashkova Ballet Company should still have needed to raise funds. Even though its season had only just started, people were agreeing that it would be a brilliant success. The Théâtre du Châtelet had been full the previous evening and the enthusiasm of the audience unrestrained, the number of curtain calls at the end of the performance seeming endless. Critics writing of the performances earlier in the week had been extravagant in their praise.

Sophia may have guessed what he was thinking, for she said, 'Boris is a fine director for the ballet. He has taste and imagination and judgement and more important than that he inspires loyalty in the people who work for him. But when it comes to dealing with finance, he is worse than a child. I found out that he was keeping no accounts at all. We had no idea how the money was being spent. So I had to insist that we appointed a business manager and of course Boris took great offence.'

Gautier had planned not to tell Sophia of Ranevsky's attack on Judge Prudhomme until after they had finished dinner, for he did not wish to spoil the pleasure of the evening. Now, since the subject of Ranevsky's behaviour had emerged in another context, he decided he had no choice but to mention it.

'Your problems with Ranevsky are not over, I regret to say,' he told her. 'Now he is in trouble with the police.'

'The police! I don't believe it!'

'This afternoon he attacked a Frenchman, a judge, with his sword-stick.'

As he described what had happened in the Hôtel Bayonne that afternoon, Gautier watched Sophia's expression. The dismay which she had shown on hearing of Ranevsky's behaviour was slowly replaced by resignation and then by weariness. He began to understand the strain which bringing the ballet company to Paris was imposing on her and which her vitality and enthusiasm for the venture had so far concealed. The importance of succeeding after her plans for the previous year had ended in failure would be exacerbating the stress.

'This will ruin all we have achieved.' She could not keep the dejection out of her voice. 'It will be a disaster for the ballet!'

'Not necessarily. Even if a judge decides that Ranevsky has a case to answer, it may well be weeks before it comes to court. Your season of ballet will probably have been concluded by then. Justice moves slowly in France.'

Sophia shook her head. 'Think of the scandal! The news will spread through Paris like a fire on a dry heath.'

'No one knows of the incident except your ballet company and some of the hotel's staff.'

'They soon will once the newspapers pick it up.'

Gautier knew that she was probably right. French journalists had an efficient network for gathering information and none more so than those who wrote for the society columns. They hired people to work for them who were a cross between reporters and spies and who scavenged for scraps of news which could be turned into scandal, hanging around the law courts, fashionable restaurants and outside the home of any hostess who might be entertaining celebrities.

'Is Ranevsky a homosexual?'

'Of course,' Sophia replied. 'In Russia he has always been reasonably discreet about it, but there seems to be something about Paris which has encouraged all the members of the ballet, not only Boris, to abandon their inhibitions. They love your city and are happy here.'

'Presumably Bourkin is a pédé as well.'

'Oh yes. He is the great love of Boris's life. In the past Boris has had affairs with any number of men, but it is only with Bourkin that he has been so passionate and so possessive.'

'Paris is not the place in which to flaunt one's homosexuality,' Gautier remarked.

The French looked with suspicion on homosexuality, linking it with the decline in national virility which they blamed for the country's defeat by Prussia in 1870. More recently this suspicion had turned into contempt following the Eulenburg Affair. Prince

Philip von Eulenburg, a married man and a friend of Kaiser William, was past sixty when he was attacked in the press for homosexuality. As Oscar Wilde had done, he sued his accusers for libel, but evidence was produced in court which justified their accusations and as a result the Prince, again like Wilde, had to face a criminal prosecution which ruined his career and his life.

'The scandal if it breaks,' Sophia said, 'will be so much worse as Bourkin is a dancer.'

'Why should that make any difference?'

'When our company arrived the French were shocked to hear that we had male dancers. In French ballet male rôles are danced by women in *transvestie*. The stage-hands at the theatre even had a protest meeting.'

'They are all French are they?'

'Yes, permanently employed by the theatre management. Anyway after our successful first week the audiences – and the critics – are just beginning to accept that men should dance on the stage. They have been amazed by the talent and virtuosity of Bourkin and the other men dancers. Now . . . ' Sophia finished her sentence with an expressive shrug of the shoulders.

While they were talking a huge earthenware dish of cassoulet and two plates had been brought to their table. As she tasted it Sophia commented that it was delicious, but Gautier could see that, as he had feared, her enjoyment of the meal had been spoiled. On previous occasions when they had dined at bourgeois restaurants, she had eaten ordinary farmhouse dishes hungrily, saying how the rough country wine had sharpened her appetite. Now they ate almost in silence and he could see that she was worried.

'In your opinion is it likely that Boris will have to appear in court?' she asked finally.

'I am afraid so. Judge Prudhomme seems determined that he should be punished.'

'Surely you could do something to prevent that happening?'

'I cannot see how.'

'Everyone knows that the police have powers which sometimes they use and which nobody questions.'

'What powers?'

'How shall I put it? Powers of silent coercion?'

Gautier was tempted to remind her that they were in France and not in Russia. In Russia, he had read, the police were at

29

the disposal of the Tsar; they were an instrument which the government used to impose its will. France on the other hand was a democracy and although political patronage could on occasions be used to influence the decisions of the judiciary, ultimately the police were responsible to the National Assembly.

'Really there is nothing I can do to prevent a process against your director, if the authorities decide that one should be instituted.'

'You were able to help the proprietor of this restaurant.'

'Yes, but that was not in a criminal matter.'

Gautier could see that Sophia was not convinced by his assurances, so he told her, 'We, that is the Director General of the Sûreté and I, will do all we can to persuade Judge Prudhomme not to press charges. That is all I can promise.'

They did not discuss the matter any further over dinner, but Gautier could sense a lingering constraint there. Sophia was not satisfied with his answers to her questions and he felt that she was being unreasonable. Their disagreement was not serious enough to be a barrier, but it might become one. His relationship with Sophia, ever since they had first made love at the hotel in Asnières, had been one of complete trust and frankness and honesty. The thought that it might now change and be infected, however faintly, with hidden reservations and suspicion, saddened and depressed him.

4

Although it was not yet eight o'clock when Gautier arrived at the Sûreté next morning, he found Monsieur and Madame Lebrun waiting for him outside the entrance. They were wearing what were probably their best clothes and he felt that this was not to impress him, but because they were determined to accept whatever sanction justice might impose on them with dignity.

'Why are you here?' Gautier asked, meaning why were they waiting outside the entrance to the building.

'We have come to tell you the truth, Inspector,' Lebrun replied.

'Then we had better go to my office.'

Once upstairs, Gautier sent for Surat and then made the Lebruns sit down facing him across his table. The worst symptoms of Lebrun's influenza appeared to have abated, for his eyes were clearer, his face less flushed. His wife would glance at him from time to time, looking for reassurance, and one could sense not only her devotion but that she was dependent on him.

'Now what have you to tell me?' Gautier asked.

'What I said about my killing our daughter was untrue,' Lebrun began.

'And I lied to you too.'

'I will hear you one at a time. You first, monsieur. Tell me exactly what happened that afternoon.'

'My wife had gone out to the shops, leaving the child with me. As you know I have had a grippe and I had slept badly the previous night. I was lying on the bed and must have fallen asleep and I did not wake until the police were knocking on our door. When I went to let them in, I did not even notice that the baby was no longer in her cot. It was the police who told me she had been killed.'

'Why did you tell the police you had thrown the child out of the window?'

31

'To protect my wife. I thought she must have done it.' Lebrun reached out and took his wife's hand in his. 'I must have been crazy to think that she had done it. I realise that now.'

'Why did you think that?'

'The door to our apartment was locked. No one else could have got in to kill the child. And anyway why should they have killed her?'

Gautier made no comment. There would be time for questions later. Instead he turned to Madame Lebrun. 'And you, madame? Tell me of your movements that afternoon. It is true, as your husband has said, that you went out to shop leaving him alone with the child?'

'Perfectly true.'

Madame Lebrun's story was that when she had left the apartment her husband was lying on the bed, not fully asleep but dozing. She could see that he was unwell, but not so unwell that he could not look after the baby, who was in any case sleeping peacefully in its cot. When she arrived back at the building, the concierge had told her that the baby had been found dead, having fallen from the window, and that the police were upstairs in their apartment.

'She said that my husband must have thrown her from the window. I was in a panic, not thinking rationally. So on my way up to our apartment I worked out a story that I would tell, pretending that I had killed our daughter before I went out.'

'But what did you hope to gain by inventing such a story?' Gautier was inclined to believe what she had told him but could see no logic in the way she had been thinking. 'If we had believed your story your husband would not have been blamed. I accept that. But you would have been imprisoned and, in all probability, put to death.'

'It would be better that way.'

'Why do you say that?'

'If my husband were' – she hesitated over the word – 'guillotined, what would become of me? Who would look after me? No, if one of us has to die it would be better that it were me.'

'What my wife has not told you, Inspector,' Lebrun said, 'is that she is pregnant again.'

Now Gautier could see a sort of logic, tortuous and confused, in the thinking of both husband and wife. He could see it, but he did not believe that any *juge d'instruction* would or, if the ultimate stage were reached, that any jury would.

'You say that the door to your apartment was locked,' he said to Lebrun. 'Do you always keep it locked, even when you are at home?'

'Usually, Inspector. I know it is unusual for people like ourselves and living in this quartier to lock their doors, but we have some books that might tempt a thief.'

'The books you sell?'

'No, the books I have decided not to sell. A few that I have collected over the years. Mine is a modest collection, but one which I would not like to lose; some first editions of writers like Sue and Tocqueville and Montalembert.'

'He is being modest, Inspector,' Madame Lebrun said. 'The books he has collected are rare and many of them beautifully bound. I am sure they are of great value.'

'Is there no one else who has a key to your apartment? A relative perhaps?'

'Only the concierge of the building.'

'Do you trust her?'

'Certainly, Inspector. She is a good woman who has always been kind to us.'

'She has often helped me to look after our daughter.'

'You have never quarrelled with her?'

'Never. If she has any fault, it is that sometimes she drinks too much and neglects her duties.'

Gautier asked them several more questions, some of which were only indirectly related to the death of their child. Often in a murder investigation it was a mistake to focus only on the event itself, the way it had been carried out and its exact timing. An understanding of the background against which a murder had been committed could well provide answers which contributed to its final solution. The Lebruns answered without any hesitation and, it seemed, with complete frankness. After questioning them for almost an hour, Gautier decided what he would do.

'We will need to investigate this matter further,' he told them.

'And in the meantime what must we do?'

'Go home and continue with your lives. You have business to do, monsieur, and you will need to make arrangements for the funeral of your child. Gather your relatives around you to lend you support at this sad time.'

When the couple had left his office, Gautier said to Surat, 'We

33

will have to make more enquiries before we can establish who killed that child, don't you agree?'

'I agree that the woman could never have killed her baby, patron.'

'Nor could Monsieur Lebrun. He is a gentle man, with a love of books; a scholar in a way.'

'Then what do you propose?'

'You and I will go to the quartier where they live. We will talk to the concierge of the building in which they have their apartment and later to the police in the local commissariat.'

Surat pulled out his pocket-watch. It was a fine watch which his father, also a policeman, had left to him and of which he was extremely proud. 'At what time would you wish to leave, patron?'

'We need not decide that now; perhaps this afternoon, perhaps not until tomorrow. My instinct tells me that the rest of this morning will be busy; busy and very probably stormy.'

The storm broke rather less than one hour later when Gustave Courtrand, Companion of the Légion d'Honneur and Director General of the Sûreté, arrived at his office. Gautier, whose own office was directly above Courtrand's, heard the explosive shouting and was not surprised when a messenger arrived, shaken and stammering, to tell him that the Director General wished to see him immediately.

Courtrand was not at his desk, but pacing up and down his office agitatedly. He was holding the brief report on the stabbing of Judge Prudhomme which Gautier had left on his desk the previous evening and when Gautier entered the room he shook it at him as he might have shaken his fist.

'Mother of God, Gautier! This is beyond belief. How can it have been allowed to happen?'

'To what are you referring, Monsieur le Directeur?'

'A senior member of the judiciary has been attacked, stabbed, and you stand there calmly as though nothing had happened. What action have you taken in this monstrous affair?'

'It is all in my report, monsieur.'

A little game which Gautier sometimes played and enjoyed was to provoke Courtrand to an uncontrollable rage. It was a modest revenge for all the indignities and unjust reproaches that he had in the past endured. Courtrand resented Gautier; he resented his youth and his success and more recently he resented having been obliged, against his will, to promote him to chief inspector.

'Then you have done nothing! Nothing! Why is the judge's assailant, this Russian, not behind bars?'

'In my judgement it was wiser not to arrest him.'

'Your judgement? Since when have you had any judgement, Gautier? Police procedures are laid down to be followed. It was a criminal attack and the man should have been arrested. This was gross negligence on your part, Gautier. So much for your promotion!'

'If we had detained the man Ranevsky, the Russian embassy would certainly have intervened.'

'On behalf of a man with a troupe of dancers? I won't believe that!'

'Ballet is highly regarded in Russia and the Dashkova Company came to Paris with the support of the Tsar.' What Gautier was saying had originally been true although he knew now that the Tsar had withdrawn his support. 'The French Government would not thank us for provoking a diplomatic incident at this particular time.'

Relations between the major European powers were delicately balanced. France, following her defeat by Prussia, understood the importance of having strong allies. One alliance had recently been cemented by the creation of the Entente Cordiale with England in 1904. The Russians were also traditional allies and even though confidence in Russia had been shaken after her humiliating defeat by Japan, the French Government was still anxious to keep her friendship.

As soon as Gautier mentioned the possibility of diplomatic repercussions, Courtrand's attitude changed dramatically. His appointment as director general of the Sûreté had been a piece of political patronage, a return for favours which he had done some government minister in the past. He repaid the gift by doing everything within the powers of the Sûreté to ensure that not only his patron but anyone from the same political and social milieu was spared any trouble or inconvenience. Any threat that a duke of royal blood or a member of the government or a cardinal might be accused of a minor infringement of the law or exposed to scandal for deviant behaviour was, if Courtrand could arrange it, quietly extinguished. He had been a great admirer of the Prince of Wales, now King Edward VII of England, and Gautier could

35

recall when he was still a junior officer in the Sûreté, being sent more than once to smooth out trouble at one of the high-class brothels which Edward liked to visit when he was in Paris.

'There may be something in what you say, Gautier,' Courtrand said cautiously. 'Even so some action will have to be taken. Judge Prudhomme will insist on that.'

'It is really most unfortunate that he went to the Hôtel Bayonne,' Gautier remarked. He had said nothing in his report of Ranevsky's allegation that Prudhomme had tried to molest the dancer Bourkin. The subject of homosexuality must be broken gently to Courtrand.

'Why did he go there?'

'The Russian ballet dancers have made a great many friends even in the short time that they have been in Paris.' Gautier had been told this by Princess Sophia. 'They are being fêted by Parisians. Society hostesses, men of letters, members of the National Assembly, musicians and journalists entertain them in their homes or go to meet them at their hotel or in cafés and restaurants.'

'What is the attraction?'

'Partly an exotic appeal. The Russians are foreigners, but unlike other foreigners, the English for example, they are full of joie de vivre, they are friendly and almost all of them speak French.'

'I would not have thought that Judge Prudhomme would be attracted by the exotic or by joie de vivre.'

'Some Frenchmen, they say, are attracted to them for another reason.'

'What is that?'

'Ranevsky, the director of the company, and the dancer Bourkin are both pédés.'

Courtrand looked at him sharply and Gautier realised at once that he had heard the rumours of Prudhomme's homosexual inclinations and believed them. 'You are not suggesting that these Russians are accusing the judge of a homosexual offence?'

'When he was attacked he was in the bedroom of Bourkin and, I understand, partly undressed.'

Courtrand said nothing but crossed the room and threw open one of the windows. It was a mannerism of his when confronted by a situation which seemed to be getting out of control. He was not a stupid man, but his mind was too inflexible to respond quickly to a development that he had not been expecting and which made him anxious. Gautier sensed that he could be looking for reassurance and he was not mistaken.

'What do you think we should do, Gautier?'

'The best thing would be to persuade Judge Prudhomme not to press charges against Ranevsky.'

'It is most unlikely that he could be persuaded to do that. He believes that the law must always be enforced.'

'Even in this case, when to do so will create a scandal?'

'The man is so intransigent. He gives the impression that his belief in the law is stronger and more unshakeable than his belief in the Holy Trinity.'

'Is he proud of being a member of the judiciary?'

'Without question; fanatically proud.'

'Then perhaps you should tell him that by provoking a scandal he would do the reputation of the judiciary incalculable damage.'

'Would he believe it? It does not seem very plausible.'

'On the contrary. Can you not imagine how the newspapers would love finding out that there is a pédé among our judges? What a story for them! Remember the Eulenburg affair!'

'I can see the logic behind what you say.' Courtrand was beginning to glimpse a way by which he might escape from what might well become a distasteful embarrassment. 'But will Judge Prudhomme see it? He is stubborn and wilful as you know.'

'Why not ask the Prefect of Police to speak to him?'

'How strange that you should suggest that, Gautier! I had just decided that was exactly what I would do.'

One of Courtrand's more irritating traits was that he hated to give anyone credit for what he realised was a good idea. He returned to his desk, took Gautier's report on the Prudhomme affair and began jotting down his own notes on it. Before he could finish, his secretary Corbin came in from the adjoining office.

'Monsieur le Directeur. Judge Prudhomme has just telephoned. He wished to speak with you.'

'What did you say to him?'

'That you were in an important meeting and could not be disturbed.'

The telephone had not long been installed in the offices of government departments. Courtrand, who distrusted telephones, had refused to have one in his office, giving as a reason his fear that it might allow outsiders access to secrets of security. So Corbin had to take all calls for him.

'Quite right. I am. What did the judge want?'

'He wishes to see you immediately in his office at the Palais de Justice.'

'Telephone him back and tell him that I'm on my way to see the Prefect of Police.'

'It is unlikely that you will be able to see the Prefect this morning, monsieur. He is in a meeting with the President's chef de cabinet and the Minister for the Interior.'

Corbin began walking back towards his office. He had obviously realised that Courtrand was trying to avoid a meeting with Judge Prudhomme and took pleasure in cutting off the path of retreat. As with many junior officials in the Sûreté, any respect and loyalty which he might once have felt for the Director had long since been stifled by Courtrand's arrogance and petty tyranny.

Before he left the room he said, 'Judge Prudhomme seems very upset, monsieur. I would say he is absolutely enraged!'

When they were alone, Courtrand looked at Gautier reproachfully. 'You see, Gautier! Once again your disregard of police procedures has placed me in an invidious position.'

'I do not agree, monsieur. You are in a position where you can save Judge Prudhomme and the judiciary from embarrassment and ridicule. You must persuade the judge to forget this absurd business with the Russians.'

5

'If the eighteenth century was the age of enlightenment,' Duthrey said, 'then it would appear that the twentieth will be the age of depravity.'

'I think you are being too pessimistic, old friend,' Gautier replied.

The two of them were sitting at a table in the Café Corneille, where more often than not they met around midday with a small group of friends. Cafés were where men went to take an apéritif and talk, about politics, literature, finance, the affairs of the day or simply to gossip. In Paris one could find cafés which catered for almost every profession or métier. There were cafés which were frequented by members of the Bourse, by bankers, hat makers, diamond merchants and music hall performers; just men of course. Usually the only woman to be seen in a café would be the wife of the proprietor, who sat behind a desk in her black dress, looking after the accounts.

The Café Corneille in Boulevard St Germain attracted mainly men of liberal views, drawn from a variety of professions – the law, politics and journalism. Duthrey himself was a journalist who wrote for *Figaro* and that morning the group in which he and Gautier were sitting included Froissart, a bookseller who also published poetry, an elderly judge and the deputy for Val-de-Marne, generally accepted as the most brilliant of France's younger politicians.

'I agree with Gautier,' the deputy said. 'Changes in attitudes to morality are cyclical. We are living at a time when the younger generation is rebelling against the old moral codes which were universally accepted only a decade or two ago, but the pendulum will swing back.'

'The influence of America is undermining French society,' Duthrey complained.

'Surely not? I have always understood that Americans have two gods; money and domestic virtue.'

'Only in America. The Americans who come to France do so to escape from the iron bands of their matriarchal society. They come to Paris to live like bohemians, flaunting their promiscuity, their perversions and their drunkenness.'

What Duthrey had said was at least partly true. In the past few years an increasing number of Americans had been coming to live in France. Some came simply for pleasure, since Paris had become indisputably the cultural and entertainment centre of the world. Others, like Anna Gould, daughter of a railroad millionaire, who married Comte Boni de Castellane, and Clara Ward, whose father owned most of the slaughterhouses of Chicago, and who became Princess Joseph de Caraman-Chimay, were heiresses looking for aristocratic husbands. A large number were aspiring writers and artists who came to Paris because there they could live cheaply, side by side with the modern painters who had made Montmartre their home, painters like Picasso, Modigliani and Utrillo.

Duthrey's complaint triggered off an argument about whether or not the influx of foreigners was damaging French life, morality and institutions. The discussion was vigorous but not passionate, for the habitués of the Café Corneille, although as suspicious of transatlantic influences as most Frenchmen, were too cultured and too liberal to be intolerant.

'I have nothing against foreigners as a general rule,' the elderly judge said, 'but we should exclude the Anglo-Saxons from our country and stick to our old friends.'

'We only have one,' the deputy for Val-de-Marne remarked, 'the Shah of Persia.'

Everyone laughed at the reference to the Shah who made frequent state visits to France. He was popular with the French, for he had been one of only two rulers who had accepted an invitation to come to Paris for the Exposition in 1900.

As the discussion continued more members of the regular group arrived at the café. One was a clever young lawyer, always popular because of his talent as a raconteur of irreverent and not infrequently bawdy stories. The second new arrival was another journalist, Michel Puy, who worked on the staff of *La Libre Parole*. Puy was a man whom Gautier had never liked. Sharp, abrasive and full of his own importance, he came to the Café Corneille infrequently and only then, Gautier suspected, when he thought he might pick up some information there which he could use in a story. *La Libre Parole* was in any case a newspaper whose style and editorial policy did not appeal to the habitués of the Café Corneille. Articles published in it were anything but liberal and, more often than not, anti-Semitic and vitriolic in tone.

Almost immediately after he arrived he asked Gautier, 'Did I see you at the Châtelet theatre on Saturday evening?'

'Very probably. I was there.'

'Yes, with that woman who has brought the ballet here and claims to be a Russian princess.'

'If you care to look in the *Almanach de Gotha*, you will find her listed and see that her late husband was indeed a prince,' Duthrey said acidly.

'The *Almanach de Gotha*!' Puy said scornfully. 'I don't waste my time on that rubbish! Where else but in France would one find a directory of the so-called aristocracy? No doubt your princess is listed in it, but that won't help her if she fails to meet her financial obligations.'

'What reason have you for thinking she might?' the lawyer asked.

'Her ballet company is seriously in debt.' Puy looked at Gautier. 'Did you know that?'

'No. And I have no reason for believing that what you are saying is true.'

'It's true all right. They have had lavish costumes made for a spectacular new ballet which they intend to present in Paris, but they cannot pay for them. The costumier has refused to release the costumes until he has been paid his five thousand francs.'

The other members of the group looked uncomfortable. They might well have known or at least guessed that Gautier had an intimate liaison with Princess Sophia and did not like to see him embarrassed.

'Did you come to this café simply to regale us with these disgraceful pieces of gossip which you have scavenged from the streets?' Duthrey asked him. 'If so you may as well know that we do not appreciate them.'

'Sadly for you and for *Figaro*,' Puy replied coolly, 'you do not realise that what you believe to be mere gossip is news and news is what people expect to read in a newspaper.' He turned to Gautier. 'Do you know anything about a fight that took place in the hotel where these ballet dancers are staying? I have heard that one of the Russians seriously wounded a French citizen.'

'If I did know,' Gautier replied, 'I would not be at liberty to tell you, would I?'

'Just as you please. I'll find out anyway. I have other sources.'

Puy left them, conscious perhaps of the hostility he had aroused. It was clear that he had only come to the Café Corneille that morning in the hope of prising information out of Gautier and the other members of the group resented it. Cafés were where men talked politics and it had been known for the authorities to send police spies or agents provocateurs to venues where they suspected that politics were turning towards sedition. In the Café Corneille Gautier was trusted by the other members of their group as a friend, but to avoid embarrassment there was a tacit understanding that no one should question him on police business and he never raised it in discussion.

Not long afterwards, when Gautier and Duthrey were leaving, they walked down the boulevard together to a corner where Duthrey could find a fiacre. His wife cooked him an excellent lunch every day and he liked to return home punctually so that he would have enough time to eat it at leisure and take a short nap before returning to the offices of *Figaro*.

'How is the Princess Sophia?' he asked Gautier.

'Very well and enjoying life in Paris.'

'And how is your relationship with the lady? Or am I being impertinent in asking?'

'Not at all. A friend always has the right to ask and I too am enjoying Paris now that Princess Sophia is here.'

'Is there any prospect that the two of you might marry?'

'Very little I should say, but as it happens Sophia did suggest marriage last year when she was in Paris.'

'And what did you say to that?'

'I laughed. The idea of a princess and a policeman marrying seemed preposterous at the time.'

'I cannot see why. If she stopped using her title people would soon forget that she ever had one.'

'I suppose that is possible.'

'You should remarry, Jean-Paul.' Duthrey was the only member of the group at the Café Corneille who addressed Gautier by his Christian name. Gautier had never felt that he should use the same familiarity with Duthrey, for he was a much older man.

'A police officer should be married. I have always felt that you have been lonely since your wife died.'

Duthrey made no allusion to the fact that Gautier's wife Suzanne had in fact left him and had only died some time afterwards. Gautier appreciated his tact.

'Although I laughed when Sophia suggested marriage,' he said, 'I did promise her that I would at least consider it.'

When Gautier arrived back at the Sûreté, Courtrand was not there. The Director General, Corbin told him, had returned to his office only briefly after his meeting with Judge Prudhomme and had then gone to get ready for a lunch which he was due to attend at the Hôtel de Ville. The lunch was in honour of a delegation of mayors from Italian cities who were on an official visit to Paris. Courtrand, who had a passion for ceremony and formal occasions, had gone home to change into his best frock coat, have his hands manicured and his beard trimmed. Before leaving he had left a message for Gautier with his secretary.

'Judge Prudhomme insists that these Russians should be charged with attempting to murder him,' Corbin said.

'He cannot insist. It will be for the *juge d'instruction* to decide whether there is a case to be made against them.'

'Technically speaking you are right, but Judge Prudhomme is in a position to – how shall I put it? – influence the *juge d'instruction*.'

'When will one be appointed?'

'No one can say. Not for two or three days anyway. As you probably know, an epidemic of influenza is sweeping through Paris and as a result there is an acute shortage of magistrates available for work. Enquiries into several cases more important than the attack on Judge Prudhomme have had to be deferred.'

Corbin's admission that Judge Prudhomme would be able to exert pressure on the Department of Justice over whether or not Ranevsky should face trial, reminded Gautier of the remarks that Sophia had made over dinner the previous evening. Perhaps she was not being so unreasonable after all. Even so there was no way in which Gautier could bring pressure on Judge Prudhomme to drop charges against the Russian. One could only hope that the judge might, on reflection, have the good sense to change his mind.

Returning to his own office, he arranged for a message to be

43

sent to Ranevsky and Bourkin, telling them that they need not come to Sûreté headquarters that afternoon and that they would be informed in due course of when he wished to interview them. Gautier believed that he had already learnt as much as he was likely to from Ranevsky and Bourkin of how Judge Prudhomme had come to be stabbed and the only purpose of bringing them to his office would be to have a formal interrogation, recorded in writing, which would later be given to the *juge d'instruction*. In view of what Corbin had told him there was now no urgency for this and, by postponing it, he would be giving Prudhomme more time for second thoughts.

After the messenger had left, he settled down to some routine work, reading the reports which other inspectors had left on his desk. A woman, a well-known anarchist who had just returned to France after being deported to New Caledonia for ten years, had been found walking up and down Place de la Concorde announcing that she was about to assassinate the President of the Republic. When a policeman, thinking she was an elderly eccentric, had told her to move on she had shot him, fortunately not fatally. A civil servant from the Ministry for War, who had been missing for several days and who, it had been feared, had stolen secret information which he could have sold to a foreign power, had been found hanged in a disused cowshed near Lille. The home of a titled Irishman in Avenue Van Dyck had been burgled. That alone would not have been enough to warrant action by the Sûreté, but the Irishman possessed a fine collection of sporting rifles and revolvers, some of which had been stolen.

One of Gautier's responsibilities was to select the reports which he believed merited the attention of the Director General and send them to Courtrand's office with a brief résumé of the remaining ones. He had just finished writing the résumé when Surat came into his office.

'I thought you should know, patron, that a demonstration is taking place outside the Palais de Justice.'

'What kind of demonstration?'

'A group of people carrying banners are walking up and down the street outside the entrance.'

'Why should that concern us in the Sûreté?' Gautier asked.

Demonstrations were commonplace in Paris at that time. A few years previously they had been organised mainly by anarchists, as a protest against low wages and poor working conditions. More recently a motley assortment of other organisations had taken to the streets, some fighting intellectual or radical causes, others from a lunatic fringe.

'The demonstration appears to be directed against Judge Prudhomme.'

'In what way?'

'I do not know exactly, patron. I have not seen it myself but a policeman coming on duty described it to me.'

'Is it violent?'

'Not as yet, apparently.'

'In that case we had better go and make sure it does not become so.'

The entrance to the Palais de Justice was only a few minutes' walk from Sûreté headquarters. When Gautier and Surat arrived there they saw a group of perhaps a score of men, drawn up in ranks, facing the entrance. All of them were dressed in judges' robes and every alternate man carried a banner made out of a sheet of cardboard attached to a broomstick. On each banner was a crude drawing of a gallows from which hung a figure of a man, also in the robes of a judge. Beneath the drawing had been written in large capital letters:

A BAS PRUDHOMME

'Do you think it is a joke?' Surat asked Gautier.

'If it is, somebody has a macabre sense of humour.'

They watched the demonstration for a minute or two. From time to time the demonstrators would chant the slogan that was written on their banners. They chanted solemnly and in funereal tones, but without any of the passion which political agitators or defenders of the rights of women showed when they demonstrated. One had the impression that one was watching the chorus in a Greek tragedy, which had been rehearsed in its rôle.

Two uniformed policemen were watching the demonstration, alert for any signs that it might be becoming violent. Gautier sent them to escort one of the demonstrators to him.

'Bring one from the back row,' he said, 'and treat him gently. Explain to him that he is not being arrested, but that I simply wish to ask him a question.'

The demonstrator whom they brought back was a small, gross man with a red beard, the colour of which did not match what little hair he still possessed on his head. He came willingly enough and smiled at Gautier cheerfully.

Gautier explained to him that he and Surat were officers of the Sûreté. 'I merely wished to ask you the reason for this demonstration.'

'It is a demonstration against Judge Prudhomme.' The man's French had no accent.

'One can see that, but why? What have you got against the Judge?'

'To tell you the truth, Inspector,' the man replied smiling, 'I'm not absolutely sure.'

'Are you by any chance an actor who has been paid to perform in this charade?'

The man looked surprised. 'How did you know?'

'I guessed.'

'That's uncommonly clever of you. Most people think I look nothing like an actor.'

'I wouldn't say that,' Gautier replied solemnly. 'You seem to have all the attributes for comic parts.'

The actor burst into laughter. 'What perceptiveness! You must be wonderful in an audience, Inspector. I shall send you a ticket for my next performance, when I'm working again that is.'

He rejoined the other demonstrators and Gautier watched them for a little longer. They might well all be out-of-work actors, he decided, for they were playing their sombre rôles with enthusiasm, as though glad to have a chance to perform, even in the streets.

As he and Gautier walked back to Sûreté headquarters, Surat said, 'Should we not have stopped the demonstration and made those characters disperse?'

'We'll allow them to continue for a little while longer,' Gautier smiled as he replied, 'just in case Judge Prudhomme is not yet aware of what they are chanting.'

6

The programme at the Châtelet Theatre that evening was to include a ballet which had been created by the Dashkova Ballet Company and which had been performed for the first time outside Russia only the previous week. *Seraglio*, set in a harem, had been a succès fou, earning notices from the critics that were lyrical in their praise.

Gautier was there to watch what was to be its second performance in Paris, sharing with four other guests of Princess Sophia the box which was permanently reserved for her use during the ballet's season. Sophia herself was not with them, for she had watched the ballet several times when it had been performed in Russia. She would be backstage, she had told Gautier, dealing with management matters, but she would join him for supper after the performance.

The programme that evening consisted of three ballets, the first a romantic story of a prince and a woodman's daughter, the second little more than a pas de deux, danced with haunting grace by a ballerina named Elena Karpovna and a young man far more handsome than Leon Bourkin, but felt not to be as talented. Both ballets were performed against pastoral stage settings, which were skilfully designed but no more than conventionally pretty. They left Gautier unprepared for the dazzling spectacle of *Seraglio*.

The scene when the curtain went up was the harem in a sultan's palace. A huge looped curtain, sky blue striped with green and patterned with peacocks' feathers, dominated the stage. Beneath it the carpet was pink and the ottomans on which the concubines of the harem reclined were heaped with cushions, yellow, green, orange and crimson, while from the ceiling hung golden lamps. Along the back of the stage Negro slaves stood silently, arms folded, wearing yellow lamé trousers to show off the glistening brown of their bare torsos.

The impression which the stage setting gave of a sensuality bordering on the erotic was a perfect complement to the story of the ballet. The central characters were a beautiful concubine named Yasmin, the favourite of the sultan, and a young man who, after catching a glimpse of her through a window, had fallen in love with her. So that he could be near her, he had disguised himself as a Negro, colouring his face and body, and taken his place among the other slaves in the harem. Yasmin had been unable to resist his charm and, with the complicity of the other concubines, they began making love behind a silk curtain held by the other slaves. At this point the sultan, who was thought to be away in another city, had come into the harem with his servants. In a fury of rage he gave orders that not only Yasmin and her lover but all the other concubines should be put to death. The ballet ended in a frenzy of barbaric but voluptuous violence.

Shortly after the ballet began, Gautier noticed a man slipping into the box. The other guests, to whom he had been introduced when he arrived at the theatre, were two married couples, both Russian and both elderly. Sophia had told him that they were émigrés who had come to live in France to escape the growing political unrest in their own country. They spoke French only haltingly, so Gautier had been able to do no more than exchange a few words of small-talk with them in between the ballets.

The man who arrived during the performance of *Seraglio* was not wearing evening dress as most of the audience were, but a pair of baggy trousers and a crumpled cardigan. He was a tall man with a stoop and the face of a scholar. Gautier noticed that he was watching the ballet intently, sometimes frowning and making small gestures of impatience, at other times nodding with approval. When the final curtain came down at the end of the performance, he looked out over the auditorium smiling and clearly delighted by the enthusiasm of the audience, many of whom were standing and cheering.

He turned to Gautier. 'They seem to like it,' he said.

'And so they should. The last ballet was superb, a tour de force. And the décor! I've never seen anything to match it!'

'Do you really think so? I detected one or two small flaws in tonight's performance, but it grows better every time they dance it.'

'You've seen the ballet before, then?'

'I created it. *Seraglio* is my ballet.'

48

He told Gautier that his name was Alexandre Sanson and that he was the artistic director of the Ballets Dashkova.

'Do you actually write the ballet?' Gautier had been wondering how a ballet was conceived.

'A ballet is not written in the way that a play is. It is created. In the case of *Seraglio*, I planned the story and suggested the music which should be used and I designed the stage settings myself.'

'From where did you get your idea for the story?'

'It is based very loosely on a story from an old collection of Eastern tales.' Sanson perhaps thought that Gautier might be disappointed to hear that the story of the ballet was not his own invention, for he added, 'All dramatists sometimes use old stories as a framework for their masterpieces. Shakespeare, as you know, borrowed from an old English chronicler, Holinshed.'

'Do you also plan the steps and movements of the dancers in a ballet?'

'No. Usually the choreography, as we call it, evolves rather than being formally composed. It is a joint effort in which the interpretation and improvisations of the dancers play a major rôle.'

Their conversation was interrupted by the arrival of one of the theatre's ushers, who came to tell the Russian couples that the carriage of Princess Sophia was waiting to drive them to their homes. As they were leaving, the Russians bowed to Gautier and Sanson, almost apologetically it seemed. Many of the émigrés now in Paris had lost all their possessions when they left Russia and had to live frugally. Gautier knew that Sophia went out of her way to be kind to them, inviting them to the opera and the theatre and dinner parties and putting her carriage at their disposal.

When they were alone Sanson said to Gautier, 'If you were impressed by *Seraglio*, then I hope you will come and see my other new ballet when it is performed.'

'Is it equally impressive, then?'

'In my view it is better; more spectacular and more moving.'

The second ballet, Sanson told Gautier, had never been performed before and the company had been working on it, rehearsing every day, ever since they had arrived in Paris. The setting would be ancient Egypt and the story was based on legends which went back to the time of Rameses III.

'When will the first performance of this ballet be?'

'Not until the end of this week. Boris does not believe it will

49

be ready until then. He's a perfectionist, you know. But it will be superb when we perform it. I am sure of that.'

The theatre had been almost cleared by this time and all the boxes were empty. In the Châtelet, like most of the other theatres in Paris, electricity had been installed not long previously to replace the gas lamps and as Sanson and Gautier sat there, the house lights were being turned down. Gautier was wondering whether he should continue waiting in the box for Sophia when Sanson made the decision for him.

'Are you taking supper with us tonight?' he asked.

'Well, Princess Sophia invited me to join her for supper.'

'Then you'll be with us. Boris is organising a supper party as he often does after the performances. There'll be a dozen of us, I suppose.'

'Do you know where it is to be held?'

'No, but the others will. Let's go and find them.'

The supper party, they discovered, was to be in a private dining-room of a restaurant near the Madeleine. They found the other members of the party downstairs in the lobby and the fiacres which would drive them to Boulevard Malesherbes were waiting outside the theatre.

Although it was Sophia who would be paying the bill for supper, Ranevsky had taken over the rôle of host and it was he who seated the party when they arrived in the restaurant. He placed Sophia on his right and Bourkin on his left and sent Gautier to sit on the other side of the table opposite him, between Sanson and Elena Karpovna, the ballerina who had danced the leading rôle in the second ballet on the programme that evening.

Unlike the dinner parties in the homes of society hostesses to which Gautier had sometimes been invited, the supper was highly informal. Three or four conversations were being held across the table at the same time, often in raised voices and with a good deal of theatrical gestures. Miming, Gautier had been told, was an indispensable part of a dancer's art and, it seemed, the members of the Ballets Dashkova used it not as a substitute for language but to reinforce it. He found himself trawling in remarks and snippets of conversations from different parts of the room.

'His interpretation of the rôle is grotesque,' one man was saying. 'He dances it with all the élan of a paralytic undertaker.'

'Missia began dancing too late in life of course,' Elena Karpovna was saying to anyone who cared to listen.

'When the orchestra at l'Opéra was asked to play a composition by Stravinsky, they burst out laughing.'

'Are we to be judged only by the number of beats we can manage in an entrechat? Is that all appreciation of ballet means?'

'That journalist was insufferable!' Gautier heard Sophia complaining. 'Finally I had to ask him to leave.'

No introductions had been made, but by listening to the conversations, by deduction and elimination, Gautier was able to identify most of the party. Both of the principal male dancers of the company were there; Bourkin, next to Ranevsky, and Serge Olenine, who had danced the pas de deux with Karpovna that evening. Nicola Stepanova, who had danced the rôle of the sultan's favourite concubine, was seated a few places from Gautier to his left. Critics said that Stepanova, besides being the leading dancer of the Ballets Dashkova, was the greatest ballerina alive.

Like Sanson all the dancers were dressed informally, for they had changed out of their costumes into everyday clothes. Ranevsky was wearing evening dress, for it would have been expected of him when he went on stage at the end of the performance to acknowledge the audience's applause; so was Gautier and so were three other men at the supper party. Gautier had concluded from remarks which Sophia had made to the grey-haired man on her right that he must be Emile Labat, the owner of flour mills who was now helping to finance the ballet company's tour. Another man in evening dress, whom Gautier had met briefly on his first visit to the Châtelet theatre, was Ivan Voynitsky, a Russian composer, who had evidently been commissioned to write the music for Sanson's new Egyptian ballet. The remaining man, also a guest, looked familiar to Gautier, but it was Sanson who, without being asked, revealed his identity.

'Do not expect our beautiful Karpovna to pay much attention to you, my friend,' he said.

'Why do you say that?'

'Don't misunderstand me. She is not unfriendly, but as you can see her attention is being monopolised by the aristocrat on her right, the Comte de Tréville.'

Gautier glanced past Karpovna towards the Comte, surprised that he had not recognised him. For many years Comte Edmond de Tréville had been one of the young lions of Paris society. As a bachelor and a descendant of a family ennobled by Louis Quatorze, he had been in great demand as a dinner guest, monopolised attention at soirées in the best salons, fought duels with the husbands he had cuckolded and for that reason been blackballed by the Jockey Club, a distinction in itself. Then the Comte had married a rich American, heiress to a fortune made in the new automobile industry. With her money he had built a splendid palace of a home and filled it with paintings and tapestries and fine furniture, but the marriage had not lasted long. In addition to his many other talents, the Comte was a successful and inexhaustible womaniser. Eventually the Comtesse had tired of his unending succession of affairs – with her friends, actresses, even the pretty little modistes who brought her new hats to the house – thrown him out of the home and divorced him.

Since then the Comte had seemed to go into a decline. Alone and impoverished, he had exhausted not only his credit with his tailor, but his credit of goodwill with friends and admirers. Now his name was seldom mentioned in society or in the newspapers, which some would think was the ultimate humiliation.

'The Comte is besotted with Karpovna,' Sanson explained, 'and she seems attracted to him. One cannot understand what she sees in such an ageing lecher.'

Since the Comte could not have been much more than a year or two older than Sanson, the description of him seemed unreasonably cruel and Gautier wondered whether there might be a motive for the malice. Was Sanson himself perhaps in love with Karpovna, besotted with her as he would express it, and for that reason jealous of the attentions which the Comte de Tréville was paying her? Untidy in his person and with unkempt hair and a straggling beard, Sanson did not seem like an ardent lover, but one could never be certain.

Then Gautier reminded himself that he should not be so ready to question a person's motives. Speculating on the reasons behind the actions and even the casual remarks of other people was becoming a habit for him and one which he must break. Speculation could easily become suspicion and suspicion, although part of the essential armoury of any good police officer, could easily filter into one's personal relationships, undermine and then destroy them.

'It is the behaviour of men like the Comte,' Sanson said censoriously, 'that has given us Frenchmen a reputation as compulsive fornicators, a reputation which we do not deserve.'

'Are you French then?' Gautier asked.

'Certainly. My family comes from Normandy.'

'I had assumed you were Russian. So many of your colleagues in the ballet speak such faultless French.'

'No, I am French. Although I have lived in Russia for the greater part of my life.' Sanson's father, he told Gautier, had been an architect who had left France to work in Russia when Sanson was still a boy. After studying in St Petersburg, Sanson had been engaged to design stage sets at the Maryinsky Theatre where he had been introduced to ballet. Then some three years previously he had been invited by Boris Ranevsky to join the ballet company which he was forming.

'And you have been working together ever since?'

Gautier's question appeared to provoke memories which were unwelcome to Sanson. His reply was almost surly. 'No, we had a disagreement and I resigned, but after a few months Boris persuaded me to rejoin the company. He said that they could not manage without me.' Then as though he felt he should justify this last remark, Sanson added, 'I think I can say without boasting that much of our success in Paris is due to me.'

'I'm sure that's true.' Gautier was not merely being polite, for he had heard Sophia express the same view.

As the evening passed, the conversation in the room grew louder, the laughter more boisterous. One reason for this might have been the wine which was being poured freely by the waiters, but it was also, Gautier decided, a symptom of the gregarious and uninhibited nature of the Russians. Just once was the noisy enjoyment interrupted and then only briefly. One place at the table had not been filled and neither the place setting nor the chair had been taken away by the waiters, which suggested that one more guest was still expected at the supper party.

The meal was more than half over when the missing guest arrived and when she appeared, the effect was dramatic. Without exception everyone stopped talking to look at her. She was a striking woman certainly, tall and slender and with hair the colour of copper. Her face was not beautiful but it compelled attention, with eyes that had been made up to seem even more enormous than they were and skin that could not have been whiter. Although the silence which greeted her was only momentary, Gautier sensed an immediate change in the atmosphere. He could not be sure whether it was hostility she had provoked or admiration. Sophia perhaps also sensed an awkwardness or constraint among the others in the room, for she was the first to break the silence.

'Missia!' she said, rising from her chair and holding out her arms in welcome. 'We had almost given you up for lost!'

'My dear, the Princesse de Polignac insisted on taking me to see her home. She kidnapped me! I only escaped by pretending to have the vapours.'

'You should avoid that woman,' Sanson said. 'She is not to be trusted.'

'Alex knows all the secrets of the French aristocracy,' Olenine remarked.

'I hope not!' the Comte de Tréville said and everyone laughed.

'Come and sit down, Missia,' Sophia said. 'The waiter will bring you some of those delicious quails' eggs and in the meantime you can drink a glass of champagne.'

'I'm sorry we have no lilies.' Stepanova's remark held no more than a hint of spite.

'The French newspapers printed a story that Missia will only drink champagne out of madonna lilies,' Karpovna explained to Gautier.

'Who is she?'

'Missia Gomolka. She joined the company only a few weeks before we came to France. She is Polish by origin and fabulously rich. She has ambitions to be a dancer.'

Ranevsky had been watching Missia's arrival with cynical boredom. One had the impression that he was preoccupied with other, more important matters and from time to time he had glanced at Gautier, as though there were some remark he wanted to make. Eventually, after Missia had settled herself in the empty chair and champagne had been poured for her, he leant across the table.

'Well, Inspector. How is your Judge Prudhomme?'

'As well as can be expected, as they say in hospitals.'

'Has he changed his mind and decided not to press for legal proceedings?'

'Not as far as I know. And in my opinion he is unlikely to be frightened into doing so by the out-of-work actors whom you hired.'

Ranevsky's questions had been put with a contemptuous hauteur. Now the sneer vanished and his face was twisted with a malice which not even his most talented dancers could have mimed.

'In that case,' he said, 'perhaps the judge needs a more intimidating warning.'

7

'My word, Inspector! I'm most impressed!'

'These are the weapons that were stolen from you, then?'

'Two of them, yes, definitely.'

The Earl of Newry took one of the two pistols which Gautier was holding and raised it, arm outstretched, as though he were going to fire it. He was an enormous man with red hair and a face that looked as though it had been carved out of a wall of rock and came to life only with geniality.

'These are a pair of flintlock pistols which belonged to my ancestor, the second earl. Where did you find them?'

'Lying in a clump of shrubs in the park behind your apartment.'

'My word! I would never have thought of looking there.' The Earl took the second pistol from Gautier. 'They are collectors' pieces, you know, and really rather valuable.'

'I understand other weapons were stolen as well.'

'Yes, two modern nine millimetre revolvers. You have not found them, I suppose?'

'No. But the park is still being searched.'

The Earl of Newry was living in a large, ground-floor apartment with a garden which backed on to Parc Monceau. Breaking into it had been all too simple. The conservatory at the back of the apartment had glass doors leading into the garden and breaking one pane had been enough.

'The glass has been replaced already,' the Earl told Gautier, pointing at the glass doors. 'A man came round and fixed it in a matter of hours. My word, you French are resourceful! Back home in Ireland we would have had to wait for a week, a month even, to get that done.'

'One can have anything done quickly in France,' Gautier agreed, 'provided one is prepared to pay.'

'My word, that's true!'

The Earl spoke execrable French. Gautier, who had only a few words of English, could scarcely reproach him for that, but some of the Earl's French puzzled him. Several times he had used the expression 'My word', translating it literally into French, and Gautier wondered whether it was meant to have any special significance. An Englishman's word, he had been told, was his bond, a guarantee of integrity. On the other hand the Earl, being Irish, would probably be a Catholic and he might be referring to the Word Made Flesh, in the same way as Frenchmen sometimes called on the Mother of God. Gautier decided it would be an interesting point to discuss with his friends at the Café Corneille.

'What else was stolen in the burglary?' he asked.

'A sizable sum in cash, gold francs mostly. The safe had been forced open, you see. In addition the thieves took a number of valuables; small items of silver, gold ornaments and jewellery. My housekeeper, Claire, made a list for the local police. I'll ask her if she has a copy she can give you.'

They were in the drawing-room of the apartment and the Earl went and tugged on a bell-pull that hung from one wall. Gautier thought that he should at least see the list of the stolen property, even though the chances of recovering any of the items were small. The burglary was clearly the work of a professional criminal, who had selected the items to take knowledgeably and would dispose of them professionally, not in any of the disreputable pawnshops in Paris, but through receivers of stolen property who knew their business. He was uneasy about the missing revolvers though.

'Were any bullets stolen with the revolvers?' he asked the Earl.

'No, but they can easily be bought.' As the Earl was replying a girl came into the room, in answer to his ring Gautier assumed. 'This is my housekeeper, Mademoiselle Claire Ryan.'

The girl smiled at Gautier. He saw then that she was not a girl but a woman of perhaps thirty, whose youthful face and figure had misled him. What struck him immediately was her extraordinary resemblance to the Earl. Her features were quite unlike the Earl's, not as prominent and not as chiselled, but the colour of her hair, the way she held her head and the humour in her eyes were startlingly the same. When the Earl asked her if she had a copy of the list of stolen property, she crossed to a writing desk on the other side of the room and fetched one.

'What I cannot understand,' the Earl remarked, 'is why they did not take more of my gun collection. Several of the fowling-pieces and shotguns in the case are extremely valuable.'

'I imagine because they would have been too heavy and awkward to carry,' Miss Ryan suggested.

'Then why did they throw the two pistols into the bushes?'

'Perhaps because when they had left the house and had time to examine them, they realised that they were museum pieces and impossible to fire.' Miss Ryan's manner when she spoke to the Earl was that of a kindly parent explaining something to a not very intelligent child.

'My word! That's very shrewd of you, Claire. I would never have thought of that.'

'It would be helpful,' Gautier told them, 'if you could tell me where in the apartment all the stolen items were kept.'

'The guns were in a glass display case in my study,' the Earl replied, 'the cash in the safe. If you wish, Claire will show you round all the rooms which the burglars visited.'

'If it is not too much trouble.'

'Of course not.'

'If you don't mind, Inspector,' the Earl said, 'I'll leave you in Claire's hands. I have an appointment at the Jockey Club shortly.'

'It was kind of you to give me so much of your time.'

'In any case it will be better if you deal with Claire over the matter of the robbery. As you will have noticed, Inspector, she speaks excellent French.'

When the Earl had left the room, Miss Ryan said to Gautier, 'You must forgive the Earl for leaving you. It is not that he thinks this robbery is unimportant, but he has only just been elected to the Jockey Club and he is delighted. He believes it is a great honour which the French have paid him.' She smiled tolerantly. 'He goes to the club every morning and spends the whole day there with his new friends.'

She began showing Gautier the places in the drawing-room from which articles had been stolen. They were few in number; a carriage clock from the mantelpiece, a gold filigree basket containing tiny gold and enamel eggs from a Louis XV table by one wall, two miniatures by an eighteenth-century Italian artist from a glass corner cabinet. One could understand why nothing else had been stolen from the room, for although it was crowded with pictures, bric-à-brac and ornaments, most of them were of little value and many of them banal and even vulgar.

From the drawing-room Miss Ryan took Gautier to the dining-room, then to the study and finally to the Earl's bedroom. The safe in the study from which money was missing appeared to have been opened without being forced and the glass case, in which the pistols had been kept together with several shotguns, had not been locked. The stolen jewellery, which consisted of the Earl's gold watch, gold cuff-links and dress studs, had been kept in a drawer of his dressing table. In Gautier's opinion the Earl of Newry had been careless with his possessions to the point of folly.

As they made their tour of the apartment, he asked Miss Ryan about the household. The Earl was a widower, he learnt, and besides Miss Ryan he had three servants to look after him; a cook, a maid and a manservant who combined the duties of butler, footman and valet. The cook came in daily and the other two lived on the premises. If the Earl entertained, the maid's brother would come to help wait at the table. By the standards of Paris society it was a modest household.

Gautier knew from the report on the robbery which he had received from the local police commissariat that it had been committed on the previous Sunday evening, at a time when there had been no one in the apartment. Miss Ryan told him that the Earl had been dining with friends that evening and she had been visiting an old schoolfriend who lived in Passy. The maid was always allowed to spend Sunday afternoons and evenings with her parents.

'Where was the manservant?' Gautier asked her.

'Walking the two dogs. He was only away for forty-five minutes, he says.'

'That was very convenient for the thieves,' Gautier commented.

'Are you suggesting that François may have been implicated in the robbery in some way?'

'Not necessarily. The thieves may have been watching the house. How long has the Earl been living in Paris?'

'For almost a year now.'

'That would be more than enough for criminals to reconnoitre the apartment as a possible target for a well-planned

58

burglary. Its position backing on to Parc Monceau makes it very vulnerable.'

'And so does its owner's carelessness.'

'I did not say that.'

'I know, but that is what you are thinking.' Miss Ryan laughed. Her laugh was rich and full, a Celtic laugh. Gautier had heard laughs like hers in Brittany, where the people were also Celts. 'Tell me, mademoiselle, if it is not impertinent to ask, why did the Earl come to live in Paris?'

'To economise.'

'Are you saying that life is less expensive here than in Ireland?'

'It is for the Earl. At home he has an estate to maintain, a large, cold baronial house and farm workers whose cottages always seem to need repair. He is weighed down with obligations.'

'He has come here to escape those obligations, then?'

Gautier knew that he should not have asked the question, for it was needlessly aggressive and bordered on insolence. He had asked it on a sudden impulse, wanting to see what reaction it would provoke in Miss Ryan. Her Celtic temper flared immediately. 'You have no right to suggest that! The Earl has always honoured his commitments and he always will, whatever the cost.'

Miss Ryan's answer, it seemed to Gautier, was illogical but he had always heard that the Irish were an illogical race, so he made no comment; nor did he ask her any more questions. The burglary was neither unusual nor particularly intriguing but untidy and he distrusted untidiness. Explanations were required but Miss Ryan was not the person to question, for her answers might be coloured by her loyalty to the Earl. Even in the few moments that they had been together he had sensed an unusually strong bond between her and the Earl. He could not help speculating on whether it might be the bond of a relationship far closer than that of employer and servant.

That afternoon Gautier and Surat crossed to the Right Bank and boarded a horse-drawn omnibus, heading for the 20th arrondissement. Horse-drawn omnibuses were rapidly vanishing from Paris, replaced by the faster though less reliable motor omnibuses. Gautier had suggested that they travelled by one, partly because it was a fine afternoon and they would have more time to enjoy the sunshine, but also to humour Surat, who had an almost pathological distrust of the internal combustion engine.

59

Monsieur and Madame Lebrun lived in an apartment on the upper floor of a building in Rue des Pyrénées which, though sombre and unwelcoming in appearance, seemed to be well maintained and clean. When Gautier and Surat arrived, the concierge came out of her lodge by the entrance to meet them. She was a stout woman whose listless eyes and mottled complexion suggested that she had long ago found an anaesthetic for the faded hopes of youth and the disappointments of middle age.

'I wondered when you flics would be along,' she said when Gautier had explained who they were. 'Come to take them away again, I suppose.' She looked out into the street. 'Where's the wagon?'

'We wish to talk to you, madame.'

'With me?'

'Privately.'

The concierge shrugged her shoulders. That the police could be obtuse as well as perverse was a fact of life. 'Come on in, then.'

They followed her through a bead curtain into the room where she spent her days, as well as a substantial portion of her evenings, watching visitors as they came and left and taking messages and parcels for the tenants of the building. Although the furniture in the room was dilapidated and the carpet threadbare, it might have had a certain air of inviting comfort, had it not been pervaded by a smell of stale wine.

'You should never have let them out of prison,' the concierge told Gautier.

'Like everyone they have a right to their freedom until it has been proved that they committed a crime.'

'My other tenants do not like having them around since they killed that baby.'

'We do not know that they did.'

'Who else could have done?'

'That is what we are here to find out. For a start, you can tell me how many apartments there are in this building.'

'Ten including Monsieur Lebrun's. None of them is large.'

'Are they all occupied?' The concierge said they were, so Gautier asked, 'Do you know which of the tenants were in the building last Saturday afternoon when the child was killed?'

'How could I possibly know that?' The woman was becoming truculent. 'I am not paid to spy on the tenants.'

'Then I'll put the question another way. Would you know if one of the tenants came into or left the building?'

'Not every time, but in most cases, yes. Very often they pass the time of day or even come in for a chat.'

'And if a stranger came into the building would you notice him?'

'That is what I'm paid for.'

'But you saw no one last Saturday afternoon? No one behaving in a suspicious way?'

'No one.'

'You told the police that you saw Madame Lebrun as she went out to shop for food that afternoon. At what time was that?'

'How can you expect me to know that? People come and go all the time.' The questions were exasperating the woman. She pointed at a clock which stood on a table in her room. 'As you can see, my clock is not working and they refuse to supply me with another one.'

'Very good, madame. That is all we wish to know for the present but we shall probably wish to speak with you again.'

Gautier and Surat climbed three flights of stairs to reach the Lebruns' apartment. On the way they met no one and Gautier was struck by the silence in the building. They heard no children crying, no dogs barking, no banging of pots and pans, no voices raised in anger. The tenants of the apartments, it appeared, were either unusually staid or unusually secretive.

When Marie-Louise Lebrun opened the door to their knock, she was wearing an apron and the smell from her kitchen suggested that she was in the middle of the week's baking. She appeared embarrassed that they should have found her working and, after taking them to the living-room, she excused herself. As Gautier had expected, the living-room was simply furnished with few ornaments, but in a bookcase opposite him he saw forty or fifty books, most of them old and some bound in leather. This, he realised, must be the collection of books of which Lebrun had spoken.

Marie-Louise returned, having taken off her apron, and she told them that her husband was at his bookstall. His influenza was only marginally better, but he had arranged to meet one of his regular customers that day, a gentleman for whom Lebrun would put aside any books that came his way on subjects which he knew interested him.

'Does your husband have many such clients?' Gautier asked.

'More than you would probably expect. They are collectors mainly and ask Jacques to help them find books on subjects in which they have a special interest.'

She was clearly proud of her husband's professional knowledge. They had met, she told Gautier, when she was working as a shop assistant in the store A La Samaritaine, which was near the Seine. Whenever she could find the time, she would walk along the river, looking at the stalls of the *bouquinistes*. Lebrun had noticed her interest in his books and had encouraged it. Gautier let her talk on about her husband and their life together, prompting her from time to time with questions, for he wanted to understand why it was that both of them had confessed to killing their child, although he was almost convinced that neither of them had done so.

'How well do you know the other tenants in this building?' Surat asked her, wishing to steer their conversation back to issues more relevant to the murder.

'Some are friends, some we scarcely know. They are all good people.'

'Do you recollect meeting any of them when you were leaving the building to go to the shops that afternoon? On the stairs for example?'

'No.' Madame Lebrun looked at Surat in astonishment. 'Surely you do not believe that any of them could have killed our baby?'

'What I wish to establish is what time it was when you went out and whether anyone saw you leaving. We have asked the concierge, but her replies are vague to say the least of it.'

Madame Lebrun hesitated and then said, reluctantly it seemed, 'That may have been because she had been drinking that afternoon.'

'What makes you think that?'

'She had a friend with her, a man. I don't know who he is, but he has been coming to see her quite often recently and they usually take a glass together.'

'And was he still with the concierge when you returned from the shops?'

Madame Lebrun thought for a moment. 'I don't think so. No, I am sure he must have gone by then.'

When Gautier and Surat left the apartment a few minutes later and went downstairs, they found the concierge in her lodge, filling a glass with red wine from a large enamel jug which she must have had concealed behind her armchair. She did not have time to hide what she was doing and looked at them defiantly.

'When I asked you earlier, madame,' Gautier said to her sternly, 'you told me you saw no one in the building last Saturday afternoon other than your tenants.'

'That is true.'

'And what of the man who was seen in this room?'

'You asked me whether I had seen any strangers. Jules is not a stranger. He is a friend.'

'What was he doing here?'

'Visiting me. He drops in for a chat most days when he is passing.'

'For a chat? Or a drink?'

'Sometimes for a drink. There is no harm in that.'

'What is his other name?'

'I only know him as Jules.' Gautier's question might have embarrassed the concierge, for she began to bluster. 'We don't carry visiting cards in this quartier, you know.'

'Tell me about him.'

By persistent questioning Gautier and Surat prised the truth out of the woman and found the facts meagre. No, she had not known Jules for long. She could not say exactly for how long, certainly not a matter of weeks. He had come to the apartment building one day looking for an old friend, he said, whom he was sure lived in that quartier. The concierge had not been able to help him, but they had begun chatting. Jules was sympathetic. He had looked in again the following day, bringing a bottle of wine for her to thank her for her kindness. Of course she had to ask him to have a glass with her. Jules had seemed to like her company even though she was older than he was and he had taken to dropping in most days. On Saturday he had even brought a bottle of calvados. She had always liked the taste of calvados, didn't everybody? When Surat asked her if Jules had ever been in the building and gone up to any of the apartments, she grew truculent.

'Why should he have? He doesn't know any of the tenants.'

'But did he?'

'I don't know. He may have taken a parcel up to one of the apartments, just to oblige me. My legs are no longer as young as they were, you know.'

When Gautier and Surat were walking along the street after

leaving the building, Surat remarked, 'She's a slovenly woman, that one. Did you notice that she was wearing carpet slippers? I wonder how that Jules could bear to sit and drink with her.'

'I agree,' Gautier replied. 'And I wonder also whether she will ever see him again.'

8

That evening, unexpectedly, Gautier met the Comte de Tréville again. Madame Labat was holding a soirée in her home and, at Ranevsky's supper party the previous evening, her husband had asked Princess Sophia and Gautier if they would like to go. Although the invitation had come so late – many would think discourteously so – they had accepted. Monsieur Labat deserved some acknowledgement for agreeing to support the Dashkova Ballet and a princess among the guests would add lustre to his wife's soirée.

Gautier was alone when the Comte approached him, for Sophia had been taken by their hostess to say kind words to a young Greek pianist who had played for the guests. Immediately he began talking about the ballet.

'What did you think of Elena Karpovna?' he asked Gautier.

'She is extremely talented.'

'You really think so?'

'I'm no judge, but I thought her dancing in that first ballet yesterday evening was most moving.'

The Comte was delighted. 'And do you find her beautiful? No, that is an absurd question. Elena is not beautiful.'

'She is certainly very attractive.'

'Agreed, but that is not the same. Elena is beautiful to me, but that is because I have invested her with beauty.' The Comte realised that he was puzzling Gautier and went on, 'Allow me to explain. You know of course that I am a great admirer of women?'

'Well, you do have a certain reputation.'

'I know that! How do they describe me? The Casanova of Paris? A philanderer? Incorrigible womaniser? Lecher even.' Gautier remembered that Sanson had called the Comte just that, but had also added an adjective which was hardly flattering. 'My taste in women is catholic, some would say undiscriminating. Have you ever wondered why?'

'Everyone has his own taste.' Gautier knew the answer was lame, but he would hardly tell the Comte that he had never given the man's obsession with women so much as a passing thought.

'The reason is this, my dear friend. I have an extraordinary power of imagination. I can see an attraction in almost every woman, even when she has none. In my imagination she becomes beautiful or seductive or graceful or intelligent, very often all of these. Do you know which women attract me most? The ones I never even meet; anonymous women, girls one sees passing in the street, behind a shop counter, in the back row of a troupe of dancers in the music hall. My imagination creates fantasies about them, investing them with all those qualities that attract me most, until they seem irresistible. I feel an urge to follow them, meet them, savour the delights of their bodies or their minds, seduce them, make them my own.'

'And what happens then?' The Comte's analysis of his erotic adventures was beginning to fascinate Gautier. 'How do these encounters end?'

'Usually I do not pursue them. There are limits to a man's time and energy' – the Comte smiled disarmingly – 'and to his purse. But when I do meet these women I have to admit things almost always end badly. Not at once, you understand, but eventually the fascination with which I have invested them has gone, slipping away almost unnoticed like leaves in autumn, leaving only the stark unloveliness of the tree.'

'And will this happen with Karpovna?'

'Karpovna?' The Comte seemed amazed at the question. 'With Elena it is different. Surely you can see that? I shall never tire of her. And she needs me. She needs help.'

'What kind of help?'

'She is being shamefully treated by that scoundrel Ranevsky. Although she is a much more talented ballerina than Stepanova, Ranevsky refuses to accept the fact. The best rôles are always reserved for Stepanova.'

'Has she complained?'

'No, complaining is not in her nature, but she deeply resents the injustice and is very unhappy.' The Comte looked at Gautier for a moment as though trying to decide whether he was ready for his next question. 'You could help the poor girl, Inspector, if you would.'

'In what way?'

'You have influence with Princess Sophia. Speak to her on Elena's behalf.'

'I really feel that I should not interfere.'

Reluctant to accept a refusal, the Comte continued trying to persuade Gautier that he should intercede with Sophia. He obviously believed passionately in Karpovna's talent and that she was being unjustly treated.

'More than anything she wishes to dance the leading rôle in the new Egyptian ballet which the company will be performing for the first time. Both Stepanova and she have been rehearsing it, but even though Sanson, who created the ballet, believes that Elena is more suited to the leading rôle, it will be given to Stepanova for the première.'

The Comte persisted in his importuning and Gautier was relieved when Madame Labat put an end to it by announcing that the Greek pianist would perform again, this time playing two pieces by Chopin. During the recital he looked around him, curious to see who had been invited to the soirée. Madame Labat's aspirations as a hostess in Paris society were relatively recent. Her husband was undeniably very rich and they had bought a fine old house in St Germain, that part of the Left Bank where the aristocracy had traditionally liked to live, but wealth and a magnificent home alone did not provide an entrée to Tout Paris. The Labats had become socially acceptable only when, to everyone's surprise, King Edward VII had accepted an invitation to dine with them during a private visit to Paris. No one knew why. Some claimed to have discovered that twenty years previously the beautiful Clementine Labat had been one of the Prince of Wales's mistresses. Whatever the reason, Madame Labat was now taking the first tentative steps towards becoming a fashionable hostess.

The guests at her soirée that evening reflected the standing of her salon in the eyes of society. They included the statutory sprinkling of writers, poets and musicians, none quite in the first flight; no members of the Académie Française but one or two celebrated artists of the old school, the 'Pompiers' as they were scathingly described by the avant-garde in Montmartre, but who still commanded impressive fees for their portraits. Most of the other guests were, like the Labats themselves, nouveaux riches on the way up or, like the poor Comte de Tréville, aristocrats on the way down.

Gautier wondered, as he had at similar soirées in the past, what he was doing there. On this occasion he had been invited only because of his friendship with Sophia, but over the past year or two he had been finding himself on the guest lists of a number of hostesses for soirées and dinners. Was it because he had become a celebrity in a small way or merely because he was useful for making up numbers, a single man and one who had from time to time been the chosen escort of beautiful and well-connected women? Whatever the reason he knew it had become a matter of speculation and perhaps surprise among his colleagues in the Sûreté and his friends at the Café Corneille.

During the piano recital the Comte had moved away and later Gautier saw him talking animatedly to the daughter of the Duc and Duchesse de Charente. The Duc's daughter was neither a pretty nor a witty girl, but Gautier supposed that she might have already become both in one of the Comte de Tréville's fantasies.

The soirée lasted until later than usual, suggesting that Madame Labat had not yet acquired the finesse that a skilled hostess shows in speeding guests who are staying too long. Sophia and Gautier were among the earlier leavers, Sophia saying that she was tired, although she showed no signs of fatigue. The carriage which, together with a coachman and footman, she had hired for her stay in Paris was waiting outside the house and as they drove away to cross the Seine, she laid a hand on Gautier's arm.

'You will think me ungrateful for not having thanked you,' she said.

'Thanked me? For what?'

'Boris has heard nothing more about the ridiculous business with the sword-stick. That can only be because you have used your influence as I asked you to.'

'The matter has not been settled yet. Judge Prudhomme is still demanding that legal action should be taken against Ranevsky.'

'I am sure nothing will happen. You have arranged it.'

Gautier sighed with resignation. Sophia seemed certain that he had the power to protect Ranevsky and he could not see how he could convince her otherwise.

'Would you like to spend the night with me at my hotel, chéri?' she asked, directly and without coyness.

'That would give me great pleasure.' Gautier knew that the

invitation was not a reward for the favour which she thought he had done her.

Sophia laughed, mocking him. 'What a reply! So French!'

'Why French?'

'So formal, so polite!'

'What did you expect?'

'A little passion at least.'

'Why waste passion on words? We can have all the passion we want later.'

They did. When they were alone in her bedroom she took her clothes off, without fuss and rapidly. Other women Gautier had known took an age to rid themselves of voluminous skirts, layers of underskirts and garments for which he could see no practical purpose. Sophia was stripped before he was and, as always, she was ready to make love, needing no stimulation. Nor was there any artifice in her. She simply gave herself to him and at once they were in harmony, their separate consciousness seeming to merge as their bodies did, reaching fulfilment explosively and together.

When the first frenzy was spent, she lay beside him, her head on his shoulder and began to talk. That was a good sign, meaning that they would make love again. Often after they had made love she would fall asleep, instantly like a child does and still in his arms. This time her curiosity needed satisfying first.

'You and the Comte de Tréville had a long, earnest discussion this evening.'

'Too long and too earnest for me.'

'I hope he was not encouraging you to share his debaucheries.'

'Nothing so interesting. He talked only of ballet.'

'So? You don't find ballet interesting?'

'I do, but not the Comte's preoccupations with ballet dancers.'

He gave Sophia a brief summary of what the Comte had told him about the rivalry between the two principal ballerinas of the Dashkova Ballet. Sophia listened to him and then commented, 'The Comte exaggerates. I know Karpovna is jealous of Stepanova, but it isn't true that she is being unfairly treated. Technically she is as good a dancer, but she does not have Stepanova's range of expression. I am very fond of Karpovna. She is a tremendously loyal person, loyal to her friends and to the company, but alas, like so many dancers she is highly-strung and neurotic. She is also very ambitious. I hope she doesn't do something foolish.'

'What might she do?'

'I don't know; walk out perhaps, resign from the company.'

'One supposes that these rivalries are inevitable in a ballet company, just as they are in the theatre. We are always reading of the jealousy between Bernhardt and Duse.'

'They are common enough, I agree, but in our company matters are made worse by Boris. He has his favourites and makes no attempt to hide the fact. And should he be crossed or spurned, he either goes into a sulk or a passion of rage. It is very unsettling for the others.'

'Last night at supper I formed the impression that Missia is not popular with the other dancers.'

'She isn't. They feel that she is no more than a gifted amateur and has no place in the company. She has not undergone the years of training and practice that the other dancers have.'

'How did she come to join the company?'

'One might say that she bought her way in. She made Boris a loan at a time when he was in pressing financial difficulties. He does not believe that she will ever be good enough to dance anything except very minor parts, but he tolerates her. Missia is content with the arrangement, at least for the time being.' Sophia sighed. 'Managing a ballet company requires a great deal of tact and diplomacy.'

'From what I have seen of your company they seem amiable enough.'

'They are, but unreliable. Often they behave like children. For example this afternoon Bourkin failed to attend rehearsal. He has not explained why. If it had been any other dancer Boris would have disciplined him. As it is—' She shrugged her shoulders. 'Every tour has its share of problems, but at times I wonder whether someone is not deliberately trying to create trouble for us.'

9

Early next morning Gautier walked to Sûreté headquarters again, following the same route as he had on Sunday, through the Tuileries gardens and down to the Seine. This time though, as it was not a Sunday, Paris was far from asleep. Tradesmen were out with their carts selling food and produce and servants, hearing their cries, came out into the streets to buy.

He was sleeping with Sophia every two or three nights now and he was sure that had he asked if he might move in to live with her in her hotel suite, she would have agreed. But he had not suggested it and, so far, neither had she. Sophia attracted him more than any woman he had met for years and the attraction was much more than simply physical. They seemed to share an unusual rapport, a meeting of minds and views and tastes that were perfectly matched. Yet he felt himself holding back from entering into too close and too binding a relationship, some inner force which he could not analyse or identify restraining him. He did not know how he would respond if Sophia did ask him to move into her suite. A man needed sex and companionship, but he also needed nights when he could sleep alone.

When he reached his office at the Sûreté, he busied himself with the papers that lay on his desk waiting for his attention. Most of them were of trifling importance and he worked through them leaving to the last a report on the Lebrun case. The previous day, after returning from visiting Madame Lebrun, he had sent two police officers to the quartier in which she lived. Their instructions were to go from door to door and from shop to shop, making enquiries about the concierge's friend Jules.

Gautier wished to know who the man was, where he came from, where he was lodging and what, if anything, he did for a living. He reasoned that even if Jules did not live in the quartier, he had been a regular visitor and so someone would remember having

71

seen him. The humbler quartiers of Paris where working people lived were small, tribal communities. Everyone knew everyone else and their relatives and their business. They helped each other, lent each other money, married each other and treated strangers with almost as much suspicion as they treated the police.

The report of the policemen who had made the enquiries might have seemed disappointing to some, for it was as meagre in facts as the concierge had been when Gautier questioned her. Several people remembered seeing a man resembling the description of Jules in the quartier and other tenants of the building recalled seeing him with the concierge, every day for the past week or so, some said. But no one knew his name and it seemed certain that he was not living locally. Only one person appeared to have spoken to him and that was the owner of a small café where Jules had eaten on a number of occasions. Whenever he had been to the café he had bought drink to take away with him, bottles of wine and once a bottle of calvados. The café owner had found him morose and unwilling to make conversation. Beyond that, all he had noticed was that the backs of Jules's hands had been tattooed and that he spoke with the accent of people from the west of France.

Gautier did not find the report disappointing, for its lack of information was revealing. Little was known about Jules because Jules had wanted it that way. He had not come to the quartier to be noticed and to make conversation and to be remembered. He had come for one purpose only, to kill the Mongol baby of Monsieur and Madame Lebrun. What Gautier had now to discover was why.

After he had read the report, he sent for Surat. Surat had also been sent on an assignment the previous evening and one which was perfectly suited to his talents. Over the years Gautier had found out that Surat had a flair for making friends with ordinary people. He was a good listener and his manner was sympathetic, so people would confide in him, unasked and sometimes to the point of embarrassment. He had spent much of the previous evening in and around Parc Monceau at a time when servants from the households in the area were free from their duties for an hour or two and would go out to the cafés.

'How did you fare on your expedition to Parc Monceau last night?' Gautier asked him when he arrived.

'One might say it was interesting. I came across the Earl of

Newry's manservant and his maid in a nearby café. It seems that they are affianced and will marry shortly.'

'What sort of fellow is this François?'

'I liked him. Too talkative, of course, but honest I would say.'

'What did he talk about?'

'His employer. Servants seldom talk of anything else.'

'Was he complaining?'

'Not at all. He and the maid like the Earl and feel sorry for him.'

'Now that is unusual. The servants of the rich usually feel sorry only for themselves.'

Surat looked at Gautier disapprovingly. 'You must not allow yourself to become cynical, patron. They are good people and they feel sorry for the Earl because they realise he is not well placed financially. For a man of his standing his household is too small and the cook has to work on a very tight budget. In spite of that, they say, the Earl is as generous to them as he can be.'

'What did they say about the burglary?'

'They seemed surprised that anyone should have felt it worth his while to break into the apartment.'

'But the Earl reports that valuable silver and china were stolen.'

Surat shrugged his shoulders. 'François and the maid do not appear to believe so. I suppose there is always the matter of insurance. To have your valuables stolen can be less embarrassing and more lucrative than selling them.'

'Now it is you, old fellow, who is being cynical!'

They continued discussing the burglary. The Earl's home had been left unattended for just long enough to allow the burglar to make his haul and Gautier was curious as to how this had come about. He knew that the British were devoted to pets and to dogs in particular, but any French servants whom he knew would not be enthusiastic about taking dogs walking at any time, certainly not at night. He asked Surat if François or the maid had spoken about the dogs.

'They did. It seems that when François was engaged he was told that his duties would include walking the dogs every day. They are two great red beasts and need exercise, but very friendly, useless as guard dogs. François says he has become quite fond of them.'

'How long has he been with the Earl?'

'Only for just over two weeks. The previous manservant left and the maid was able to secure the position for François.'

'Do we know why the man left?' Gautier asked. Discontented servants sometimes revenged themselves on their former employers.

'He found a better position. It was quite amiable.'

'Does François often walk the dogs at night?'

'Always. At ten o'clock precisely. The Earl insists on that.'

Surat left and Gautier began preparing his own reports for the Director General on the cases which he was investigating. He kept the report on the death of the Lebrun baby short. Even though it was a case of murder, Courtrand was not likely to take any great interest in the affair, because it involved ordinary working people. On the other hand he would insist on knowing that everything possible was being done to solve the robbery at the Earl of Newry's home and to recover his property. Gautier preferred it that way. He wished to postpone the appointment of a *juge d'instruction* in the Lebrun case for as long as he could, so that he would have a free hand to conduct his own enquiries.

When he had finished the reports he took them up to the Director General's office where, to his surprise, he found that Courtrand had already arrived. Another surprise was that Courtrand was in an unusually jovial mood. The reason for his good humour was the arrival that morning of an invitation for the Director General and Madame Courtrand to dine at the home of the Minister for Justice. Courtrand had never before been honoured in that way and not even the fact that his wife insisted on having a new dress made for the occasion was allowed to infect his good spirits.

He read the reports and then, as Gautier had expected, put the report on the Lebrun affair to one side without comment. After reading the report on the burglary at the Earl of Newry's home for a second time, he asked Gautier, 'What exactly is an earl? Obviously it is a title of some importance, but what standing does an earl have?'

'I believe that in Britain an earl ranks immediately below a duke.'

'Then he would be more important than an ordinary English milord?'

'So I understand.'

'You see, Gautier, even the English nobility come to us for help!'

Gautier restrained a smile. Courtrand might find satisfaction in knowing that the privilege of being burgled in Paris was not reserved for the French or the poor, but he did not suppose that the Earl of Newry would share that view. They were discussing the burglary and the prospects of recovering the Earl's property when Corbin came into the room from his office next door.

'I apologise for disturbing you, Monsieur le Directeur,' he said, 'but I have just been told some news that I am sure you would wish to hear at once.'

'What is it?'

'Judge Prudhomme has disappeared.'

Judge Prudhomme lived in a modest bachelor apartment on the Left Bank in Rue de Grenelle. Like the Earl of Newry, he employed a woman to cook for him and the rest of his needs were attended to by a manservant who lived in the apartment. He could certainly have afforded a larger apartment and a household establishment to match, but Prudhomme had a reputation for being careful with his money, a failing which Gautier had noticed in many bachelors. It had been the manservant, Bernhard, who had gone to the local police commissariat to report the judge's disappearance – there was no telephone in the apartment – and it was he who opened the door to Gautier and Courtrand when they arrived.

'Now what is the meaning of this?' Courtrand demanded at once, as though suggesting that the manservant himself was responsible for Prudhomme's disappearance.

'My master the judge has not come home. We have not seen him since yesterday at midday.'

They were standing at the entrance to the apartment. Courtrand waved the man aside and led the way into the living-room. It was a room that to Gautier seemed both unwelcoming and lacking in personality, a room that might equally well have been lived in by an ascetic or a traveller who used it only as an occasional resting place.

'Did the judge not spend the night here?' Courtrand asked.

'No, monsieur. When I went to his room to rouse him this morning the bedroom was empty and his bed had not been slept in.'

'Then why did you not inform the police at once?'

'I thought he might have spent the night with a friend. He

75

sometimes does.' There was a sly innuendo in the last remark which Courtrand did not appear to notice.

'Perhaps he did just that and has gone straight to his office in the Palais de Justice.'

'The judge would never do that. He would return home to bath and change his linen. That was his habit. In fact I had put the bath ready in his room to fill with water as soon as he returned home.'

Courtrand snorted contemptuously. One could not be sure whether it was because he disbelieved the manservant or because he was scornful of Judge Prudhomme's fastidious habits. He looked around the room suspiciously as though it might offer up a clue to explain the judge's disappearance.

'Did you say that your master was here at midday yesterday?' Gautier asked Bernhard.

'Yes, monsieur. He returned home for his lunch as usual.'

'Did he say anything which might have suggested that he would not be sleeping here last night?'

'Nothing. He was due to dine with friends in the evening and I laid out his evening clothes ready for him. When I found them there, still laid out, this morning I began to be worried.'

'Then he did not come back here at the end of the day?'

'I cannot say, monsieur. I was not here.'

The man explained that as Prudhomme had planned to dine with friends, he had told the servants that he would not need them that evening. So the cook had gone home and Bernhard had taken the opportunity to go with a friend to a music hall.

'Surely when you returned home you checked to see whether your master was here?' Courtrand asked.

'No, monsieur. I came back earlier than he would have done,' Bernhard replied. Then he added with an insolent smile, 'Also it would have meant looking in his bedroom. I would never do that!'

The insinuation in the remark was that it would be tactless to go to Judge Prudhomme's bedroom at night, because one could never be sure who one would find there. Again, Courtrand either did not understand the innuendo or chose to ignore it. He and Gautier asked the manservant some more questions and then made him show them round the rest of the apartment, but they found nothing which might explain why Prudhomme had not returned home the previous night or where he had gone. Both Bernhard and the cook agreed that there had been nothing, either in their master's manner or in what he had said, that would account for his disappearance.

From Rue de Grenelle Courtrand and Gautier drove in a fiacre to the Palais de Justice. It was not often that they drove anywhere together, but when Courtrand had heard of Judge Prudhomme's disappearance, he had at once decided that he would take charge of the investigation personally. The idea that a judge might have been the victim of a kidnapping or some other brutal crime shocked and enraged him. He was determined to show those who had appointed him to head the Sûreté that he had the ability and the resolution to prevent such an affront to the judiciary and to the law or, if that were now too late, to avenge it. Gautier would have preferred to work alone, for what little talent Courtrand possessed lay in administration, but he took comfort in the knowledge that the man would soon tire of the painstaking and patient routine of a criminal investigation.

At the Palais de Justice, however, the respect which Courtrand's position commanded proved useful. He was able to bypass the network of guards and minor civil servants which a lesser police officer would have had to penetrate one at a time and he and Gautier were taken at once to Judge Prudhomme's office. There they were met by his secretary Pierre Mathurin.

Prudhomme's office was just as austere and cheerless as his apartment, with few concessions to luxury or even comfort, reinforcing the impression which Gautier had formed of him as a man without humour and with very little compassion. The desk was bare except for a silver inkwell and a silver tray with a supply of pens and pencils. The nibs of all the pens were clean, all the pencils freshly sharpened. On one side stood two piles of documents, neatly stacked.

Mathurin answered their questions with precision. The judge, they were told, had returned to his cabinet the previous afternoon after lunch as usual. He was not in court that afternoon, but was studying the dossier of an important case which he was due to try that morning, but which had been postponed when he failed to arrive.

'Did he give you any indication that he might not be here today?' Courtrand asked.

'None. That is what I find so strange. When he left here yesterday afternoon, he told me that he would be here early today, as he had not finished reading the dossier.' Mathurin pointed to the pile of documents on the desk.

'What time did he leave?'

'Unusually early. He was in his office for not much more than an hour.'

'Have you any idea why?'

'No, unless it was because of the letter he received.'

Gautier was instantly alert. Instinct told him that this letter which Prudhomme had received would explain his disappearance. He realised that he had been expecting something of the sort; a letter, a false message, a threat. At the same time he felt a curious and irrational uneasiness.

'What letter?' Courtrand demanded.

'I am assuming it was a letter. It came in an envelope that was delivered by hand.'

The envelope, Mathurin told them, had been delivered to the law courts by a messenger and brought up to the judge's office directly. As far as Mathurin could tell, it contained only a brief note.

'How did the judge behave when he read the note?' Gautier asked.

'What do you mean?'

'Did he show any emotion? Was he surprised? Agitated perhaps?'

Before replying, Mathurin thought for a while. One sensed that he was remembering, trying to recreate in his memory the exact moment when Prudhomme had opened the envelope.

'Surprised? No, I would not say so. He seemed to have been half expecting the letter, but even so there was something in his manner which I find hard to describe. Yes, I suppose you could say that he was agitated.'

'How soon after receiving the note did he leave here?'

'Very soon. He tidied up the papers he was reading and left. I did not connect the letter with his early departure, but now that I think about it I am sure it was the reason for his leaving.'

'Is there nothing more you can say that will help us?' Courtrand was growing impatient. The significance of the letter had escaped him, Gautier decided.

'Nothing, monsieur. The judge took the note with him, leaving only the envelope on his desk.'

'Do you have it?' Gautier asked quickly.

'As a matter of fact I do, or at least I have put it in a drawer of the desk for safe-keeping.'

The envelope which he produced for them had been slit open. Judge Prudhomme's name was written on the face of it in block capitals, which seemed to Gautier curiously immature, the writing of a child or someone of little education. He had one last question to ask Mathurin.

'Has the judge ever received letters like this before?'

'It is very possible, Inspector, although I cannot be certain. A good many letters and notes are sent to him here, from advocates, clients, even friends. People always seem to be in a hurry when they are dealing with judges.'

As they were walking the short distance from the Palais de Justice to Sûreté headquarters, Courtrand appeared to be in a more contented mood than he had been earlier. He remarked to Gautier, 'I think we can assume that there is nothing sinister in this business.'

'Why do you suppose Judge Prudhomme has disappeared then?'

'That note he received must have told him that a relative of his was ill. He has an elderly uncle in Poitiers, I understand.'

'If he has had to go to Poitiers surely he would have told his secretary and his servants that he was going? It would mean his staying there overnight.'

'Then what alternative reason can you suggest for his sudden disappearance?'

'I am inclined to worry about his safety. That note could have been a threat.'

'A threat?'

'On his life; or at least a warning. If it was, he may well have taken fright and gone into hiding. The judge does not strike me as a courageous man.'

Courtrand looked at Gautier sharply. He was not always obtuse and at times could be surprisingly sharp. 'Ah! You are thinking of those Russians!'

'It is a possibility.'

'Mother of God! This is all your fault, Gautier! That man Ranevsky should be behind bars, but you persuaded me otherwise against my better judgement. Well, we'll soon put that right. Have him arrested immediately!'

10

The theatre, its auditorium in darkness, the stage empty except for four figures, without scenery and only partly lit, seemed not so much lifeless as unreal. Sitting alone towards the back of the stalls, Gautier was struck by the incongruity of what was a kind of paradox. That evening with the auditorium full, the make-believe of the ballet would become reality, vital and alive, but now in its emptiness, sounds and voices echoing, the theatre was unreal, a world that had no purpose, no meaning.

On the stage two dancers, Stepanova and Bourkin, were rehearsing sequences of steps which, he decided, must be from the dances of the new Egyptian ballet, soon to be performed in public for the first time. They were being watched and, from time to time, corrected by Alexandre Sanson and another man, the maître de ballet. The orchestra was not present and music was being provided by a pianist on one side of the stage. Gautier noticed that when either of the dancers jumped or leapt, he could hear the thud of their feet landing on the boards of the stage, something he had never noticed during an actual performance.

He had come to the Châtelet not to watch rehearsals but to interrogate Boris Ranevsky. That morning at the Sûreté, after returning from the Palais de Justice, he had managed to persuade Courtrand that Ranevsky should not be arrested. Courtrand had given way only reluctantly even though Gautier's arguments were sound. What charge could be brought against Ranevsky? They had no proof that Judge Prudhomme had been the victim of any criminal act, that he had been abducted or even threatened. Ranevsky could not even be charged over the business of the sword-stick, for Prudhomme was not there to lay a complaint.

Eventually Courtrand had said, 'You will go at once and interrogate him. I insist on that. Show him no mercy, no matter what the Russian ambassador may say, and you may well get a confession out of the scoundrel.'

So, learning that Ranevsky was at the Châtelet, Gautier had come there and been told that the director was in an important meeting, but would see the Inspector when he was free. Rather than waiting in the foyer, Gautier had come into the theatre to watch the rehearsals.

Minutes later he heard a voice behind him. 'Inspector Gautier! How good to see you!'

Looking round he saw Elena Karpovna. She was dressed for rehearsal, in a leotard with a cardigan over her shoulders. Because she was wearing ballet shoes he had not heard her coming down the aisle. As she slipped into the seat beside him, Gautier noticed for the first time how similar she was in build and appearance to the company's other principal ballerina. Both she and Stepanova were dark and tiny, not much bigger than small girls, with Slav faces that seemed prettier at a distance than they really were. He had also noticed that off stage both of them walked with their toes turned out, the result one supposed of their ballet training.

'You have not come here simply to watch us rehearse, surely?'

'No, I fear not.'

'I hoped that perhaps you had become a devotee of the ballet after watching me dance.'

'If anything could fire the thoughts of a dull old man like me,' Gautier replied, 'it would be your dancing.'

'My dancing? Not me?'

'You of course. That goes without saying.' She pinched his arm and he added, 'Sadly I must be honest and confess that I have come to speak with Boris Ranevsky.'

'Have you not found him?'

'He is in a meeting but will see me later.'

'Then his loss is my gain!' She pinched his arm again.

As they watched the rehearsal, Gautier wondered why Karpovna was teasing him flirtatiously. She had showed no particular interest in him when they met at the supper party. He had encountered women before who remained formal and correct in public, but once alone with a man could not resist acting as though they were inviting him into a private world for two.

'Have you been rehearsing too?' He pointed at her leotard.

'Practising and rehearsing. This morning, as I do every morning, I spent three hours doing the exercises that a dancer must do, to retain her form. That was at l'Opéra where they have a properly equipped dance studio. Now I am waiting my turn to rehearse on the stage.'

Gautier nodded towards the two dancers on the stage. 'Is that Alex Sanson's new Egyptian ballet that they are rehearsing?'

'One of the dances from it, yes.'

'Sanson tells me that it will be even more spectacular than *Seraglio*.'

'Not only more spectacular, but more moving and more artistic.' Karpovna was silent for a time, a cloud of gloom darkening her face. 'Did Alex tell you that he created the ballet for me?'

'No. Is that true?'

'It is, but Stepanova will be dancing the principal rôle in the première and again at the gala performance.'

'But you are rehearsing it as well, are you not?'

'Of course. The principal dancers must be able to dance all the leading rôles in the company's repertoire of ballets, in case one of us is taken ill. But we will be giving only two performances of the new ballet while we are in Paris – the première and the gala performance before the President – and Stepanova will dance the leading rôle on both occasions, so inevitably it will become known as her ballet.'

'Who decides these things?'

'Boris ultimately and he always gives in to Stepanova. Alex is most displeased. As I say, he created the ballet for me.'

Gautier had already felt himself being drawn into the life of the Dashkova Ballet. He did not mind that, for he was enjoying learning about the art of ballet and he found the members of the company stimulating. What he did not want was to become involved in the jealousies and intrigues of the dancers, but that was going to be hard to avoid. He tried to think how he could divert their conversation away from the subject of the new ballet.

'Alex seems to be very fond of you,' he remarked.

'He is, and I of him.'

'I hope he will not be jealous when he sees us here together.'

Karpovna laughed. 'Jealous? Alex would never be jealous!'

'I believe he was a little envious of the attention that the Comte de Tréville was paying to you at supper the other night.'

Karpovna made a little noise to show her disbelief, but she still seemed pleased at the idea that she might be the cause of such rivalry. 'Edmond likes to imagine himself as a Casanova, but really he is harmless. In any case Alex would not be jealous. Our relationship is not romantic and certainly not physical. One might say he is an uncle to me, a devoted uncle.' She paused and then added, wistfully it seemed, 'It was not always that way.'

'No?'

'At one time we were lovers. That was in the old days when Boris had just started putting the company together.'

'Before Alex left it?'

'Yes. When he came back things had changed. Alex had changed and so had I. He still loves me but in a different way.'

'Why did he leave the company and then return to it?'

'It's a long story.'

But Karpovna told him the story which, in truth, was not so long. Sanson had left the company after a bitter quarrel with Ranevsky over a new ballet of his. Bourkin had just been recruited to the company and he helped with some of the choreography for the new ballet. When it was performed for the first time Ranevsky, carried away by his infatuation, had it billed in a way that suggested it was entirely Bourkin's creation and gave Sanson no credit at all. Sanson had left the company in a fury and returned to live in France.

'What made him rejoin the company?' Gautier asked.

'Both he and Boris realised that they needed each other. Alex is the finest stage designer alive and yet there is no other ballet company good enough to use his talent. Since he came back the company has been revitalised and every ballet he has created has been a sensational success.'

While they had been talking, Stepanova and Bourkin had stopped dancing and were talking to Sanson. The discussion lasted for some minutes and Gautier could see Sanson emphasising the points he wished to make with gestures and once or twice even with a clumsily executed ballet step. Presently the three of them walked towards the wings.

'I will have to leave you now, Jean-Paul. Olenine and I must take our turn to rehearse.' Before leaving her seat, Karpovna leant over and kissed Gautier lightly on the cheek. 'But we will meet again, will we not? Soon?'

As she walked away, without thinking Gautier touched his cheek. The kiss was not a gesture which any well brought up French girl would have made, but ballet dancers were bohemian, he was realising, and Russian ballet dancers doubly so. Karpovna

83

had taken the trouble to find out his Christian name and no doubt in due course he would discover whether she wished to share only a mild flirtation or some more serious liaison.

Restless and wondering how much longer Ranevsky would keep him waiting and whether he should tolerate it if he did, he left the auditorium and went into the foyer. The staff had not yet arrived to get the theatre ready for the evening's performance and the foyer was deserted, except for a lone watchman asleep in a chair by one of the doors that led out into the street. He had decided that he would wait no longer and was about to wake the watchman up and demand to see Ranevsky, when Michel Puy, the reporter from *La Libre Parole*, came out of the theatre manager's office. When Puy saw Gautier he came over towards him.

'Inspector! Are you waiting for your fairy princess?'

'As it happens no,' Gautier replied ignoring the sneer.

'By the way you were right about the ballet company's finances. It seems that Emile Labat has come to their rescue.'

'He is to be one of the sponsors of the tour, if that is what you mean.'

'Tell your princess to be watchful. Labat is a Jew and Jews as you know expect a return for their money. If he feels she is taking advantage of him, there is nothing he will not do to have his revenge.'

Gautier was not surprised that Puy should choose to attack Emile Labat. *La Libre Parole* was unswerving in its anti-Semitism and had been violent in its denunciation of all those who had supported Captain Dreyfus and eventually secured a pardon for him. So he made no comment.

Instead he asked Puy, 'If, as I suspect, you came here to see Boris Ranevsky, would you be kind enough to tell me where I can find him?'

Puy smiled. 'As always, Inspector, your suspicions are well founded. I have just interviewed Monsieur Ranevsky who told me a very interesting story, which you will learn tomorrow. You will find him in the manager's office.'

After Puy had left the theatre, Gautier went to the manager's office and found Ranevsky studying a pencil sketch of what appeared to be a stage setting. Three or four similar sketches lay on the desk in front of him.

'Inspector Gautier!' Like Puy, Ranevsky appeared to be in a good humour. 'Have you come to arrest me at last?'

'No, monsieur, merely to ask for your help.' Notwithstanding what Courtrand believed, Gautier was sure that Ranevsky was a man who would respond better to politeness than to bullying.

'Evidently the wheels of justice turn slowly in France. In Russia by this time I would be in a dungeon or on my way to Siberia.'

'May I sit down?'

'By all means.' Ranevsky pointed to the chair opposite him. Then when Gautier was sitting down he passed over the sketch he was holding. 'What do you think of this?'

The sketch was, as Gautier had guessed, of a stage setting. The scene was dominated by a temple, its portals flanked by huge pillars, with a river in the background, across which a majestic barge rowed by slaves was approaching the shore. Soldiers in armour stood on each side of the entrance to the temple. The style of the sketch and the figures of the soldiers reminded Gautier of Egyptian wall paintings and frescoes he had seen in the Louvre.

'Is this a scene for your new Egyptian ballet?' he asked Ranevsky.

'Yes. Splendid is it not?'

Gautier looked at the sketch more carefully. Two dancers, a man and a woman, were pictured in the foreground, the ballerina poised in an arabesque, the man with his hands on her waist. The figures of the dancers had been drawn only in outline, but even so, Gautier thought he could see a resemblance between the ballerina and Stepanova. The male dancer, on the other hand, could have been almost anybody.

Ranevsky took the sketch back from Gautier. 'I must not get carried away by my enthusiasm. You did not come here to talk about the ballet, Inspector, I am sure of that.'

'No, monsieur, about Judge Prudhomme.'

'What of him?'

'Have you had any contact with the judge since the incident in your hotel?'

'None. I had expected he might have written to apologise to me.'

Gautier was not surprised by the man's effrontery, for he realised it was in character and was probably one reason for his success as an impresario. 'You have not spoken to the judge then, or sent him messages?'

'What kind of messages?'

'Threats.'

'Why should I threaten the creature? He is beneath my contempt.'

'The demonstration which you arranged outside the Palais de Justice was intended to frighten the judge, to dissuade him from taking legal action against you for assault.'

'That was nothing!' Ranevsky said dismissively. 'No more than a practical joke.'

'And at supper the other evening you made a remark which implied a threat. As I recall you said that the judge needed to be intimidated.'

Ranevsky's expression hardened and Gautier could see that he was beginning to lose his temper. 'This conversation is becoming boring and wearisome. If you have come here to accuse me of an offence, may I know what it is?'

Gautier knew that he was on weak ground. He could not accuse Ranevsky directly of sending Prudhomme a threatening letter which he had never seen and which might not even exist. At that stage he did not even want Ranevsky to know that Prudhomme had disappeared. So instead of answering the question he asked one.

'I would like you to give me a sample of your handwriting, monsieur.'

Immediately Ranevsky was watchful and suspicious. He did not ask, as most others would have done, why Gautier wanted a sample of his writing. Instead he replied brusquely, 'I regret that I do not have one with me.'

'In that case perhaps you would be so good as to provide me with one.'

An inkwell stood on the manager's desk with a glass tray of pens and pencils. Gautier had come prepared with a sheet of plain paper, which he now took out of his pocket, unfolded and laid in front of Ranevsky.

'I'm damned if I will! You have no right to ask it. Who do you think you are dealing with? A common criminal?'

Gautier had begun by treating Ranevsky politely. Now it was time to be firm. 'Monsieur Ranevsky, you have made it clear that you are contemptuous of French justice, but I can tell you this. Should you continue to be obstructive, I have the power to arrest you and, if necessary, to have you expelled from France.'

Ranevsky stared at him, his fury checked only by doubt and a suspicion that Gautier might mean what he was saying. For a man who came from a branch of the Russian aristocracy deference was synonymous with humiliation, but eventually he capitulated, picked up a pen and dipped it in the inkwell.

'What do you want me to write?'

'Simply Judge Prudhomme's name.'

When Ranevsky had finished, Gautier looked at what he had written. The script was large and flowing, the handwriting of an extrovert, confident in himself and in the world's appreciation of his ability. Gautier turned the sheet of paper over and laid it in front of Ranevsky again.

'Would you be so good as to write the name once more? This time in block capitals.'

Unexpectedly Ranevsky smiled. 'You're thorough, Inspector. I'll say that for you.'

Gautier could detect no resemblance between Ranevsky's writing of Prudhomme's name and that on the note which the judge had received. He was neither surprised nor disappointed. In his view writing menacing letters, even supposing that Prudhomme's letter had been menacing, was not Ranevsky's style. He would prefer a more subtle – and a more flamboyant – way of making his point.

'Is that all you want from me, Inspector?'

'For the time being, yes.'

'I am certain that before long this judge of yours will realise that the silly business at the hotel is best forgotten.'

'What makes you so confident?'

Ranevsky smiled, with the condescending arrogance of a man who believed the situation was now under his control. 'You will find that out in due course.'

After leaving the Châtelet theatre, Gautier walked down to the Seine and along the embankment to where the *bouquinistes* had their stalls. He was looking for Jacques Lebrun, for he wished to tell him that he would no longer be in charge of the investigation into the death of the Lebruns' child. That had been the outcome of a decision by Courtrand. The best of the resources and talent of the Sûreté, the Director General had decided, would immediately be concentrated on finding Judge Prudhomme. With some reluctance he had agreed that Gautier might continue to supervise the enquiries into the robbery at the Earl of Newry's home, a concession which recognised the Earl's rank and standing as a distinguished foreigner. In Courtrand's view the murder of the

Lebrun baby, although a criminal act, was a routine, commonplace enquiry on which Gautier should not be allowed to waste too much of his time.

Lebrun was not at his stall, although it was open, its cover removed and books on display, and the *bouquiniste* with the next stall was looking after it. He told Gautier that Lebrun had gone to a café just along the street with a customer for whom he was trying to find early editions of Balzac novels. Gautier thought of following to the café, then changed his mind and was heading for the Sûreté when he saw Claire Ryan. She was standing by the stall of another of the *bouquinistes*, reading a book which she had picked up and was holding in one hand. In her other hand she held a parasol, using it to shield herself from the pale afternoon sunshine. She was wearing a green dress, a rather brighter green than most Frenchwomen would have worn in daytime, and her parasol was of a russet colour. Together they showed off her red hair which one could just glimpse, pinned up beneath her toque hat.

She was standing very still, with the Seine behind her, and for a moment Gautier had the impression that he was looking at a painting, not one by the old school of portrait painters but more colourful and alive, the work of one of the better Impressionists, Degas perhaps or Renoir. He walked towards her and when she saw him, the painting dissolved and came to life.

'Enchanted to see you, mademoiselle. You are a lover of books, then?'

'Not exactly a bibliophile, but I come here sometimes; to browse rather than to buy.'

'What kind of books interest you most?'

Miss Ryan hesitated and Gautier wondered whether the question had embarrassed her. He noticed that she had replaced the book she had been reading quickly and in the back row of those laid out on the stall, in such a way that he could not see its title.

'Almost any kind. I have catholic tastes.'

'What a coincidence meeting you here!'

Miss Ryan smiled at him disarmingly. 'I have to be honest and say that it was not entirely a coincidence.'

'No? How is that?'

'I was looking at the books only as I tried to pluck up the courage to come and see you in your office.'

'Why did that need courage? Am I so forbidding?'

'Not at all, you are very sympathetic. No, it is the Sûreté that makes me nervous. The law, justice, retribution all appear so sinister to me.' Miss Ryan laughed. 'Will you suspect me now as by nature not law-abiding, a potential wrong-doer?'

'Who knows?' Gautier teased her. 'But if you are brave enough to come to my office I guarantee you safe passage.'

'Could we not talk here? Perhaps we might take a stroll by the river.'

'Willingly.'

They left the row of *bouquinistes'* stalls and walked by the Seine, Miss Ryan with her face in shadow beneath her parasol. Gautier remembered being told that red-haired people frequently had very fair skin, which was easily burnt by exposure to the sun. Glancing at her face, he saw that her skin was fair but covered in freckles.

'Now, how can I help you?' he asked her.

'Perhaps it is I who should be helping you.'

'In what way?'

'Yesterday morning you remarked that it must have been very convenient for the thieves to find our apartment unattended.'

'Perhaps "convenient" was not the word I meant to use.'

'I have been thinking that, in fairness to our manservant, François, I should have explained that he has instructions to take the dogs out walking every evening. That is one of his duties. So you should not imagine that he might have taken them out that evening by prior arrangement with the thieves.'

Gautier might have told her that what she had said did not in itself clear François of any involvement in the robbery. Servants who knew that the home in which they worked was left unguarded in the evenings could easily tip off criminals and they frequently did. He made no comment, preferring to wait and hear what else Miss Ryan might have to tell him.

'You should also know that François has only been with us for two weeks.'

'Do you think that is significant?'

'He would not have been able to plan a burglary in such a short time, surely?'

'Do you know where he was employed before?'

'He was in service with a good French family.'

'Why did he leave them?'

'I am told he quarrelled with the family's butler,' Miss Ryan replied and then she added hastily, 'but it was not a serious matter. No dishonesty was involved.'

That appeared to be all the information she had to offer and Gautier was curious. Why had she come to see him? Although she seemed anxious that the police should not believe that François might have been implicated in the robbery at the Earl's home, what she had said did not divert suspicion from him. If anything the reverse was true. In any case she had told him no more than the police already knew. Gautier wondered whether Miss Ryan had somehow found out about Surat's conversation with her servants.

They parted soon afterwards, Gautier finding her a fiacre and helping her into it. She drove away without looking back at him. When he reached his office in the Sûreté, he found a note waiting for him which, he was told, had been delivered by hand less than an hour previously. The note was from Sophia.

Chéri,
I will not be able to have supper with you tonight, as we have decided to hold a meeting of the entire ballet company immediately after this evening's performance. This is needed as there are disciplinary matters which have to be dealt with. You could come round to my hotel later if you wish. I hope you will!
Affectionately, Sophia

After he had finished reading the note, Gautier remembered the envelope which Judge Prudhomme had received which was in his pocket. When he compared it with the envelope in which Sophia's note had arrived, he realised why the writing had seemed familiar. Sophia always addressed envelopes in block capitals and her writing too seemed unusually immature.

11

Judge Prudhomme's body was found that evening in a small hotel near the Gare du Nord. He was lying face down on the floor, a bullet wound in his head and a revolver in his right hand.

Gautier, reconciled to spending the evening alone, was eating in the café in Place Dauphine, after which he planned to return to his apartment where there were several domestic tasks awaiting his attention. He did not mind being alone, for Sophia's return to Paris and the busy social life in which he had become enmeshed were leaving him little time for the kind of thinking that was needed to analyse and disentangle the enquiries for which he was responsible.

The way in which he had become involved in three cases in quick succession had also prevented him from devoting as much thought to planning their investigation as he would have liked. He thought of them as three cases only – the murder of the Lebrun baby, the robbery in Parc Monceau and the disappearance of Judge Prudhomme. In his view the stabbing at the Hôtel Bayonne was a trivial business which need not be treated as a separate investigation. In any case he was satisfied that it must be connected in some way with the sudden disappearance of the judge.

Although he was no longer responsible for investigating the death of the Lebrun baby, he still thought about it. He was convinced that neither of the parents had killed the child, but the problem would be to prove their innocence. Courtrand had reassigned the case to Inspector Lemaire, who was an amiable fellow, and Gautier resolved to speak to him the following morning and tactfully suggest the lines that his enquiries might take. In the meantime he began rethinking his strategy for dealing with the other investigations.

Before he had done much more than review the problems, his plan for an evening of constructive thought and domesticity was

91

demolished. He had scarcely finished his meal when an officer from the Sûreté came looking for him. That he could be found so easily was his own fault, he recognised that, for he had become a man of fixed habits and ate more often than not in the same cafés or restaurants. He did not mind being traced, for domestic tasks could wait and the news that Prudhomme was dead quickened the sense of expectation he had felt when he had learnt of the note that the judge had received at the Palais de Justice.

The Hôtel de Valence, in which Prudhomme's body had been found, was known to the police, not because it was one of the many scores of *hôtels de rendez-vous* in Paris, but because almost all of those who used it for assignations were homosexuals. As in more conventional establishments, a room could be rented there for as long or as short a time as the client required and questions were not asked or answers volunteered. The police kept an unfriendly eye on the hotel, because they suspected that it was being run as a male brothel, providing partners for foreign visitors, particularly from England and Germany, who were not in Paris long enough to find their own. This the authorities could tolerate, but brothels of any type could become breeding grounds for more sinister offences.

When Gautier arrived at the hotel, he was taken by the proprietor to the room where Prudhomme's body had been found. Brunet, the proprietor, was a stout, balding man with an unmistakable Alsatian accent, whose breath and clothes smelt of ether. A uniformed policeman was standing on guard outside the room and another was inside with a doctor, who had been called when Prudhomme's body was discovered. The doctor was finishing his examination when Gautier went into the room.

'There's no mystery about how this man died,' he told Gautier, pointing to the body. 'By his own hand.'

Gautier looked at the body which lay fully clothed, head twisted to one side, in a pool of congealed blood. The fingers of the right hand were curled around the butt of a revolver, loosely, as though it had slipped from their grasp. There was a bullet wound in the head, a few centimetres behind and below the right ear.

'Have you any idea when he may have died?' Gautier asked the doctor.

'Several hours ago, I would say. Perhaps yesterday evening, but one cannot be precise.'

'Do you know when this man arrived at the hotel?' Gautier asked Brunet.

'Yesterday, in the afternoon.'

'Who found the body?'

'One of my maids. She knocked on the door to see if it was still occupied and when there was no reply, she looked inside.'

'When was this?'

'Soon after five o'clock today. The police were called immediately.'

'Why did no one check the room before? He must have been here for more than twenty-four hours.'

'Our guests do not like to be disturbed. They can stay for as long as they wish and we do not disturb them.'

'I shall leave you now, Inspector,' the doctor said. He had done what he had been called to do. The man was dead and he was impatient to be gone. 'An ambulance will be here directly to take the body to the mortuary.'

After he had left, Gautier looked around the room. It was furnished more luxuriously than one would have expected in a hotel in that quartier, with a double bed, a chest of drawers, a table and two chairs. The china jug and bowl on the wash-stand were of a good quality and two clean towels hung over a rail at one end of it. A framed pencil drawing of Michelangelo's statue 'David' hung on one wall. An open bottle of champagne, still more than three parts full, but with the champagne flat and lifeless, stood with two glasses on the table. Some dregs of champagne remained in one of the glasses; the other had not been used.

'When this man arrived at your hotel, I assume he was not alone.'

'He was then, but when he paid me for the room he told me he was expecting his friend.'

'At what time did the friend arrive?'

'I cannot say. I did not see him arrive.' Brunet paused before adding, 'Or leave. One of my staff may have seen him. I am not always in the lobby downstairs.'

'We can check on that in due course. Do you know the dead man?' Gautier was not ready to reveal Prudhomme's name. The world would know soon enough.

Brunet's hesitation in replying was long enough to show that he was not going to tell the truth. 'Not by name, but he has used my hotel before.'

'How often?'

'I cannot say.'

Gautier began to lose patience with the man's evasiveness. 'Look, my friend. We have the power to shut this hotel at any time we choose. It may be that we should have done so before, but I can tell you this. If you refuse to cooperate, it will be closed tonight, permanently.'

Brunet accepted the ultimatum and answered Gautier with surly resignation. The dead man, he said, had been coming to the Hôtel de Valence every five or six weeks for almost two years. He and his friend met there by arrangement, usually in the afternoon and occasionally staying for the night. It was always the same friend, a man who spoke with an English accent and usually arrived carrying a valise with a label on it, which suggested that he had arrived from England by steamer and train.

'In my opinion the man was an English aristocrat,' Brunet concluded.

'What makes you think so?'

'His manner. He had the apologetic politeness one finds in a person of good breeding who is now impoverished.'

'Is he a young man?'

'By no means. He cannot be more than ten years younger than his friend there.'

Gautier knew that many Englishmen had mistresses in Paris, who offered an escape from the stifling conventions of English morality. He supposed it was not inconceivable that an English homosexual might have similar arrangements with a friend of the same inclinations.

As they were talking, their voices were almost drowned by the noise of a passing train and, looking out of the window, Gautier saw that the hotel stood on the edge of the railway tracks which led out of Paris towards the north and the Channel ports. That might explain why the shot that killed Prudhomme had not been heard elsewhere in the hotel and why his death had remained undetected.

'How long is it since these men were here last?'

'It cannot be more than about two weeks. So I was surprised yesterday when this one arrived.' Brunet added inconsequentially, 'They always insisted on having one of my best rooms.'

Gautier began examining the body more closely. Only one bullet had been fired from the revolver, even though it had been fully loaded. He handled the revolver with care, for it would have to be sent to the government laboratories, even though he did not

94

believe that scientific examination would reveal anything germane to Prudhomme's death.

Prudhomme had been wearing a frock coat and Gautier had to roll his body to one side in order to search the pockets of his waistcoat. In one of them he found a pocket-watch with Prudhomme's initials engraved on the silver case, in another a small folding pocket-knife. It was in one of the remaining pockets that he found what he had been hoping he might find, the note that Prudhomme must have received in his office the previous afternoon. The note had been written on a single sheet of plain paper folded once and the message was brief.

I arrived on this morning's boat train. Will be waiting for you from 3.30 as usual.
F.

The paper on which the note had been written looked ordinary enough, although not quite of the quality which one might have expected an English aristocrat to use for personal correspondence. The envelope which Prudhomme's secretary had given him was in Gautier's pocket and taking it out, he compared it with the note. As the envelope had been addressed in block capitals, it was not possible to decide whether the handwriting was the same, but he could detect no similarity in the shape of the letters. When he turned the note over, he noticed that the back of the paper was discoloured, with a slight brownish tinge.

Brunet had been watching him. 'Another note?' he asked.

'Another? You've seen one before?'

'After they had left we would find notes like that one, which had been thrown into the wastepaper basket. It must have been their way of communicating. Just short notes, no signatures, only initials. Very discreet, I must say.'

'Did you keep any of them?'

'No. Why should I?'

'And you were never able to find out their names?'

'I never bothered to try. Clients come to my hotel because they know their privacy will be respected.'

Gautier knew he was lying. By his own admission Brunet had taken the trouble to find out what the two men had left in the wastepaper basket of the room. He would certainly have tried to find out who they were, if only to protect himself

95

if there were any trouble or, at some time in the future, to blackmail them.

He did not press Brunet, for that could be done at another time in Sûreté headquarters if it were felt to be necessary. In the meantime the routine procedures of a police investigation must be followed and the room in which Prudhomme had been found must be sealed once his body had been taken away. It was not far short of midnight by the time he left the hotel.

Earlier in the evening he had almost, but not finally, decided that he would not take up Sophia's invitation to join her at her hotel. Now he decided that he would. He did not try to analyse his motives for doing so, although he knew that they were prompted by more than just sexual desire. When he reached the Hôtel Cheltenham, the concierge, an old friend, was on duty and he stopped to chat with him.

After they had exchanged a few words, he asked the man, 'Has the Princess Sophia returned from the theatre?'

'Yes, monsieur, some time ago.' The concierge hesitated before he added, 'She has a gentleman with her.'

'In that case I will not disturb her.' In spite of himself Gautier could not resist putting the question. 'Do you know who the gentleman is?'

'Yes, monsieur. The Comte de Tréville.'

12

The staff conference in the office of the Director General of the Sûreté next morning was one of the infrequent occasions when Gautier felt sorry for Courtrand. When taking charge of the investigations into the disappearance of Judge Prudhomme and the robbery at the Earl of Newry's home, Courtrand had decided that every morning he would hold a staff conference of all those working on the two cases at which, in the style of Napoleon with his generals, he would map out the strategy of that day's work. This plan, he had been confident, would soon produce results and both cases would be solved. Now, almost before the investigations had been started, Judge Prudhomme had been found dead. Courtrand was not only deflated, but filled with gloom.

'For a man of the judge's stature to kill himself in that hotel,' he complained, 'is beyond comprehension.'

'If it had to be in a *hôtel de rendez-vous*, why choose one for pédés?' one of the inspectors sitting at the table remarked.

'Precisely.'

Any Frenchman, a judge, a government minister, even the President, might have occasion to take a woman to one of the many such hotels to be found in Paris and would not earn disapproval. He might even shoot himself in one of them and not be accused of any offence except eccentricity, but Courtrand could not see Prudhomme's behaviour resulting in anything but an unpleasant scandal.

'What I keep asking myself,' Gautier said, 'is why he used a hotel at all.'

'What do you mean?'

'If he intended suicide, he could have done it anywhere; at his home, in his office.'

'His choice of place does not strike me as significant,' Courtrand replied.

'The Chief Inspector may be suggesting that perhaps the judge's death was not suicide at all,' Surat commented. He knew better than anyone in the room how Gautier's mind worked.

'You cannot believe that he was murdered, surely?' another inspector said.

'I am just wondering, that's all. There are questions that need answering.'

'What questions?'

'First there is the question of the bullet wound. It is a full ten centimetres behind the right ear. A man who wishes to kill himself will almost always shoot himself in the temple or the mouth. To fire a revolver into one's head from behind the ear requires an extremely awkward bending of the wrist.'

Using his right forefinger as though it were the barrel of a revolver, Gautier demonstrated what he meant.

'Are you saying that the judge may have been shot by someone else and the revolver placed in his hand afterwards?'

'It is at least a possibility.'

'But who could have done it?'

'Let me pose another question,' Gautier said. 'We know that Judge Prudhomme went to the hotel to meet another man. He received a note suggesting that they should meet and we know that the hotel was their regular meeting place. Where is this man? What happened to him?'

'Perhaps they did meet there, quarrelled and the man stormed out, breaking off their relationship for ever. The judge was so upset that he shot himself.'

'You have a vivid imagination, my friend! Of course that is a possibility, but then we must ask ourselves did Judge Prudhomme take a revolver with him to the assignation? And if so, why?'

'This is all idle speculation,' Courtrand said impatiently. 'What should be concerning us is how we can minimise the scandal. We must try to conceal the name and the nature of the hotel in which the judge was found dead.'

'I fear that will be impossible, monsieur.'

Their discussion was interrupted by one of those apparent coincidences which seem bizarre at the time but are really not so remarkable. Courtrand's secretary came into the room carrying a copy of a newspaper. Another man might have waved it excitedly, but that was not Corbin's style. He carried it still folded and placed it on the table by Courtrand's elbow.

'I apologise for interrupting, monsieur, but I believe you will wish to see this.'

The newspaper was *La Libre Parole* and the article to which Corbin wished to draw Courtrand's attention had been printed in a prominent position. Its headline was calculated to intrigue: 'A Tale of an Apple Peel Judge'. Courtrand read the article, his expression changing from gloom to anger, and then he passed it around the table.

A Tale of an Apple Peel Judge
Friends of Judge Théo Prudhomme will be desolate at the misfortune which has befallen him. The judge, well known for the savagery of the sentences on any wrong-doers who come before him and, until now at least, for his stern moral rectitude, has been recently seen with his left forearm heavily bandaged. The explanation he gives to his friends is that he cut himself while peeling an apple. This, he says, happened the other afternoon in the Hôtel Bayonne near Boulevard St Michel where, it so happens, the Russian Ballets Dashkova are lodging.

Although the judge had not admitted this, we are reliably informed that this unfortunate accident occurred in the bedroom of one of the company's dancers. We may ask ourselves why Judge Prudhomme was peeling an apple in these unusual surroundings. Was he thinking of his health, following the old adage to keep the doctor away? Or was the apple, as it was with Adam, a temptation, an invitation to explore new worlds of knowledge? If the latter were the case, he can scarcely blame Eve, for the bedroom where the apple was peeled was that of a male dancer. If there is a moral to this tale, it is to tell us that the judge is clearly neither a prude nor even, it seems, a man.

While the newspaper was circulating, Courtrand said angrily, 'How can any newspaper be allowed to publish such filth? Now Judge Prudhomme's reputation will be besmirched for ever.'

'Can you imagine what they will print now, when they hear that he has killed himself?'

'Is it possible that he knew this story was to appear today and shot himself because he could not face the scandal?'

'That would not explain the note which was found on his body.'

Gautier could have told the others that Prudhomme would not have known what *La Libre Parole* would be publishing that morning. He was reasonably sure that Michel Puy had written the piece and that it was based on information given to him by Ranevsky at the Châtelet theatre the previous afternoon. By that time Prudhomme was already dead. He could also have told them that the article must have been inspired by Ranevsky to prevent Prudhomme taking legal action in the matter of the stabbing. Once he had been ridiculed in print, no man, however stubborn he might be, would risk making himself look foolish for a second time by taking such a matter to court.

He did not tell them because it would achieve nothing and only muddy a discussion which had already lost its way. In any case it was clear that Courtrand, dejected by the news of Prudhomme's death and worrying about how it might affect his own reputation, had no wish to prolong the conference. He knew that in view of Courtrand's apathy, if any action were to be taken in either the matter of Judge Prudhomme's death or the robbery at the Earl of Newry's home, he would have to take it.

Before that, though, he wished to speak with Inspector Lemaire about the Lebrun affair. Lemaire was a competent enough police officer and an intelligent man, but Gautier had found from experience that he was inclined to look for an easy solution to any problem which faced him. They were good friends and Gautier was sure Lemaire would not resent a suggestion on the line that his investigations might follow.

Lemaire had already read all the written reports in the dossier of the case and now listened while Gautier told him of the efforts that were being made to trace the concierge's friend Jules.

'If what you suggest is true,' he said, 'then this man must have been sent there to kill the child.'

'Yes. I believe he may have been hired to do just that.'

'But who would wish to kill the child? And why?'

'It would be a neighbour or perhaps a *bouquiniste*, one of Lebrun's competitors. You know as well as I do that finding some apache or *voyou* who will kill for money is easy enough in Paris. The motive could be spite or jealousy or revenge for some grievance or wrong.'

'I'll do my best to find the man,' Lemaire said but one could see that he did not find Gautier's theory convincing.

After leaving Lemaire, Gautier sent for Surat and told him what he wanted done. The first priority was to trace the 'friend' whom Prudhomme was to meet at the Hôtel de Valence. At the Gare du Nord they would have a list of the passengers who had made reservations on the cross-Channel steamer and train. If Brunet was right and the man was an English aristocrat, he might well have a title. Brunet had also given Gautier a description of the man and either the conductor of the train or one of the sleeping car attendants might remember a passenger who matched the description. At the same time all the members of the hotel's staff must be questioned to find out whether the friend had kept his rendezvous with Prudhomme, whether he had been seen arriving or leaving and if so at what time. Finally Gautier told Surat to go himself to Prudhomme's home. It was possible that one of the judge's domestic staff might have heard of the friend, even though Prudhomme had kept their relationship a secret. Alternatively Surat might be able to find something in the apartment, letters perhaps or a present, which would provide a clue to the man's identity.

After giving his instructions, Gautier found a fiacre and had himself driven to l'Opéra where, he had already learnt, Leon Bourkin would be found. Parisians were proud of the magnificent opera house which stood at the head of Place de l'Opéra facing down the broad avenue of the same name towards the Louvre. That had not always been the case, for the building had been commissioned in 1861 by Napoleon III who, before it was finished, had led France to a humiliating defeat in a war with Prussia and been forced to abdicate. These memories had been slow to die, but as the nation's confidence was restored, l'Opéra became an institution and an indispensable part of social life in Paris.

Gautier made his way from the foyer with its imposing marble staircases, painted ceilings and chandeliers to the Foyer de Danse, where during the opera season certain privileged gentlemen were allowed to meet the ballerinas before or after performances. Adjacent to the foyer was a large room, equipped with a barre and mirrors, where dancers could exercise and practise steps and movements. There he found more than a score of dancers from the Dashkova Ballet, members of the corps de ballet as well as principals, at work under the supervision of the maître de ballet. He did not see Stepanova among them, but Karpovna was there and so was Leon Bourkin.

When he told Bourkin that he wished to speak with him in private, alarm flared in the Russian's eyes. At first he seemed to be searching desperately for any excuse which would allow him to escape the interview. Then, still frightened, he agreed and the two of them went together to the Foyer de Danse.

'I cannot help you, Inspector,' Bourkin said hastily.

'How can you tell, monsieur, until you know what I am going to ask you?'

'You have come about that newspaper article, I suppose.'

'No, what I am investigating is far more serious.'

'What is it then?'

'Judge Prudhomme was found dead last night.'

Bourkin was stunned. His expression, a mix of astonishment and fear, might have been comical in any other circumstances. 'Dead!' he gasped. 'How did he die?'

'A bullet in the head killed him.'

'Why are you questioning me about this? I know nothing of the matter. Why should I wish to kill the judge? He and I were friends.' Words spilled out of Bourkin as his panic heightened. 'Why do you accuse me?'

'I am accusing no one as yet.'

'Then what do you want of me?'

'Information. Would you tell me where you were the day before yesterday?'

'At what time?'

'In the afternoon and evening.'

'In the evening I was performing. Everyone knows that. In the afternoon I was rehearsing.'

'Monsieur Bourkin, I know for a fact that you did not appear for rehearsals that day, even though you were expected to. Where were you?'

The panic in Bourkin's face turned into something bordering on terror. He looked around him, fearful that one of the other dancers might have heard what Gautier was saying to him, even though there was no one within earshot. At the same time he was frantically searching for an escape, for a lie or prevarication which would satisfy Gautier's question.

'Where were you?' Gautier asked again.

'Inspector, I cannot answer that question.'

'Why not?'

'I spent the afternoon with a lady.' Gautier sensed that Bourkin was improvising. 'You cannot expect me to give you her name. As a Frenchman, you will understand that.'

At any other time Gautier might have found it amusing to hear a homosexual pretending that he was protecting the reputation of a lady, but he needed answers and was not willing to be deflected from the line he was pursuing.

'Clearly you do not appreciate that this is a serious matter, monsieur, a case of violent death. I must insist that you give me the name of this lady.'

'I refuse. You have no right to question me. After all it was not I who stabbed the judge at our hotel.'

'Refusing to give me the name will achieve nothing. We can find out by other means.'

'I still refuse. And I shall answer no more questions.'

Bourkin turned and hurried away back to the dance studio, running lightly on his toes, a ballet dancer's run across a stage. Gautier did not follow him, for he did not seriously believe that Bourkin might have shot Judge Prudhomme. At the same time his visit to l'Opéra had not been wasted. Bourkin's behaviour had given him an insight into the complexities and tensions in the relationship among members of the Dashkova Ballet. There had been no fire, no offended indignation in Bourkin's refusal to answer Gautier, only fear. And he had been ready to divert suspicion for Prudhomme's death from himself to Boris Ranevsky.

As he was leaving the opera house, an automobile pulled up in front of the entrance and he stopped to look at it. Automobiles were becoming part of daily life in France, not yet replacing coaches and carriages, but every day noisily claiming their place on the boulevards. Every year new models were being produced and shown in the Salon de l'Automobile, vying with each other in the novelty and luxury of their fittings and accoutrements. The model which drew up outside l'Opéra was the latest Panhard-Lavassor, beautifully appointed with brass headlamps and polished woodwork.

A chauffeur in brown and blue uniform came round to open the door and Emile Labat climbed out and then turned to offer his arm to a woman companion. She was wearing a veil tied under her chin as many women did when they went motoring and it was only when she stopped in front of Gautier that he realised it was Nicola Stepanova. She smiled at Gautier, allowed Labat to kiss her hand and then left them, passing through the entrance into the opera house.

'Inspector Gautier! I did not expect to find you here. There has been no trouble, I hope.' Labat nodded in the direction of the opera house.

'Not so far as I know.'

'And where are you going now? Back to Quai des Orfèvres? If so, would you care to ride with me?'

'That is very kind, monsieur. I would not wish to put you to any trouble.'

'You would not be doing so. I am heading for the Faubourg St Germain.'

'Then I accept your offer with pleasure.'

They drove away, watched by a small crowd of urchins who had gathered as they always seemed to in Paris, whenever there was anything to admire. The smell of leather inside the automobile suggested that it was a very recent purchase.

'We French are taking a long time to accept the automobile,' Labat said. 'My wife humours me over having one, thinking of it only as a small boy's plaything. And every day we read passionate articles in the newspapers attacking the internal combustion engine and defending the horse.'

'It is certainly a convenient and comfortable way of travelling.'

'There is another benefit of the automobile which everyone appears to ignore. As coaches and carriages disappear, it will mean an end to the dreadful pollution of the city.'

'Pollution?'

'By horses. When they vanish, the streets can be kept clean.'

Gautier had never thought of the automobile as a force of cleanliness. Too often people walking in the street would recoil from the fumes and smoke as one drove past.

'It is seldom that I have the good fortune to escort a beautiful young lady to her work,' Labat remarked. He seemed to believe that he should explain Stepanova's presence in his automobile. 'I went to see Boris Ranevsky at his hotel this morning and when I was leaving I saw Mademoiselle Stepanova looking for a fiacre.'

'She would be grateful for the ride, I am sure. It is an awkward journey and the other dancers are already hard at work practising.'

'Quite so. Everyone is working very hard to make sure that

the gala performance is a success.' Labat smiled. 'Even I am in a small way.'

'You, monsieur?'

'Yes. I have been given the responsibility for seeing that all goes well.'

The gala performance, as Gautier knew, was in aid of charity, to raise money for the victims of a recent earthquake in North Africa. So that all the money raised from the sale of tickets should go to this fund, the sponsors of the Dashkova Ballet were meeting all the expenses of the performance, including the cost of decorating the theatre with flags and flowers and the printing of a special programme. Labat was looking after all these arrangements.

'In addition a special protocol has to be observed on all occasions when the President of the Republic is to be present,' he added. 'Yesterday this was explained to me by one of the President's aides and I went to the Hôtel Bayonne this morning to pass the instructions on to the company. Let us hope nothing occurs to ruin the performance.'

Before making his last remark, Labat glanced at Gautier, which made him wonder whether it was an oblique reference to the enquiries he was making and how much Labat knew of Ranevsky's attack on Judge Prudhomme. It was possible, he supposed, that Labat might have read Puy's article although it was unlikely that he would subscribe to a paper with such a poor reputation as *La Libre Parole*. That made him wonder too whether Sophia would have read the article and what effect it would have on her.

What Labat said next showed that he had trouble of a different kind in mind. 'When I reached their hotel this morning,' he remarked, 'I found the company in a state of extreme agitation.'

'Why was that?'

'You know Alexandre Sanson, do you not? Well, he had been dreadfully ill during the night and they thought he had been poisoned.'

'What symptoms did he show?'

'Violent stomach pains and all the signs of internal bleeding. Fortunately the fellow had the good sense to take a strong emetic and after prolonged vomiting he recovered.'

'Does he know what caused the attack?'

'Eating oysters apparently. The company had a meeting last evening, after which they ate oysters and drank champagne.'

'Were any of the others affected?'

'No, but as you know, a single bad oyster can be enough to poison one. It was a very distressing experience for Sanson and when I left the hotel he was sleeping, absolutely exhausted.'

The traffic was heavy that morning and after manoeuvring carefully down Avenue de l'Opéra through a throng of coaches, fiacres and an occasional omnibus, Labat's chauffeur passed the Palais Royal and turned into Rue de Rivoli, heading for the Place du Châtelet.

'Are you sure I am not taking you out of your way, monsieur?' Gautier asked.

'Not at all. My wife is expecting me at home, for I promised to drive her to the Hôtel Ritz, where a group of ladies are holding a luncheon in honour of the poetess Comtesse Anna de Noailles.' Labat smiled. 'After that I shall be able to take refuge in the Jockey Club.'

'No doubt you will see the Earl of Newry there.'

'No doubt. He has recently been elected a member.'

'He must be glad that he can still follow his British style of life in Paris. I understand he spends most of his day at the club.'

'On the contrary, the Earl seems to have adopted our French habits very quickly.' The irony in Labat's tone was very gentle. 'Like most of us he comes to the club at midday and sometimes lunches there. He spends his afternoons at his little bachelor apartment nearby, entertaining his *petite amie*. I understand that she too is a dancer.'

Gautier was sitting alone at the Café Corneille, for he was the first of the group of friends to arrive. As he waited for the others, he found himself thinking of Judge Prudhomme. In spite of the scepticism of his colleagues at the staff conference that morning, he was still inclined to believe that the judge had not shot himself. The position of the bullet wound was only one of the things that bothered him. An absence of any plausible motive for suicide was another. He was curious too about the friend whom Prudhomme had been meeting in secret. Early reports from the enquiries that were being made at the Gare du Nord and the Hôtel de Valence were not encouraging. No one knew of any Englishman who had arrived on the boat train, nor had one been seen arriving at the hotel for a rendezvous with the judge. Only forty-eight hours before he died, Prudhomme had been attacked with a sword-stick and Gautier believed that the two events must be connected. Of course it might be no more than coincidence, but he had always distrusted coincidences.

He tried imagining how anyone who wished to kill Prudhomme might plan the murder. If he knew or had found out about the judge's secret assignations in the Hôtel de Valence, he could trick him into going there. Then, because of the secrecy in which the meetings were held, it would not be difficult to lie in wait for him, kill him and escape undetected.

He could see one flaw in the theory and that was the note which Prudhomme had received making the assignation. The judge would have accepted the invitation only if the note had been written in a handwriting which he recognised. Gautier had the note with him and taking it out of his pocket, he examined it. The script was too bold and confident to be a forgery and yet there was something about the note which worried him. The paper on which it had been written had been folded once to fit into the envelope, but Gautier thought he could detect very faint traces of other folds or creases. There was also that slight discolouration on the back which made him uneasy. He had experienced the same uneasiness in other investigations in the past, a feeling that he had overlooked or misunderstood some simple fact which would explain other contradictions and so unlock the truth.

He was still studying the note, waiting for inspiration which would not come, when Duthrey arrived at the same time as Froissart and an elderly judge who sometimes joined them at the café. Almost immediately they began talking of the scurrilous article about Judge Prudhomme in *La Libre Parole*.

'That man Puy is a scoundrel,' Froissart exclaimed. 'This must be the story which he was trying to uncover when he was here the other day and behaved so offensively.'

'Newspapers should not be allowed to assassinate a man's character in this fashion,' Duthrey said.

'I fear there may be at least a basis of truth in the article's allegations,' the judge said sadly.

'Even so, the laws of libel in our country should be far more stringent. In England, for example, Judge Prudhomme would be able to take the newspaper and the man who wrote the article to court and win substantial damages.'

'I am not sure as to that. Look what happened to Oscar Wilde.'

'This will damage Prudhomme's career as well as his reputation,' the judge said. 'He may be obliged to resign.'

'There is no chance of that now.' Gautier had not wished to discuss the Prudhomme affair with his friends, but he felt he had no option now but to tell them the facts. 'Judge Prudhomme is dead.'

'Dead? How did that happen?'

'It would appear to be a case of suicide.'

He explained how Prudhomme's body had been found in a hotel room, a bullet wound in his head and a revolver in his hand. The full story would be in the next day's papers, so he gave no more details nor did the others ask for them.

'Might this newspaper story have driven him to kill himself?'

'No. He died well before it appeared.'

'Then might he not have been forewarned that it was to appear?'

'He would not have killed himself on that account,' the elderly judge said. 'I knew Prudhomme for many years, ever since he first began studying law. He would never allow himself to be intimidated by threats or even by the prospect of impending disgrace. Some people would call that stubborn conceit. I prefer to think that he had great moral courage.'

Their conversation slipped quickly into another subject. The habitués of the Café Corneille were not the kind of men who would derive any pleasure from the sensational or the macabre. They began talking about literature, of articles that had been published in *La Revue des Deux Mondes*, the leading literary review to which many prominent authors contributed. From literature they turned to old books and particularly to first editions, on which Froissart was recognised as an authority.

'Talking of books,' the judge said, 'reminds me that I saw you, Gautier, strolling along the Seine by the stalls of the *bouquinistes* yesterday afternoon.'

'Are you starting a collection?' Froissart asked.

'Possibly, but not of books,' the judge said slyly. 'He was enjoying the sunshine in the company of a most attractive young woman. Not a Frenchwoman, I fancy. Maybe Scottish.'

'You are very observant,' Gautier told him. 'You should have been a detective. But she is Irish, not Scottish. Miss Ryan is the Earl of Newry's housekeeper.'

'Is that the poor man whose apartment was burgled?' Duthrey asked and when Gautier told him it was, he added, 'Then I hope his property was insured.'

'Why do you say that?'

'Because he has been trying to sell his collection of fire-arms.'

'How do you know that?'

'One of my colleagues in *Figaro*, who writes a weekly feature on shooting, told me so.'

'Are you saying that the Earl has advertised his collection for sale?'

'Good heavens, no! Nothing so vulgar as that. His wish to sell was mentioned, very discreetly, in an article on shooting in another paper.'

'I must say,' Froissart remarked, 'that I find this new craze for imitating the customs of the English quite absurd.'

He was referring to the enthusiasm with which the French were taking up English country sports. Gautier too found it extraordinary that Frenchmen, who were not a sporting race and who netted or shot any birds or animals that could be eaten, without regard for any rules of sport, should have begun to dress and arm themselves like English gentlemen and discuss the mysteries of pheasant, partridge and woodcock. They had even started hunting with foxhounds in the Bois de Boulogne.

The conversation at the Café Corneille that morning was stimulating and wide-ranging and Gautier thought no more of either Judge Prudhomme or the ballet until he returned to the Sûreté. There he found another communication from a lady waiting for him; not a letter this time but a *petit bleu* or message sent through the city's pneumatic postal system. It was from Missia Gomolka and composed in a curiously stilted French.

Mademoiselle Gomolka wishes to see Inspector Gautier with urgency. Is it possible that they can meet this afternoon? The matter is one of importance and concerns the death of the judge. She will wait on the inspector with impatience at the Hôtel Meurice from three hours onwards.

13

Gautier did not arrive at the Hôtel Meurice until well after three o'clock and he expected that Missia Gomolka would be waiting for him in the lobby. She was not and when he asked for her, a page took him up to a suite on the second floor. The drawing-room of the suite was immense, larger than the whole of the Lebruns' apartment in the 20th arrondissement, and its windows offered a fine view of the Jardin des Tuileries across Rue de Rivoli.

Missia did not get up from the chaise-longue on which she was reclining, but held out her hand to be kissed. She was wearing a bizarre outfit of tight leopard-skin trousers, a black blouse and a yellow belt with a large buckle in the shape of a death mask on one hip. Her copper coloured hair was concealed beneath a wig that had been powdered blue and entwined with silver necklaces, which gleamed like snakes in a blue jungle. Her eyes were green flecked with yellow and she had blackened the lids with kohl and painted her lips a bright vermilion. The effect was startling.

Deciding that he was supposed to be startled, Gautier deliberately showed no surprise as he bent over her hand to kiss it. Disappointed perhaps, she asked him, 'Do you not find my trousers elegant?'

'Very,' Gautier replied, truthfully, because he did think they were elegant, though not in any way seductive. The only other time he had seen a woman in trousers was on the stage when Sarah Bernhardt was playing one of the masculine rôles of which she was so fond.

'This is the fashion of the future,' Missia assured him. 'Before long women everywhere will be wearing trousers as elegant and colourful as these.'

'You may well be right, mademoiselle.'

'I am. Just remember that.'

'Are you living in this hotel?' Gautier had no wish to start any discussion on women's fashions.

'Yes, there was no room for me at the hotel where the rest of the company is staying.' Missia smiled. 'But don't tell the others about my suite. They probably believe that I have a little attic room here, but I am afraid I cannot stand discomfort. For one thing I must have my own bathroom. You see I take a herbal bath every day. Now promise you won't give my secret away!'

'Of course, if that is what you wish.'

'I expect you are wondering why I asked you here, Inspector.'

'In your *petit bleu* you said it was to tell me something of importance.'

'That's right, but I am not certain where to start.'

Missia hesitated. If it had been any other woman, Gautier might have thought she was embarrassed by what she had to say, but he did not believe that anything would ever embarrass Missia. She had all the confidence that charm and great wealth can provide. Presently she decided where she should start.

'You spoke to Leon Bourkin this morning, did you not? About the death of that judge person?'

'I asked him some questions, yes.'

'And he refused to tell you where he was on the afternoon of the day before yesterday?'

'He did.'

'I can tell you where he was, Inspector – here in this very room, with me; all afternoon. That was the reason why he missed rehearsals at the Châtelet theatre.'

'In that case why did he not tell me?'

'Don't you understand?' Missia gave Gautier the pitying look which she would have given a half-wit. 'Poor Leon! He is terrified in case Boris finds out. Boris would kill him. He's insanely jealous!'

'Even of women?'

'Especially of women. He would imagine the worst, even though Leon only came here to help me with my dancing. He is so sweet-natured. And it makes a pleasant change to find a man who does not immediately want to start wrestling on the chaise-longue!'

Her last remark made Gautier wonder whether Missia thought that he had sexual ambitions on her. He had not, because although he was aware of her intense personal magnetism, he did not find her physically attractive. Her exotic clothes and bizarre colouring camouflaged any seductiveness that she might have possessed and he supposed they might even have been a deliberate device to frighten away predators.

'Do you not train and exercise with the other dancers?' he asked her.

'I do of course. This morning I arrived at l'Opéra just after you had left. But Alex says I need extra tuition because I started dancing later than most ballerinas. It was Alex who persuaded Bourkin to help me.'

'Would it not be better if Bourkin gave you this extra tuition in the dance studio?'

'He does and so do the other dancers. Everyone is so kind. But on top of that Leon has been giving me some' – Missia hesitated, as though looking for words – 'extra classes which Alex says I need. I realise that I shall never be so accomplished as Stepanova and Karpovna.'

'And recognising that, you still persevere with ballet dancing?'

'I must. For me dancing is only one part of my apprenticeship in the theatre,' Missia said. 'Before starting dancing I studied acting and before that the piano and singing. It is all part of my ultimate plan.'

Missia's ambition, she told Gautier, was to be recognised as an actress as well as a dancer. One day she intended to have her own stage company and to produce, direct and perform in plays and ballets. She would commission leading playwrights and poets to write dance dramas based on the great legends and myths of history and stage them as brilliant spectacles in Paris, Moscow, London and Vienna. Gautier could see that as she described her plans she was already acting, playing a rôle that she had fashioned and fired by her enthusiasm. Yet for Missia the drama was real enough.

'Do you think I am being too ambitious?' she asked him.

'Not if you have the talent,' Gautier replied. He knew she possessed the other prerequisite for her plan which was wealth.

'I have, but first I must school and discipline my talent, learn my art and make my reputation.'

When he had first entered the room, Gautier had been aware of an unusual and not altogether pleasant smell. The smell still lingered and seemed if anything to have become stronger and more pervasive. It was a smell which he had difficulty in identifying but which reminded him of visits to the circus as a child, when he had walked round the cages of the animals before the performance. Both his sense of smell and his memory were proved right when suddenly, while Missia was talking, a leopard came out from behind the sofa on which he was sitting and began walking slowly across the room.

'Rajah!' Missia exclaimed. 'So you're awake.'

She held out a hand towards the leopard in much the same way as she had greeted Gautier and, when the animal reached her side, began stroking its head. Gautier noticed that the beast was wearing a leather collar which was studded with jewels.

'Rajah is my pet leopard, Inspector,' Missia told Gautier. 'Don't be nervous. He is quite tame.'

'I would hope so!'

'I walk him in the Tuileries every day. When we appear in Rue de Rivoli it creates a sensation.'

'Is it not tactless to wear those trousers when he is around?'

'Tactless? I see what you mean. No, I am sure Rajah won't—' Missia stopped in mid-sentence, looked at Gautier and then laughed. 'You're teasing me!'

'I had been wondering what the smell in the room was.'

'Smell? You must have a very sensitive nose. Do you find it offensive?'

'Not offensive, no. Oppressive maybe.'

'Then open a window. Please do.'

Gautier crossed the room and opened one of the windows. The afternoon was warm and children were playing in the Tuileries gardens, watched over by their governesses. Small boys in sailor suits and girls in straw hats were bowling hoops and playing prisoners' base. A small writing desk stood against the wall between two windows and as he passed it on his way back to the sofa, Gautier noticed a watercolour painting lying on it. The painting was not framed and was similar in size to the sketches which he had been shown by Boris Ranevsky at the Châtelet theatre. He could see that it was a painting of an Egyptian scene.

Noticing him glance at the painting, Missia said, 'You are not supposed to see that!'

'Is it not a scene from Sanson's new ballet?'

'How did you know that?'

'Boris Ranevsky showed me a series of sketches similar to this one yesterday afternoon.'

'Those were just Alex's first rough pencil sketches. From them he did working drawings for the scenery builders and the costumier. The watercolour over there he painted specially for me.'

'May I look at it?'

'Yes, now that you have seen it, but don't tell anyone. Alex wants to keep his designs secret, for the time being anyway.'

Gautier picked up the painting. The stage scene it portrayed was similar in outline to the one he had seen in the sketches Ranevsky had shown him but different in details. The entrance to the temple, flanked by soldiers, was the same, but instead of a barge painting on a backcloth, a real barge was moored at the river bank. The figures of the two dancers in the centre of the stage were missing and instead a small procession was moving from the barge towards the centre. At its head was a queen, followed by two slaves holding palm leaves over her to protect her from the sun, with courtiers and handmaidens making up the procession.

All the figures were painted in more detail than in the pencil sketches. Even though they were too small for one to make out their faces, Gautier decided that the Queen, tall and slender, was meant to be Missia.

'One day, when Alex's genius is recognised,' Missia told Gautier, 'that watercolour will be a collector's piece. His work will hang in galleries and museums.'

'He certainly has talent. No one can dispute that.'

'Alex is more than just talented. He is completely obsessed with his work. Boris gets impatient with him, for he always wants everything in a hurry, but Alex will never be rushed. He spends days laboriously working out every detail of the ballets he creates and checking the accuracy of everything. An infinite capacity for taking pains. Is that not a sign of genius?'

'One of them perhaps.'

'He has helped me so much. Of course the rest of the company have too, everyone. I know how fortunate I am to be one of them. They are also so charming, so friendly.'

Gautier found it hard to believe that Missia's last remark could be sincere. Could she be so insensitive that she had not noticed the feelings of resentment that she had aroused in other members of the Dashkova Ballet? What Sophia had told him too suggested that there was a lack of harmony and discipline in the ballet company. Missia must be aware of this even if she were not the cause of it.

'Were you at the meeting of the whole company which was held after last night's performance?' he asked her. 'From what Sophia told me I gathered it might have been stormy.'

'Not really. Boris said some hard words to us. He told us that we were not working hard enough, that we were allowing ourselves to be distracted by the attractions of Paris and the wonderful reception that the people of Paris have given us. He gave us a severe lecture and a warning. So did Alex and so did the maître de ballet. We were told that anyone who misbehaves in future will be sent home.' Missia laughed, showing that she for one had not taken the warning too seriously. 'We all promised to be good and the meeting ended happily. Alex sent out for oysters and champagne for the whole company. Even the stage-hands who were still in the theatre joined in. I really enjoyed the evening.'

'Did you hear that the oysters made Sanson sick during the night?'

'Yes, the Comte de Tréville told me. He came round to see me earlier today. Poor Alex!'

They chatted for a little while longer, not about the ballet but about France. Missia was enchanted by Paris, with the style of life, the luxury, the women's fashions and the freedom of thought and expression. Many Frenchmen with avant-garde ideas criticised their countrymen for their bourgeois mentality and slavish adherence to outmoded conventions, but for Russians, accustomed to the moribund conservatism of their own country, France was modern and uninhibited and excitingly alive.

When he was leaving, Missia said to him, 'You won't tell anyone of Leon's secret visits to me, will you?'

'Not unless the question is raised by my colleagues at the Sûreté, which is unlikely.'

'And don't mention Alex's gift to me of his painting.'

'Not if that is what you wish.'

'It might also be prudent not to tell the others that you came here to see me – alone.'

On his way downstairs, Gautier reflected that Missia seemed to enjoy hedging her life around with secrets. Was this another protective device? He decided that he would prefer to treat it as a warning. People who made much of secrets and the importance of keeping them, he had observed, did not always have the same regard for telling the truth.

* * *

From the Hôtel Meurice, Gautier walked along Rue St Honoré looking for a fiacre to take him to Parc Monceau. For some reason none of the many thousands of fiacres in Paris was to be found and reaching Rue Royale, he turned northwards in the direction of the Madeleine. Seeing the church with its imposing classical façade reminded him of the suggestion which Sophia had made more than once now, that the two of them should marry. Whenever she mentioned it, he thought of Guy de Maupassant's novel *Bel Ami*. The central character in the book, a selfish and unscrupulous journalist, had used his powers of seduction and deceit to become editor of an important newspaper and then to marry the proprietor's daughter in the Madeleine. When Gautier tried to picture himself coming out of the Madeleine with Princess Sophia on his arm to face a crowd of spectators, he wanted to laugh. Sophia had not raised the subject of marriage during the last week or so and he wondered whether that was because she was immersed in the problems of the ballet company, or whether the idea might have lost its appeal.

In Boulevard Malesherbes he at last found a fiacre which took him to the Earl of Newry's apartment. François, who answered the door to his ring, told him that the Earl was not at home, but that Mademoiselle Ryan would see him. As he was following François across the hall to the drawing-room, he thought he caught a glimpse of Miss Ryan hurrying out of one room and into another, but he could not be certain that it was her.

She kept him waiting for several minutes and he spent the time walking round the room. He saw several photographs in silver frames, most of them taken some time previously so that their sepia tints had faded. Three of them were photographs of a young man, as tall as the Earl, but with a weak chin and prominent cheekbones. In one of them he was posing in evening clothes, in another on horseback waiting for a hunt to move off and in the third he was standing up to his thighs in a river with a fly rod in his hands.

Gautier also counted four paintings of horses, all executed in a peculiarly English style, the bellies of the horses not far off the ground, their legs fully stretched forward or back in a position which, one might think, would have made galloping an anatomical impossibility. Gautier wondered why it was that the English, so devoted to horses, always portrayed them as though they had no more life than the wooden animals to be found in a child's nursery.

In spite of its name, the Earl's drawing-room was clearly a man's room. Such ornaments as had been left after the burglary were what a man would choose; china wild fowl, silver hip-flasks, ashtrays fashioned out of sporting trophies and a paper-weight made from an elephant's foot. Almost the only concession to femininity was an oil painting of a hawkish woman, with a smile that was no doubt meant to be amiable but which might well have rivalled Medusa in turning men to stone.

When Miss Ryan came into the room, she was wearing a dark blue dress. The figure Gautier had seen in the corridor had been wearing brown and he wondered whether she had hurried to change and if so why. At the same time he could not help thinking what a pleasant and restful contrast her appearance presented with the extravagant oddity of Missia Gomolka's.

'I did not expect to see you again so soon,' she told him.

'Have I called at an inconvenient time then?'

'Not at all. Please sit down. The Earl is not at home, I am afraid.'

Gautier smiled. 'Is he at the Jockey Club? I could go to see him there.'

'He is, but it would be better if I were able to help you.'

'Perhaps you can. I intended to ask the Earl whether it was true that he had been trying to sell his collection of weapons.'

'Where did you hear that?'

'I am told it was reported in a newspaper article.'

Miss Ryan did not reply immediately. She closed her eyes briefly, as though she was trying to mask an expression of tired resignation. Then she smiled brightly. 'Yes, it is true. The Earl no longer has the same interest in shooting as he once had.'

'One supposes that he cannot find the same facilities for that sport in France as you have in Ireland.'

'That is not the reason. The collection was started by the Earl's father and he added to it, intending to create something special, a heritage which would pass on to his son and then to his descendants. Now all that has changed.'

'Why is that?'

'The Earl's only son, Viscount Craigavon, has left home permanently. He has emigrated to the United States and has even applied for American citizenship. The Earl is desolate. He feels he has lost his son for ever and that his family dynasty is at an end.' Miss Ryan looked at Gautier as though she were trying to guess how he would react to what she was about to say. 'That was the reason why he came to live in Paris.'

Gautier might have told her that on his last visit to their home, she had given him a different reason why the Earl had come to live in exile in France. He did not, because he felt a sudden sympathy for Miss Ryan, sensing that through loyalty she was making excuses for the Earl, trying to present his reason for deciding to leave Ireland in the best possible light. At the same time he could not help speculating on the reasons for her loyalty.

'Did the Earl get any enquiries from people wishing to buy his collection?' he asked her.

'Now it's strange that you should ask that. I told the Earl only this morning that we should tell you about the man. We agreed that we should, at the first opportunity.'

'What man was that?'

'An antique dealer. I forget his name; Colibri or something like that.'

'He made enquiries about the collection?'

'Yes. He came to the apartment and asked if he could view it. The Earl was not here at the time, so I showed it to him. He seemed very interested and told me he would speak to his client, who would certainly wish to make an offer for the collection.'

'His client?'

'Yes. He said he was acting on behalf of a wealthy Frenchman who was a passionately enthusiastic collector of weapons.'

'Have you heard from him again?'

'Not so far.'

'How long ago was it that he called?'

'I cannot say exactly but it must be at least three weeks, perhaps four.'

'Could you describe the man to me?'

'He was short and round-shouldered and had dark hair and a black beard. Oh yes and he walked with a limp,' Miss Ryan replied. Then she added, 'That description is not very helpful, is it?'

'It is better than the ones which witnesses usually give us. Did he tell you the name of the client for whom he was acting?'

'I am sure he did, but the name escapes me now.'

'The guns are in the study. Did he go in any other rooms while he was here?'

'When he arrived he was shown into this room. He would have

been able to see what was in here while he was waiting. Why? Do you think he planned the robbery?'

'That possibility had occurred to me.'

'I only wish I could tell you more about the man. You'll be thinking I am very feckless.'

'His visit must have seemed innocent enough. There was no reason why you should have taken any special notice of him.'

'I wish I had though,' Miss Ryan replied. Then immediately she clasped her hand over her mouth, as though she had committed some dreadful indiscretion. 'What am I saying? I asked Monsieur Colibri for his card. I remember that now.' She jumped to her feet. 'And I put it away in the writing bureau for safe-keeping.'

She spent some minutes searching in the disorder of the bureau before she found the card and gave it to Gautier. It gave no more information than any business card was likely to, a name and profession, GERARD COLIBRI – ANTIQUAIRE, and an address in Montparnasse. Gautier turned the card over and found another name written in block capitals on the back, LE DUC DE BEZIERS.

'Whose name is this?' he asked Miss Ryan.

Taking the card from him, she looked at it. 'Of course! Now I remember. I asked Monsieur Colibri for the name of the person for whom he was acting and he wrote it on the back of the card.'

Miss Ryan kept producing little snippets of information from a memory which appeared to be almost as untidy as the writing bureau. Gautier supposed that he should not be surprised, for he had always heard that an incompatibility with orderliness was part of the charm of the Irish.

'May I keep the card?' he asked her.

'I cannot see why not, but perhaps I had better make a note of Monsieur Colibri's name and address in case the Earl should require it.'

After more shuffling in the bureau, she produced a sheet of paper and a pencil. Gautier watched her as she wrote. She was left-handed and, as left-handed people sometimes do, wrote awkwardly with her hand curled round the back of the pencil, so that in effect she was writing from right to left. She must have realised that he was watching her, for suddenly she switched the pencil to her right hand and finished writing with it.

'I am ambidextrous,' she told him. 'When I was tiny and they saw I was naturally left-handed, my teachers insisted that I wrote with my right hand. I always found it difficult.'

When he was leaving, Miss Ryan accompanied him to the door of the apartment. It might have been a subtle indication that she knew her place in the household. The Earl or a member of his family would have asked one of the servants to show him out. On the other hand it might have been intended as a compliment to him. In the event it proved to be neither. Miss Ryan had a favour to ask of him.

'May I ask you a personal question? Is it true that you have friends among the members of the Russian ballet company?'

'One might say so. Why?'

'If it is not too presumptuous, I was going to ask whether you could help to obtain a seat for the première of their new ballet. Places are very scarce, it would appear,' Miss Ryan said and then as though to explain her presumptuousness she went on, 'I was at the first performance of *Seraglio*. It took my breath away! The colour, the movement, the grace!' She shook her head as though she still could not believe what she had seen.

They chatted a little longer about the ballet before Gautier left, promising to do what he could to secure a seat at the première for Miss Ryan. On his way into the centre of Paris, he thought about her. She appeared to give him scraps of information about the robbery at the Earl's home piecemeal and only when he was on the point of discovering them for himself, although that might be no more than coincidence. He wondered too how she had heard of his association with Sophia's ballet company and how much she knew. He found Claire Ryan's lack of affectation appealing, but he had the feeling that she was not as artless and as vague as she appeared.

14

'My first husband always maintained that brandy was bad for one's heart,' Sophia remarked.

She was pouring a glass of cognac for Gautier from a bottle which a waiter had brought up to the drawing-room of her hotel suite. Her own drink, an infusion of hot water, fruits and herbs, had been prepared to a recipe which, she said, she had brought with her from Turkey.

'What was your husband's favourite drink?' he asked her.

'Ouzo – a Greek drink which tastes not unlike absinthe.'

'And from what did he die?' Gautier knew that Sophia's first husband, although a good deal older than her, had died at a relatively early age.

'A heart attack.' Sophia shook her head and laughed. 'You have a flair for asking incisive questions, Jean-Paul, as sharp and penetrating as a surgeon's knife.'

They had met at the Châtelet theatre after that evening's performance of the ballet had ended and had driven straight to the Hôtel Cheltenham, refusing an invitation to join other members of the company for supper. At the hotel, while they had waited for the drinks to be brought up, Sophia had changed into a négligé.

As she handed him the glass of cognac, she said teasingly, 'You ignored my invitation last night. Does that mean your ardour is cooling?'

'In no way. And I did not ignore the invitation. After I had finished working I came here.'

'Then why did you not come upstairs?'

'When I arrived I was told you were entertaining a gentleman.'

'The Comte de Tréville?' Sophia looked at him in astonishment. 'You went away on his account!'

'Would it not have been tactless to interrupt you?'

'Don't be absurd!'

'The Comte has a reputation, you know.'

'For what?'

'As a ladies' man. Alex Sanson described him as an elderly lecher.'

'That's rather a harsh judgement. Perhaps Alex resents the attentions which the Comte is paying Karpovna. He dotes on her, watches every performance she gives, is always round at the hotel, brings her flowers.'

'Karpovna told me that she and Alex used to be lovers, but that now they are just good friends.'

'That's true. At one time, so they tell me, Alex was very much of a ladies' man himself, a very persistent and passionate suitor. Now he is a reformed character and lives for his work.'

'I wonder why he has changed.'

'Exhaustion maybe.' Sophia was enjoying her bantering. 'Don't you men say that it isn't love which wears you out, but the pursuit of it?'

Gautier was glad to see that she was in good spirits. Over the past few days he had seemed to notice a tension in her manner, a fraying of her nerves, which had made him believe that her responsibilities as patron of the ballet's tour in Paris were imposing too great a strain upon her. The final rehearsal for the new Egyptian ballet had been held that afternoon and he guessed that it must have been successful.

'How was the rehearsal?' he asked her.

'I thought it was excellent, faultless, but Boris was upset by one or two trivial things, mostly tiny mistakes by the corps de ballet, which no one in an audience would ever notice. So he has called another rehearsal for tomorrow morning. He is a perfectionist of course.'

'What did Alex think of it? He seems to expect high standards as well.'

'Poor Alex! He was in no condition to be critical.'

'Because of his food poisoning?'

'Yes. You heard about that, did you? Alex should never have come to the rehearsal, but he insisted.'

'Why did the Comte de Tréville come to see you last night anyway?' Gautier felt that she would expect him to ask the question.

'You have no cause for jealousy, chéri. He came to intercede for Karpovna. She wants desperately to dance the leading rôle in the new ballet.'

'She told me that Alex had created it for her.'

'That is nonsense! Alex has not even pressed for her to play the leading rôle.'

'Do you think that Stepanova is better suited to it?'

'I do. Technically she is no better a dancer than Karpovna, but the leading rôle in the new ballet is not technically demanding. What it does require is sensitivity and superb acting and that is where Stepanova excels.'

Gautier had finished his cognac and Sophia took the glass from him to refill it. As she did so she glanced at him and he felt immediately that her mood had changed. He supposed that being reminded of the squabbling in the ballet company over the new ballet had irritated her, but it was something else.

She approached what she wished to say obliquely. 'Why do you never talk to me about your work, Jean-Paul?'

'Perhaps because I feel it would not interest you.'

'Is it that or is it that you do not trust me?'

'Of course I trust you!'

'You did not tell me that the judge whom Boris attacked was dead.'

'Had I seen you last night I would have done.'

'Then tell me about it now.'

He described the circumstances of Judge Prudhomme's death, explaining that although it had the appearance of suicide, he had not ruled out the possibility of murder. The position of the bullet wound still worried him and he found it odd that no one had seen the judge's friend arrive at the hotel or leave. He could see no harm in telling her because the whole story would be in the newspapers in due course.

When he had finished, Sophia asked him indignantly, 'And is this the reason why you questioned poor Bourkin this morning?' Without waiting for his answer, she went on, 'Surely you cannot possibly believe that Leon killed this man?'

'I agree it is most unlikely, but I had thought it might have been Bourkin who went to meet the judge at the hotel.'

'And Boris? Do you suspect him as well?' Sophia demanded angrily.

'If Ranevsky is under suspicion, then it is his own fault. He has behaved very foolishly.'

'In what way?'

Gautier told her of Ranevsky's clumsy attempts to frighten Judge Prudhomme out of taking legal action over the stabbing fracas, of the demonstration by out-of-work actors and of the article in *La Libre Parole*, which Ranevsky had inspired. As she listened Sophia's anger seemed to be turning slowly into dismay.

'To involve a journalist in what was really only a private quarrel was folly,' Gautier concluded. 'Now, when Puy learns that Prudhomme is dead, Ranevsky will inevitably be suspected. God only knows what scandalous innuendoes and rumours Puy will publish!'

Sophia covered her face with her hands. Gautier thought she was going to weep, but she controlled herself. 'I should have expected this,' she said bitterly. 'It's typical of Boris! What is he trying to prove? That he is clever enough to outwit anyone? His arrogance and conceit are insufferable!'

'This time he may have been too clever.'

'The scandal will ruin our season in Paris. And now, when we have only one week left.'

'It may not be as bad as you suppose. The publicity may well attract more people to your performances.'

Gautier knew that many people in the theatrical world sought publicity avidly and would make themselves notorious just to get it. Sarah Bernhardt, the greatest actress in France, slept in a satin-lined coffin and even let it be known that she once had a crocodile as a lover. What he had seen that morning suggested that Missia Gomolka too was not averse to drawing attention to herself by sensational behaviour.

'We have no wish for that kind of publicity. I want our season in Paris to be a succès d'estime, to be praised by the critics and win the hearts of the people. Ballet is art, not a peep-show.'

'Can no one restrain Ranevsky? Have you no influence over him?'

'Me! You don't understand, Jean-Paul. Much of what Boris does is aimed at me, is meant to hurt and humiliate me.'

'But why?'

'Because he is in my debt. Without my money he could not have brought his ballet company out of Russia; he could not have shown the world his talent. In St Petersburg he was charming to me, paid me compliments, praised my intelligence and good taste, but as soon as I had agreed to support him and the contracts had been signed, he changed.'

'Has he no gratitude?'

'None. He would have preferred me to have stayed in Russia where he could have forgotten me. In Paris I am a constant reminder of his obligation to me. Boris cannot endure being under an obligation to anyone. He finds it a humiliation.'

'And so he repays the debt by humiliating you?'

'Yes,' Sophia replied in a small, strangled voice and then she did begin weeping, softly, with sobs that were barely louder than sighs.

Gautier found it hard to understand the strength of her feelings. She had beauty, intelligence, wealth and more freedom than most women would ever know. Why did she lay so much importance on her involvement with the ballet company and the success of its season in Paris? He would have asked her, but abruptly, without brushing away the tears that were coursing down her cheeks, she held out her arms to him.

She said, almost brusquely, 'Take me to bed. Comfort me!'

He awoke when the first light of dawn was edging the curtains of the windows and lay in bed listening to Sophia breathing. She had wept as they had made love, convulsive sobs, full of anguish, her unhappiness seeming only to sharpen the violence of her desire. Then, as her passion diminished, so did her grief and she began to talk. She told him of her life in Russia, how when she arrived in society, first as the wife and then as the widow of the prince, she had been treated as a parvenue and an upstart adventurer. Only gradually had she been able to break down the barriers of resentment and snobbery and it had been her patronage of the arts and her culture that had won her acceptance.

As she talked, Gautier had begun to understand why the success of the Dashkova Ballet meant so much to her. After the failure of her attempt to bring an opera company to Paris the previous year, it was all the more important to her that the tour of the ballet company should not be tainted by scandal. Sophia had talked of it passionately and then suddenly she had fallen asleep, in mid-sentence like children sometimes do, finding refuge in sleep from the disappointments and fears of her day.

Now as he lay there Gautier, even though he was touched

by the sight of her, found himself thinking analytically of their relationship. It was changing. That was inevitable of course. Any emotional relationship between a man and a woman always changed, slowly and often imperceptibly, as the first enchantment mellowed into familiarity. But the change which he observed in Sophia's attitude to him was different. The previous evening, for the first time since they had met, she had been impatient with him, relapsing into an indignation which had bordered on temper. That in itself was not significant, but he saw it as a harbinger of change, the first signs of a tiny rift between them. The thought saddened but did not surprise him. The talk of their marrying had been no more than a fantasy and Gautier had long ago disciplined himself to forgo the luxury of fantasies.

As if in response to that discipline, his train of thought switched tracks and he began thinking of Judge Prudhomme's death. The previous afternoon when he had returned from seeing Claire Ryan, he had made enquiries about the antique dealer who had inspected the Earl of Newry's collection of fire-arms and who had claimed to be the agent of the Duc de Béziers. He had not been surprised when he learnt that there was no Duc de Béziers and that the address on the business card given to Miss Ryan was not that of an antique dealer, but of a modest grocer's shop. One could safely assume that the purpose of the man Colibri's visit had been to reconnoitre the Earl's house for the burglary which followed. Now at least they had Miss Ryan's description of the man to circulate to dealers in antiques and weapons.

As he thought about his conversation with Miss Ryan, Gautier remembered the awkward way in which she had copied the name and address on the business card on to a sheet of paper. Were all left-handed children bullied into using their right hands as she had been, he wondered? Although the motives were praiseworthy, he thought of it as an act of cruelty which might well have a permanent effect on the child's personality. Yet Miss Ryan appeared normal enough.

Suddenly the picture of her writing the name provoked another idea and another picture in his memory. On the desk in Judge Prudhomme's office there had been a silver inkwell and pentray. He could picture the pentray now and the pens and pencils that had been lying in it, three pens all with nibs that had been carefully wiped clean ready for use and two freshly sharpened pencils. At the time he had decided that the judge's secretary looked after him well. All the pens and pencils in the tray had been lying with their points towards the right, he was certain of that. Only a left-handed person would lay them down in that way. Could that mean that Judge Prudhomme had been left-handed or was it Mathurin? With a growing excitement Gautier tried to recall the occasions when he had met Prudhomme, but he could not remember noticing whether he was left-handed. Certainly it had been his left forearm that had been wounded by Ranevsky's sword-stick, probably because he had instinctively used his left arm to ward off the blow.

The evidence that Prudhomme had been left-handed was slight. His secretary would be able to say whether he had been, but that would have to wait for a couple of hours or so until the Palais de Justice opened. In the meantime Gautier decided he would assume that he had been. A left-handed man might conceivably use his right hand to shoot himself in the head, but it was highly unlikely. If one followed that train of reasoning, then the assumption must be that Prudhomme's friend had shot him, for it had been the friend's message that had taken him to the Hôtel de Valence. The possibility that the note had been a forgery must be discounted, for the handwriting was too flowery to forge.

Even so, the note still bothered him. He remembered the slight brownish discolouration on the back of what otherwise appeared to be a new sheet of paper. Gautier had the feeling that there was something about the note the significance of which had escaped him. Restless now, he knew he would not sleep any more so he climbed out of bed, went barefoot into the drawing-room of the suite and drew the curtains to let in the light. Hearing footsteps in the corridor, he smiled, wondering what one of the hotel maids would think if she came in to tidy the room and saw him standing there naked. The maids in the hotel would rise early as his mother always had done at home, starting the day's work of cleaning, polishing, washing and ironing well before the sun rose.

The memory of his mother triggered off another idea in his mind. Returning to the bedroom, he dressed quickly, took two sheets of paper from the writing desk in the drawing-room and went into the corridor. Presently he saw one of the maids come out of a room a short distance away from him. When he asked her if she had an iron which he might use, she led him into a small room at the far end of the corridor in which the clean bedlinen was kept and where the maids did any sewing or pressing that might be needed. Another maid was pressing a frock belonging to one of the guests and she smiled with amusement when Gautier asked if he might borrow her iron.

He folded one of the sheets of paper which he had brought with him three times, then smoothed it out as well as he could, spread it on the ironing board and began pressing it with the hot iron. Only after repeated presses with the iron were the folds in the sheet of paper all taken out and by that time its surface had begun to scorch, turning a slight mottled tinge of brown very similar to the discolouration on the note which he had found in Prudhomme's waistcoat pocket.

Leaving the maids enjoying the joke and grateful for the pourboire which this eccentric gentleman had given them, Gautier returned to Sophia's suite. She was stirring now and, drawing back the bedroom curtains, he watched her waken. She smiled drowsily, happy to find him there, and held out her hand.

'You always wake so early, Jean-Paul,' she complained. 'It makes me seem like a lazy good-for-nothing.'

'Blame my policeman's training.'

'That? Or is it a bad conscience that prevents you sleeping?'

'We are not allowed consciences. Police regulations do not permit them.'

Any talk of consciences might stray dangerously close to their disagreement of the previous night, so Gautier rang for breakfast. They took it together, freshly baked bread and coffee, she in bed and Gautier sitting on the edge.

'The breakfasts in France are the finest in the world,' Sophia said contentedly.

'That is because our bakers stay up all night baking.'

'I wonder if Monsieur Labat stays up to supply them with flour.'

'You cannot seriously be suggesting that!'

'No. He tells me that his sons are running the business now and he spends most of his time on his collection.'

'His collection?'

'Of antiques.'

The mention of antiques reminded Gautier of Miss Ryan and of his promise that he would see whether he could find her a seat at the première of *Le Spectre du Nil* that evening. He asked Sophia if she knew whether any seats were available and told her that he wanted one for a friend.

'I very much doubt it. Who is this friend?'

'She is not exactly a friend; an Irish lady whom I met while investigating a robbery in the apartment of her employer.'

'Then why not invite her to my box for the gala performance on Monday. The box will be full tonight, but there are at least two places free for Monday.'

'Then I will. Thank you.'

Sophia smiled. 'And I thought you might be jealous of the Comte de Tréville,' she teased him. 'It would seem as though I may be the one who has cause for jealousy!'

15

When Gautier arrived at Sûreté headquarters he learnt that there was to be no staff conference that morning. Corbin explained that the Director General did not believe that sufficient progress was being made in the cases under investigation to justify holding a daily conference. Gautier was not surprised by the decision. Courtrand was fond of making bold pronouncements and taking what he believed were strong measures, but he would soon abandon and even disown them when they failed to produce dramatic results. In this instance what must have discouraged him was learning that Judge Prudhomme had apparently not been abducted or kidnapped, and he would wish to dissociate himself from what he would see as a sordid suicide in disreputable surroundings.

The cancellation of the conference suited Gautier, for it meant that he could now conduct the enquiries in his own way, without interference from Courtrand. From the Sûreté he went straight to the Palais de Justice. Mathurin had already been told that Judge Prudhomme was dead and when Gautier arrived he was still shaken by the double blow of that news and of reading Puy's article in *La Libre Parole*. Like so many of the *petits fonctionnaires* in government service, he was a man of integrity, loyal to and proud of the department which he served. When he had recovered his composure, he confirmed that the judge had in fact been left-handed.

'That almost certainly proves what I had suspected,' Gautier said. 'The judge could not have shot himself.'

He explained his theory of how Prudhomme had been tricked into going to the Hôtel de Valence with an old note which he had thrown into the wastepaper basket on a previous visit and which his murderer had retrieved.

'The address on the envelope in which the note was sent and

130

which you gave us,' he added, 'was written in block capitals, presumably because the murderer did not have an old envelope he could use.'

'Whoever it was certainly went to a great deal of trouble to kill the judge.'

'Have you no idea who it might have been? Do you know of any enemies he had? Did he ever receive threatening letters?'

They discussed the matter for some time, but Mathurin was not able to help. Upset though he still was at his chief's death, one had the impression that he was relieved to know that it had not been suicide. Gautier was aware that for most people suicide was associated either with an ignoble attempt to escape the disgrace of bankruptcy or fraud or with mental instability. In either case it carried a stigma.

As he walked back to the Sûreté, Gautier thought of other ways by which Prudhomme's killer might be traced. One possibility might be through the murder weapon which had been sent to the government laboratories for scientific examination. On an impulse he took a fiacre which was standing on the corner of Quai des Orfèvres and had himself driven to the laboratories. He was not very hopeful that he would learn anything of value, for he could scarcely remember any investigation which he had handled in which science had contributed to the solution of a crime. Even in cases of suspected poisoning, medical autopsies could often not establish whether a poisonous substance had been the cause of death or identify it.

At the laboratories he was shown the revolver with which Prudhomme had been shot. A number of fingerprints had been found on it, but none of them could be identified. The classification of fingerprints was a new science, which had originated in British India and then been adopted by the British police in 1901. The French police had followed the example of the British, but the 'library' of prints they were building up was not yet large enough to be of any practical value in tracing criminal offenders.

Gautier looked at the revolver. He could see only one thing by which it might be identified and that was a small silver plate which had been set in the butt. The initials H.M. were engraved on the plate.

'Is there anything unusual or special about this gun?' he asked the man who had brought it out to show him.

'Nothing at all. It is a well-known make of nine millimetre revolver.'

'Did you say nine millimetre?' Gautier asked quickly.

'Yes. They are common enough.' The man laughed. 'People say that every American sleeps with one under his pillow.'

'May I take it with me?'

'Of course, Inspector. If you sign for it.'

The fiacre which had brought Gautier to the laboratories had waited for him and he told the driver to take him to the Earl of Newry's house. On the way to Parc Monceau he reproached himself for his carelessness, for neglecting to make what was no more than a commonsense check. Was it because he was allowing himself to be distracted from his duties by the attractions of social life, by the ballet and supper parties and by Sophia? The success which had marked his career in the Sûreté and won him promotion at an unusually early age had been achieved by singlemindedness, self-discipline and hard work. Talent, flair, a skill in deduction, whatever one chose to call it, could help but was no substitute for them.

The Earl of Newry had not yet left his home for the refuge of the Jockey Club and he received Gautier in his study. He recognised the revolver immediately as one of those which had been stolen from his collection.

'Do you see the initials?' He pointed to the silver plate. 'H.M. stands for Homer Marsh, my wife's father. The two revolvers were a matched pair which had been presented to him by the Lions or the Buffaloes or the Elks or one other of those beastly American societies. He had been President of his local branch.'

'And he gave the revolvers to you?'

'He left them to my wife and me in his will.' The Earl smiled boyishly. 'I was never sure whether they were intended for my wife as protection against me or vice versa.'

'Is the other gun identical with this one?'

'It is. You have not found it yet then?'

'Not as yet. I regret to tell you that this one was used to kill a man.'

'My word, how dreadful! Was it by any chance that judge who was found dead in an hotel? I read about the affair in the newspaper.'

'I am afraid it was.'

'Then I hope you catch the scoundrel who shot him.'

The Earl showed Gautier out of the apartment himself. On the way Gautier asked him, 'Is Mademoiselle Ryan at home?'

'Not at present. She has taken my dogs for a walk.'

'Then would you be so kind as to give her a message from me?' Gautier explained that he had been unable to procure a seat for Miss Ryan for the première of *Le Spectre du Nil* that evening, but that she was invited to watch the gala performance from the box of Princess Sophia Dashkova.

'That's uncommonly good of the Princess and of you. Claire has little social life in Paris. In a way I feel guilty about that.'

'Why should you feel guilty, monsieur?' Not many of the Parisians whom Gautier knew would be concerned about the social life of their housekeepers.

'It was I who brought her here.'

When he arrived back at Sûreté headquarters, Gautier sent for Surat. For the plan he had in mind he would need Surat's help, but first he wished to have a report on the enquiries that were being made at Prudhomme's home and the Gare du Nord and the Hôtel de Valence. He had the feeling that they would all have been abortive, for the murder of Prudhomme had been carefully planned and executed. Surat confirmed his fears. Nothing of any consequence had been discovered. Next Gautier outlined his plan.

'For a start,' he said, 'we need to make a list of all the criminal cases at which Judge Prudhomme presided.'

'But patron, there must be scores of them! He has been a judge for at least twenty years.'

'Not scores; dozens perhaps. They will all be listed in the legal gazette. We do not have to check the transcripts of the trials. All we need to know is the year in which the trials took place, the verdicts, the names of the accused and, in cases where they were found guilty, the sentences they received.'

'Are you looking for someone who might have had a grudge against the judge?'

'More than a grudge; a passion for revenge and enough hatred to wish to kill him.'

'Then you believe Judge Prudhomme was murdered.'

'I am satisfied now that he was.'

Briefly Gautier explained to Surat his theory of how the judge's murder had been planned, how the murderer, having read in a newspaper of the Earl of Newry's collection of weapons, had reconnoitred his apartment, broken in and stolen the revolvers; how he had followed the judge to study his habits and so learnt of the assignations in the Hôtel de Valence; how he had tricked Prudhomme into going there and then murdered him in circumstances which strongly suggested suicide.

'Why did he steal the silver and jewellery as well?' Surat asked.

'Either to conceal his real purpose or, more probably, for money. My guess is that, having murdered the judge, he will have sold the stolen property and used the cash to get out of Paris.'

'Then we should be looking for someone who was recently released from jail?'

'A few weeks ago, I would say.'

'Are you ruling out the possibility that the man who stole the revolvers might have been hired to kill the judge? By those Russians perhaps?'

'I believe it's extremely unlikely. The ballet company have only been in Paris a short time and Prudhomme could not have met the dancers more than about ten days ago. The man who stole the revolvers had already reconnoitred the Earl's apartment by that time.'

The work of sifting through all the criminal trials at which Prudhomme had presided was laborious. In a large majority the accused had been found guilty. This was not surprising, for suspected offenders were put on trial only after a lengthy examination by a *juge d'instruction* and after all the evidence had been reviewed by the Chambre de Mise en Accusation, which was the body that decided whether there should be a prosecution. What did surprise Gautier was the number of convicted offenders who were still in prison, some of them in the penal settlement on Devil's Island. Studying the summaries of the cases, he realised that Prudhomme's reputation for giving harsh sentences had been well deserved.

Knowing that he would not have time to visit the Café Corneille that morning, he took a quick lunch at the café in Place Dauphine with Surat. Over the meal Surat talked of his family. He had a daughter who was proving herself to be an exceptionally gifted mathematician and he wished to give the girl an education which would help her develop her talent. He knew that would be difficult, for girls were not expected to be highly educated. Secondary education had been introduced for them only within the last thirty years and middle-class parents preferred to have their daughters at home, where they could be taught sewing, cooking and other domestic skills. Gautier promised that he would have a word with Professor Racine, a brilliant but eccentric mathematician at the university, to see what might be done for Surat's daughter.

Back at the Sûreté after lunch a further two hours of research produced a list of fourteen men sentenced by Prudhomme who might now have been released from prison. Against each name on the list they had noted the offence for which the man had been found guilty and the length of sentence he had been given.

'I suggest we eliminate all those who served sentences of more than ten years,' Gautier told Surat.

'Why? Do you feel that a man could not nurse a grudge for longer than that?'

'That is one reason. More importantly, I do not believe that after ten years in one of our prisons, a man would have either the spirit or the energy to plan a murder as clever and as ruthless as this one.'

After narrowing the list of names in the way that Gautier had suggested, they were left with only three likely suspects; Arnaux, who had been sentenced to ten years in prison for armed robbery, Maubet, who had served eight years for manslaughter, and Groeningen, who had been given a similar term for wounding a police officer.

'Do you remember any of these men?' Gautier asked Surat.

'I remember Arnaux. He was vicious that one. He screamed at the judge when he was sentenced and swore to have his revenge.'

'In that case he is probably the least likely to have murdered Prudhomme. I can remember both Maubet and Groeningen, for I arrested them both. Maubet was a small, inoffensive Corsican sailor, who was attacked with a knife by an apache in a dance hall on the Butte. He defended himself with a broken bottle and by a mischance severed his attacker's jugular vein. Prudhomme gave him first a lecture on taking the law into one's own hands and then eight years in prison.'

'That seems a little harsh if it was accidental. What about Groeningen?'

'He's a Dutchman who married a French girl and made his home in France. The girl was a waitress in a disreputable brasserie

135

and one of their neighbours accused Groeningen of living on her immoral earnings. When a police officer went to bring him in for questioning, Groeningen went berserk; attacked the man with an axe and nearly killed him.'

'It sounds as though he was lucky to get only eight years.'

'Not really. We found out afterwards that the neighbour's story was totally untrue. Although she had been a *putain* before she met Groeningen, the girl had changed her ways after she married him. I heard later that she had died in childbirth soon after he was locked up.'

'I would think that any of the three might have wished to kill Judge Prudhomme.'

Gautier remembered that Claire Ryan had given a description, though not a very detailed one, of the man who had gone to inspect the Earl of Newry's collection of weapons. 'Miss Ryan told me that the man who went to see the Earl's guns was short, dark and round-shouldered and that he walked with a limp.'

'That would rule out Arnaux. As I remember he was a monster of a man and almost bald, but what hair he had left was red.'

'The Dutchman was tall as well; tall and blond.'

'So we are left with the Corsican?'

'It would be unwise to eliminate the other two. Hair can be dyed and it is not difficult to feign a limp.'

The dossier of Prudhomme's trials which they had been studying gave the addresses in Paris at which each of the three men had been living at the time of his arrest. Gautier told Surat to contact the local police in each arrondissement to find out whether the men had returned to their former homes after being released from jail and if anything were known about what they had been doing.

'In the meantime I will speak to Miss Ryan,' Gautier added, 'to see if she can add anything to the description she gave of the soi-disant antique dealer.'

As Surat was leaving, a messenger came into the room and told Gautier that a lady was asking for him downstairs, a Mademoiselle Ryan.

'What a coincidence!' Surat exclaimed.

The news did not surprise Gautier. Miss Ryan had no doubt come to give him another of the little scraps of information which she had been handing out to him and, with the uncanny sense of timing which she seemed to possess, she had come just as he had decided that he would go and question her. He went downstairs and found her waiting by the entrance to the building. He could see she was reluctant to come inside.

'Have you come to walk by the river with me, mademoiselle?' he asked her, smiling.

'You're laughing at me!' she said reproachfully.

'Yes, but not unkindly.' He took her arm and they crossed the street towards the embankment of the Seine.

'I have a deep-rooted aversion to police stations,' Miss Ryan said, 'which I cannot seem to conquer.'

'Many people have and not always because of a guilty conscience.'

'When I was a girl I had a harrowing experience at the village police station. One day I was collected from school by the police, the Garda as we call them, and taken to the station. When we arrived I found my mother there dead.'

She told Gautier that her family had lived in the country. One day her mother, while walking from their cottage to the village, was attacked by a drunken farm labourer and brutally murdered. Since there was no hospital or mortuary in the village, her body had been taken to the police station. Claire Ryan had been taken there without being warned of what she would find.

'What a horrifying experience! Why did your father not come to fetch you from school?'

'My father was not there at the time,' Miss Ryan replied.

They walked along by the river in silence for a time, Miss Ryan perhaps allowing the pain of memory to subside, Gautier feeling that words of comfort would be of little help and might seem insincere.

'Have you come to tell me something more about the robbery?' he asked her.

'No. I am here to thank you for the invitation to the gala performance of the ballet.'

'I am delighted that I could be of help.' Gautier hoped that his disappointment did not show in his reply. He had been hoping that Miss Ryan would have something more interesting to tell him.

'I am very grateful to you, but I cannot possibly accept the invitation.'

'Why ever not?'

'I have never met Princess Sophia or any of her friends. It would be embarrassing.'

'The Princess may not even be in her box, for she usually prefers to be backstage on these occasions. As for her friends, I probably will not have met them before either.'

'Then you will be there?'

'Certainly. A gala performance is not to be missed.'

'In that case I shall accept the invitation. Please thank the Princess for me.'

They paused on the embankment to watch a sailing barge on its journey down the river. To see a vessel with sails on the Seine was rare now, for they had all but disappeared. Even so in some ways the river still clung to its past; horses would be brought to drink in it, women washed clothes on the *bateaux-lavoirs* and a few optimists still fished in it.

'My mother's death was the reason I learnt French,' Miss Ryan said. 'That sounds bizarre, but it's true. Since there was no one to look after me, I was sent first to convent school in Ireland and then to a finishing school in Switzerland. That's where I learnt my French.'

'Not only do you speak our language fluently, but you have a Frenchwoman's accent. That's what astonishes me.'

'A facility for languages is a gift; rather like an ear for music, I always think. At school in Switzerland we spoke French all the time, but girls from several countries were studying there and I found I could pick up their languages quite easily.'

'What other languages do you speak besides French?'

'Italian reasonably fluently and Spanish moderately well, but I can also make myself understood in German and Dutch.'

'A very useful gift.'

'And when a foreigner is speaking English, or French for that matter, I can always tell what country he comes from. It isn't only the accent that gives him away, but the way he constructs his sentences and the words he uses when there is a choice.' Miss Ryan made the claim without boasting, simply to explain her gift. 'For example, that man who came to view the Earl's collection of fire-arms was Dutch.'

'Are you sure of that?'

'Oh yes. Did I not mention it before? Monsieur Colibri spoke French fluently, but he was a Dutchman. I would swear to it.'

'We may ask you to do just that,' Gautier said.

16

Miss Ryan left after Gautier had promised that he would meet her at the entrance of l'Opéra on the Monday evening and escort her to Sophia's box. She seemed nervous at the prospect of meeting Sophia and any other guests who might be sharing the box and Gautier began to think that the self-assurance she had always displayed when she was with him must be no more than a façade, concealing a natural shyness. He supposed it was possible that even girls who went to expensive finishing schools in Switzerland might be shy and self-effacing.

On his way back to Sûreté headquarters he made a detour in order to pass the stalls of the *bouquinistes*. He had not seen Inspector Lemaire at all that day and was anxious to know what progress had been made in tracing Jules, the concierge's friend. When he reached Lebrun's stall he was surprised to find Madame Lebrun there. She was talking to a passer-by who had stopped to examine one of the books. Eventually the man decided to buy the book, paid Madame Lebrun for it and left.

When she saw Gautier, Marie Lebrun said, 'This is the third book I have sold this afternoon, Inspector, and the most highly priced. Jacques will be pleased.'

'Where is your husband? He is not ill again, I hope.'

'No. He is being held in prison.'

'On whose orders?'

'The *juge d'instruction*. He says that the offence is too serious for Jacques to be allowed to remain at liberty. So, as long as he cannot run the business I shall do my best.'

Marie Lebrun looked at Gautier calmly. He realised that what she was doing was not a gesture of defiance or even of courage, but a means of fighting off despair. Once again he felt a rush of sympathy for the Lebruns, compounded this time with remorse and a wish that he could have done more for them. He might well have been able to persuade Courtrand that he should be allowed to continue handling their case.

'Who is the *juge d'instruction*?' he asked.

'Judge Ducasse.'

She told Gautier that she and her husband had been before Ducasse that morning. After questioning them, first separately and then together, for more than three hours, Ducasse had told Madame Lebrun that she might return home but that Lebrun would be required for further interrogation and would be held in prison until he was called again. Other witnesses, the concierge of the building in which they lived and police officers from their local police commissariat, were also being questioned.

In Gautier's opinion Ducasse was the worst choice that could have been made for examining magistrate in the case. Ducasse was a small man in all senses of the word, full of his own importance and totally without imagination. Once in charge, he would give the police officers working on the case no freedom and his method of examining witnesses was to hector them mercilessly in the hope that they would confess. In this case he had probably already decided that Lebrun had killed his child and was merely building up the prosecution's case against him.

After trying to reassure Marie Lebrun that all would still be well and that her husband would be released, Gautier returned to Sûreté headquarters. There he learnt that Surat had already contacted the local police in each of the arrondissements where Arnaux, Maubet and Groeningen had been living before they were imprisoned. Maubet, Surat told him, could be eliminated from their list of suspects, for he was in hospital and in a coma. On his release from prison, he had quarrelled with his wife, accusing her of being unfaithful to him, which was true, and she had attacked him with a kitchen knife.

'We can rule out Arnaux as well,' Gautier said. 'Groeningen is our man.'

He told Surat briefly of his conversation with Claire Ryan and added, 'Contact the local police again and tell them that if they can find Groeningen, they should arrest him. I imagine though that we may be too late.'

'Too late, patron?'

'He could easily have gone straight from killing Prudhomme and boarded a train for Holland. That would be the clever move and if his wife is dead, there's nothing to keep him in France.'

'Shall I alert the frontier police?'

'You may as well. It will do no harm.'

After Surat had left him, Gautier wrote a concise report on the recent developments in the Prudhomme affair and handed it to Courtrand's secretary. The Director General had already left his office for the day to change his clothes before going to some social function. That reminded Gautier that he too should soon be returning home to change for the evening at the ballet. He still had enough time, though, to do something which might help the Lebruns.

Finding that Inspector Lemaire had already left for the day, he decided that even though the investigation was not his responsibility he must act, and found a fiacre to take him up to the building where the Lebruns had their apartment. The concierge seemed more alert than on the last occasion when he had seen her and her face was a better colour, which made him hope that perhaps she had not been drinking. Alcohol made her truculent and he needed her cooperation.

'Monsieur Lebrun has been arrested for killing the child,' she told Gautier as soon as she saw him.

'He is being detained while the *juge d'instruction* is examining him.'

'You don't believe he killed that child, do you, Inspector?'

'No. Do you?' The concierge only shrugged her shoulders, so Gautier continued, 'I find it strange that you should dislike Monsieur and Madame Lebrun. They don't speak ill of you.'

'I don't dislike them.'

'They say that you helped them with their child.'

'Poor little mite!'

'They both loved the baby. How could you possibly think that they would have killed her?'

'Who else could have done?'

'I believe the man Jules did it. I believe he came here just for that purpose, that he deceived you and took advantage of your good nature.'

Gautier knew he was taking a gamble. Many women, most women perhaps, would resent any suggestion that they had been duped by a man, that a man had paid them attention simply to exploit them. The concierge, he believed, might react differently. Remarks she had made suggested that she distrusted men and might even feel that she had been badly treated by them.

'What are you saying?' she demanded.

'Have you seen Jules since the day the baby was killed?'

'No, not yet.'

'I do not believe that you will ever see him again,' Gautier told her.

'Why not?'

He explained his theory that Jules had been paid to kill the Lebruns' child, that he had invented an excuse for coming to see the concierge and became friendly with her simply so that he could learn more about his victim and engineer an opportunity to carry out his commission. As he was speaking he could see from the woman's expression that his gamble had succeeded.

'So that was why he came,' she said when Gautier had finished, and added an epithet which most women would never have heard, but which summed up her opinion of all men and of Jules in particular.

'Of course I could be wrong.'

'No. What you are saying makes sense. I never did trust the man.'

'If I am right, we must catch the villain. That's the only way to prove that the Lebruns are innocent. Will you help?'

'Willingly, but how?'

'We believe that by now he will have left Paris and returned to wherever his home is. Can you think of anything he may have said that would help us trace him? He probably gave you a false name and what we need is any detail, however small, that might help us to identify him.'

The concierge thought for a while. She was a bulky, slow-moving woman and her brain was equally ponderous. Finally she said, 'There was one thing which seemed strange to me. He said he came from Marseilles, but he would tell me how he would sit in cafés by the docks, watching the big liners coming in from America, with rich Americans abroad. He was always talking about America and said he would go there one day when he had the money. But the big liners from America don't sail into Marseilles.'

'Some do, I believe.'

'Maybe, but I think he was lying when he said he came from Marseilles. I believe he is from Le Havre. Remember that bottle of calvados he brought me.'

The calvados Jules had brought her, the concierge told Gautier,

142

had been particularly good. There had been no label on the bottle and when she had commented on this, Jules had told her that his cousin had distilled it.

'Calvados is made in Normandy. Everyone knows that. No, I think the lying swine came from Le Havre.'

'If you're right that may be very helpful. Can you think of anything else that would help us trace him?'

'Did I tell you he has a hare lip?'

'You did not. Are you sure of that?'

'Absolutely. It was partly hidden by his moustaches, but you could spot it if you looked carefully.'

Gautier asked her to repeat the description of Jules which she had previously given. Then he left, satisfied that now there was at least a chance of finding Jules. If he had been hired to kill the Lebruns' child, he would have at least a reputation for violence and very possibly a criminal conviction and there would not be many such men in Le Havre who also had a hare lip.

Back at the Sûreté he found that Surat had left for home, so he hurriedly composed a telegraph message to the police in Le Havre, asking for their help in tracing the man who had posed as Jules. By the time it had been despatched, the performance of the ballet was almost due to begin, but evening dress was de rigueur for the occasion, so he had to return to his apartment to change. He did it as quickly as he could, persuading the driver of the fiacre which took him there and back to drive much faster than he would usually do, but even so when he reached the Châtelet he was told that the première of *Le Spectre du Nil* had started some minutes previously.

Up in Sophia's box he saw that there were two seats unoccupied and slipped into one of them. The two Russian émigré couples with whom he had shared the box when watching *Seraglio* were there again and he kissed the ladies' hands and nodded to their husbands before turning his attention to the stage.

A résumé of the story of that night's ballet was given in the programme, presumably since it was felt that an untutored audience would not be able to follow the plot merely by watching the dancing and miming. From this Gautier learnt that it was a full-length ballet in three acts. The central character in the story was the Queen of Egypt. In the first act the Queen makes a triumphant return to her country from a visit to Rome where she has been fêted by the Romans, after being betrothed to a young man of noble birth, a son of the Caesar. She arrives sailing up the Nile in her royal barge and as she steps ashore is greeted by her subjects who celebrate her return. Among those waiting for her are her cousin and his wife, a beautiful princess from Ethiopia, and the Queen is unaware that they have been plotting to kill her, so that they can succeed to the throne.

When Gautier arrived, the prince and princess were dancing in honour of the Queen, a pas de deux, graceful and beautifully executed, but full of a sinister menace. He thought at first that this might be the dance which he had seen portrayed in one of the sketches that Ranevsky had shown him, but the costumes of the couple were different and the rôles were being played by two dancers whom he could not recall having seen before. The Queen watched them, sitting on a throne of gold which had been placed for her at the foot of steps leading up to a temple, and Gautier saw with surprise that the rôle of the Queen was being danced by Elena Karpovna and wondered whether perhaps it was not, as he had assumed, the leading part in the ballet.

The stage setting was stupendous in its impact and Gautier felt that Alex Sanson's designs surpassed even those he had done for *Seraglio*. The brilliance of the colours, the vast, towering pillars of the temple, the extravagant richness of the awnings of the barge, the gleaming armour of the soldiers, gave an overwhelming impression of the wealth and splendour and of the traditions of antiquity.

The Queen was dancing now, a solo made up of simple steps but full of a dignity and poise in keeping with her royalty. But the atmosphere of menace could still be felt, the tension mounting. Then, as she was mounting the steps that led to the entrance of the temple, one of the soldiers from the guard leapt forward and drove his spear into her breast.

As the curtain was lowered, the door of their box was opened. Turning round, Gautier saw Sophia coming in and she sat down beside him. Even in the dim light he could see that her face was distorted with anguish.

'What's the matter?' he asked at once. 'What has happened?'

'Nicola Stepanova is dead.' One could sense that Sophia was using all her self-control to keep emotion out of her voice.

'Dead! How did she die?'

'She took poison, we believe.'

144

17

Stepanova's body lay on the floor of her dressing-room, naked except for brief undergarments and covered with a blanket. She had vomited before she died and her face was distorted with pain. Someone had closed her eyes.

'When did this happen?' Gautier asked Ranevsky, who had brought him and Sophia to the dressing-room.

'Immediately before she was due to go on stage.'

'Then she was to dance tonight?'

'Of course. The leading rôle. When she collapsed we had to send Karpovna on in her place.' Sophia glanced at Stepanova's body and flinching, turned her head away. 'We didn't realise then that she was dead. It was dreadful!'

'I sent for a doctor at once.' Ranevsky was clearly shaken. 'It's scandalous that he should be taking so long to come. I shall make an official protest.'

Gautier knelt over the body and drew back the blanket. There were no wounds to be seen. Looking round the room, he noticed that there were two dressing tables and two large mirrors on the wall, suggesting that it was meant to be shared by two performers. A tray with the remains of a meal stood on each dressing table.

Noticing him look at the trays, Sophia said, 'Stepanova always took a light meal before she danced. She preferred to have it here rather than at the hotel.'

'And the other tray?'

'That was for Karpovna. They shared this room.'

'Where is Karpovna?'

'In another dressing-room, changing her costume for the second act of the ballet. We could not expect her to come in here.'

'I shall have to speak to her,' Gautier said, 'but that can wait until the performance is over.'

'I should hope so!' Ranevsky said. 'Can you imagine what she must be feeling? Seeing her friend die and then being thrust on to the stage, quite unprepared to perform a ballet for the first time?'

'Was there anyone else here when she died, apart from Karpovna?'

'Only the dresser.' Ranevsky pointed towards a middle-aged woman who was sitting in a corner of the dressing-room, and whom until then Gautier had scarcely noticed.

Gautier looked at the trays on the dressing tables. On the one nearest to Stepanova's body there was a plate which held the remains of salad and a cup, empty except for two or three centimetres of a dark brown liquid.

'Do you know what the demoiselle had to eat?' he asked the dresser.

'Only a tiny slice of ham with the salad. She complained that the salad was not fresh and ate hardly any of it.'

'Who provided the meal?'

'A café in the square outside the theatre. A waiter brought the trays in.'

'We had a standing arrangement with the café,' Sophia explained.

Gautier picked up the cup from the tray on Stepanova's dressing table and sniffed it. He was certain that the ballerina had been poisoned, for he could think of nothing else which would kill a healthy young woman so quickly. He had no idea what the poison might have been and there was no certainty that they would ever know. Although many advances had been made in recent years, medical science was rudimentary and there were still many poisons which had not been identified.

'What did the demoiselle have to drink?' he asked the dresser.

'She would never take wine before she danced, not even a single glass – only herbal tea and she always made that herself with hot water that I brought her. She kept the herbs in that canister.'

The dresser pointed towards the dressing table where, among the bowls of powder and little pots of rouge and cream, stood a small, green tin canister. Inside there appeared to be a mixture of herbs, all chopped small and some of which he thought he recognised by their scent – rosemary, thyme and camomile. They would have to be analysed in due course, but they looked and smelt innocent enough.

146

'Were you in the room when the demoiselle died?' he asked the dresser.

'I came in just as she collapsed.' The woman shook her head, as though trying to free her memory of the horror she had watched. 'The other demoiselle had asked me to go and fetch some pins which she needed.'

'Did she say anything as she was dying?'

'Nothing. She was vomiting and clutching her stomach. Then she seemed to lose all her strength and just collapsed. Her breath was coming in great heaving gulps.'

'Where was the other demoiselle when this happened?'

'In the room. When I came in, she was trying to help her friend, but could do nothing for her.'

Recounting what she had seen was too much for the dresser and she began to weep, hiding her face in her hands. While Gautier was waiting for her emotion to subside, Sanson entered the room. He was dressed informally, wearing the same cardigan that he had the first time Gautier met him. His face was drawn, his manner that of a man trying to put on a façade of composure and authority, but the façade seemed to be cracking at the edges.

'The second act is about to begin,' he told the others in the room.

'How is Karpovna bearing up?' Sophia asked him.

'Magnificently! When she came off stage she was emotionally drained and we thought she was going to collapse, but she recovered. What courage that girl has!'

'As you can see, my dancers are totally dedicated to their art,' Ranevsky said to Gautier. He may have felt he was obliged to defend his company against the high-handedness of the police.

'What will you do now?' Sanson asked Gautier.

'The inspector has said that he will take no further action until the ballet is over.'

'That is very considerate of him.' Sanson turned to Ranevsky and added with a little spurt of malice, 'So you will get your curtain call after all, Boris.'

'Should you not go and make sure that the set is ready for the next act, Alex?' Sophia asked him quickly.

When Sanson had left, Gautier told the others that they too need no longer stay in the dressing-room. Once the doctor had arrived and made his examination, the room would be kept locked, with a police officer on guard, until the following day when it could be thoroughly searched for clues or evidence.

'You are treating this as a case of murder then?' Sophia asked.

'I have no choice. It is most unlikely that Stepanova would have taken poison deliberately just before a performance and here in the theatre.'

'Could it not have been accidental?' Ranevsky suggested. 'I warned her more than once against meddling with herbal remedies. You have no idea how many peasants in Russia die from eating poisonous fungi and berries, in the belief that they will cure minor ailments. Superstitious nonsense!'

'Let us hope you are right, monsieur, but for the present I must follow police procedure.'

They all left the dressing-room and Gautier locked the door, asking the dresser to wait outside and to call him as soon as the doctor arrived. Then he found a messenger, a young lad who did odd jobs backstage and who agreed to go to Sûreté headquarters and ask for two policemen to be sent to the theatre. Ranevsky hurried away and Gautier wondered whether, having been reassured that he would be going on stage at the end of the performance, he had gone to make sure that he was looking at his best. Ranevsky, he had observed, was a vain man, whose clothes were well made and immaculately pressed and who wore discreet touches of powder and rouge during the day.

'Was Elena Karpovna supposed to be dancing tonight?' he asked Sophia.

'Not in the première, but she danced in a short ballet which we put on before *Le Spectre du Nil*. She was also supposed to be standing by in case Stepanova could not go on for any reason. Karpovna is the only other dancer who knows the rôle of the Queen. Of course we never dreamt anything like this would happen.' Sophia looked hard at Gautier and he saw the first faint lines of anger at the corners of her mouth. 'Why? For heaven's sake, don't tell me you suspect Elena of poisoning Stepanova?'

'I suspect no one.'

'Or everyone?'

Gautier might have pointed out that Stepanova's death had come at a remarkably opportune time for Karpovna, allowing her to dance the leading rôle in the première of *Le Spectre du Nil*, an ambition of which she had made no secret and for which

148

she and her admirers had canvassed so insistently. He recognised even so that Sophia's remark was well timed, reminding him that he was in danger of slipping too readily into assumptions.

'I have never been backstage at a theatre before,' he said.

Sophia took the remark for what, in a way, it was, an apology. She said, 'We can watch the second act from the wings if you like.'

'Willingly.'

'But please do not let the dancers see you. They know you're a policeman and will wonder why you are here. None of them knows of Stepanova's death.'

Alex Sanson had been premature in telling them several minutes previously that the second act of the ballet was about to begin, for even now the stage was not ready. Gautier could see that the setting for the act was of an Egyptian burial chamber. The scenery was austere and the lighting subdued, which would have given an impression of funereal gloom had it not been for the splendour of the riches which, following Egyptian custom, went with the Queen to her last resting place. Stage-hands were carrying them on to the stage, a gold and blue death mask, vases, urns and ornaments, necklaces and amulets and jewels, all piled high and looking real enough, even though they were no more than stage props.

As Gautier stood watching, a passing stage-hand bumped into him. The man was carrying what looked like a coffin, fashioned out of gold and inlaid with jewels, but which must have been made of papier-mâché, for he was carrying it unaided without difficulty. The man seemed to stare at Gautier as he passed and smiled apologetically, but said nothing. His face was vaguely familiar, but Gautier could not recall having met him before.

'We had better move further forward,' Sophia said. 'Standing here we are in everyone's way.'

Their move was timely, for at that moment dancers from the corps de ballet began filing on to the stage, taking up their positions for the start of the second act. They were mourners, men as well as women, the men dressed in black, the women in purple robes. Presently the orchestra began to play and as the curtain was raised, the mourners started dancing, not moving their feet at first, but swaying and bending and moving their arms, miming grief. After a time they began moving across the stage, unhurriedly, forming elaborate patterns of black and purple as they crossed and recrossed. Then the prince and princess came on stage and danced with the mourners, slowly and gracefully, echoing their grief, but with a sinister undercurrent to their miming. After a time the mourners filed off the stage, disconsolate and dejected. Left alone, the prince and princess threw off pretence and their dance became one of triumph around the coffin of the dead Queen.

When their dance ended, they left the stage laughing.

Immediately the mood of the music changed. A fanfare of trumpets was followed by a march as four Roman legionnaires came into the burial chamber followed by Marcus, the son of the Caesar to whom the Queen had been betrothed. He gazed at the Queen's coffin, ordered the soldiers to leave and then began to dance, expressing his inconsolable despair.

As his dance ended, once more the mood of the music changed. First the cellos recapitulated the mournful theme of the young Roman's dance and then a solo oboe came in with an eerie melody, full of mystery and suspense. Presently from the coffin in the middle of the stage the spirit of the dead Queen arose, dressed in a billowing robe of silk, her face whitened to ghostliness. Marcus watched her, incredulous at first and then joyfully. They danced and Gautier recognised the movements which he had watched Stepanova and Olenine rehearsing in the theatre only a few days ago.

He was not able to watch the whole dance or see what followed, for at that moment the ballerinas' dresser came to tell him that the doctor had arrived. Returning to the dressing-room to unlock the door, he found that the two policemen from Sûreté headquarters had also arrived. The doctor apologised for his tardiness, explaining that the influenza epidemic which had seized Paris was making it impossible for him to meet his commitments on time. He examined Stepanova's body as Gautier watched.

'Was anyone present when the woman died?' he asked Gautier.

'Another dancer and the dresser.'

'Did they say in what way she died and how quickly?'

Gautier repeated what the dresser had told him of the events that had led up to Stepanova's collapse and death and of the meal she had eaten. Then he asked, 'Was she poisoned, do you think?'

'Almost certainly. Of course we shall have to carry out certain tests, but the way she died suggests that she probably took aconite. It is one of the fastest poisons that we know and there is no antidote.'

'In that case the poison might well have been in the food or drink she took just before she died.'

'Very probably. It has little taste and in liquid form is colourless. On the other hand that would be immaterial if she took it deliberately.'

'I would say that's most unlikely. She was about to go on stage, to dance in the première of a new ballet which everyone believed would be a great success. Why do you suspect suicide? Is the poison difficult to obtain?'

'Aconite? Not particularly. It is derived from the root of a plant, but it is uncommon.'

'Then it is not likely that the dead woman took it by accident?'

'I doubt it very much.'

The doctor locked his bag, for he had seen all he needed to see. The woman was dead and it was not for him to say whether she had poisoned herself or had been murdered. At night in Paris there would be other victims, other dead bodies waiting to be examined.

'Can the body be taken to the mortuary?' Gautier asked him.

'I will arrange it.'

'Would you be kind enough to ask those who come to fetch the body to remove it discreetly? There will be onlookers outside the theatre and we do not wish to arouse a morbid sensation.'

After the doctor had left, Gautier relocked the dressing-room and left one of the policemen on guard outside, with instructions that he should admit no one except the mortuary attendants when they came for Stepanova's body. He stationed the other policeman outside the stage door entrance to the theatre. There was always a possibility that newspaper reporters might learn somehow that there had been a death in the theatre and try to force their way backstage. The policeman would see that they did not succeed. Then he walked to Sûreté headquarters and telephoned the Russian embassy. He supposed that senior officials from the embassy might well be at that evening's performance of the ballet, but any attempt to locate them in the theatre might cause a stir, so he spoke to the duty officer, telling him only the bare facts of Stepanova's death. Finally he wrote the same information on a form used by the Sûreté for reporting a homicide of a foreign national. The demands of bureaucracy had to be met.

When he returned to the theatre, the performance of *Le Spectre du Nil* was ending and he was glad to see no signs that the audience was aware of what had been happening off stage. Ranevsky was in the wings, waiting for the curtain calls which would follow.

'As soon as the performance is over,' Gautier said to him, 'I shall have to speak to Elena Karpovna.'

'Good God, man, have you no sensitivity?' Ranevsky protested. 'The girl will be physically and emotionally exhausted. Can't your questions wait until tomorrow?'

'Not possibly.'

'Then at least give her time to compose herself and change out of her costume.'

Gautier agreed to that. 'It would also be better if I did not interview her in front of the other members of the company.'

'Then I shall bring her to the theatre manager's office. You have no objection to my being present?'

'None, monsieur.'

Gautier watched the ending of the ballet from the wings. Since he had missed the end of the second and almost all of the third act, he could not follow what was happening on the stage. Sophia was no longer backstage and he supposed that she must have gone round to her box so she could be with her guests at the end of the performance. Once again he was surprised by her calmness and by her composure after the death of Stepanova, for he knew it would inevitably create exactly the sensation and scandal of which she had been so afraid throughout the ballet company's tour.

The manager of the theatre was not in his office, presumably because he was out making sure that his staff were in their places, ready to usher the audience out of the theatre and close it now that the performance had ended. As he waited in the empty room, Gautier realised that the manager must be an orderly and methodical man. On a board behind his desk were posted the names of all the theatre's employees, listed according to their duties, foyer attendants, auditorium attendants, stage-hands, scene shifters, cleaners and catering staff who served refreshments during the intervals.

Changes in the staff had been carefully noted. Against the name of one of the foyer attendants was the word 'Deceased' followed by the date, and another name had been added at the bottom of the list, with the date when the newcomer's employment had commenced. One of the scene shifters had been dismissed and another was apparently sick and new names

152

had been added to replace them, one of whom was listed as being temporary.

Around the walls of the office bills advertising productions at the theatre were displayed, including several plays that had won acclaim among Parisian audiences over the previous two decades; *Cyrano de Bergerac* by Edmond Rostand, *La Rafale* by Henry Bernstein, *La Course de Flambeau* by Paul Hervieu. The names of famous actors and actresses topped the bills: Lucien Guitry, Réjane, Bernhardt.

Gautier was reading the bills, savouring the nostalgia aroused by memories of the Paris he had known as a young man, when Elena Karpovna came into the office, escorted by Ranevsky and Sanson, both of whom looked defiant, as though determined to protect her from any police intimidation or bullying. Gautier offered her a chair and she sat down, looking neither defiant nor nervous, but weary and resigned.

'Mademoiselle, I realise that you must be tired after your performance,' he said, 'but I have to ask you some questions about the death of your colleague, Mademoiselle Stepanova.'

'Of course, Inspector. I understand that.'

'A medical examination suggests that she probably died from poison.'

'Yes, it would seem so.'

'Have you any idea, mademoiselle, how she came to take poison?'

Karpovna looked at him steadily. She was pale and drawn, but seemed from some inner reserves to have summoned the strength for what she had to do.

She said simply, 'Yes, Inspector. I gave it to her.'

18

On Monday afternoon, sitting in his office, Gautier felt restless. The feeling was one which he often experienced when a criminal investigation on which he had been working had reached a stage where the processes of law had been put in train and there was no further action that he could take. In this case that stage had been reached in the enquiry into the death of Nicola Stepanova. Immediately after the première of *Le Spectre du Nil*, Elena Karpovna had been taken to the St Lazare prison, where she had spent the last two nights. Ranevsky had protested and Sophia had been indignant, but after she admitted giving poison to Stepanova, Gautier had no alternative but to arrest her.

That morning she had appeared before a *juge d'instruction* who had been appointed to handle the case. The examination had continued until midday and a transcript of it lay on Gautier's desk. Judge Lacaze was a man whom Gautier liked and respected and he had questioned Karpovna courteously and fairly, not attempting to bully her as some other judges might have done. Flipping through the pages of the transcript, Gautier remembered listening to the answers that Karpovna had given to Lacaze's questions.

Question: Do I take it that you admit that you were responsible for the death of the woman, Stepanova?
Karpovna: I do, yes.
Question: Then it was you who administered the poison that killed her?
Karpovna: It was.
Question: How did you administer the poison?
Karpovna: When she was not looking I poured it into the cup from which she was about to drink.
Question: You did that deliberately?
Karpovna: Yes and no.

154

Question: What does that answer mean?

Karpovna: I deliberately poured something into the herbal drink she had made for herself, but not with the intention of poisoning her.

Question: Then what was your purpose?

Karpovna: I wished to make her ill, so ill that she would not be able to dance that evening. She had no right to dance the leading rôle in the première of that ballet. It had been created especially for me.

Question: Are you saying that you killed the deceased simply to prevent her performing on that one occasion?

Karpovna: I repeat, I had no intention of killing her.

Question: What was the substance you added to her drink?

Karpovna: I do not know its name, but I believed it would make her vomit, nothing more.

Question: Do you really expect us to believe that?

Karpovna: It is the truth. I had no wish to kill Stepanova. She was my friend.

Question: From where did you get the poison that killed your friend? (*The prisoner made no answer.*) Did you not hear my question? From where did you get this liquid which you poured into the herbal drink?

Karpovna: I purchased it in a pharmacy.

Question: Then where is the bottle in which it was sold to you? If you bought it at a pharmacy, the liquid must have been in a bottle, but the police found no bottle in your dressing-room at the theatre.

Karpovna: I must have thrown it away.

Question: Where did you throw it?

Karpovna: I forget.

Question: Then answer me another question. What was the name of the pharmacy where you purchased it?

Karpovna: I do not remember the name. It was a small shop not far from the theatre.

Question: In what street?

Karpovna: I do not know the name of the street. I am new to Paris.

Question: If, as you have claimed, you do not know the name of the liquid you poured into the deceased's drink, then how could you have bought it in a pharmacy? What did you ask for?

Karpovna: I suppose I must have known the name at the time, but I forget it now. It was a French name and my knowledge of your language is limited.

Question: Your French seems excellent to me. Why do you persist in lying?

Judge Lacaze had continued questioning Karpovna about the poison, trying to establish the truth which she was concealing with her evasions. He had asked her about the colour of the liquid, whether it had any smell, the size and colour of the bottle and whether there had been a label on it, but it was obvious from her answers that Karpovna had persisted in lying.

As he remembered the course that the *instruction* had taken, Gautier's restlessness was compounded with uneasiness. His inclination was to believe that Karpovna had not meant to kill Stepanova, but only to prevent her dancing in the première of *Le Spectre du Nil*. It would have been a foolish and irresponsible thing to do, but Karpovna, like many stage performers he had met, was impulsive and he could well imagine that her behaviour would be dictated not by her intellect but by her emotions.

She had admitted putting aconite, or whatever other poison it might have been, into Stepanova's drink, so it was inevitable that she would have to face a criminal trial. Unless she was prepared to give a convincing explanation of where she had obtained the aconite and why she had believed it was not a poison, no jury was likely to believe her protestation of innocence. Weeks, perhaps months would pass before she was brought to trial and she would spend them in the St Lazare prison for women, sharing a cell with a dozen or more felons, murderesses and street-walkers. For a sensitive, cultured woman, it would be a harrowing experience that might destroy her talent as well as her spirit. And when her case finally came to court, she might well be sentenced to the guillotine. Although he knew it was not his responsibility, he could not help feeling that he should save her from herself.

He had another reason for his uneasiness. His enquiries into the death of Judge Prudhomme had been progressing satisfactorily and all the evidence suggested that the Dutchman, Groeningen, had committed the murder. If that were the case, it would be only a matter of time before the man was found and brought to justice. He was also reasonably satisfied that the man Jules had been in some way involved in the killing of the Lebruns' child and that he too would be tracked down, wherever he might have gone. What worried Gautier was a feeling, not strong enough even to be called intuition, that both crimes might be in some way linked with each other and with Stepanova's death. He told himself that the idea was far-fetched, even ludicrous, but his uneasiness persisted and with it a suspicion that he had overlooked some facet of all three cases which would provide the link.

To appease his restlessness, he left Sûreté headquarters, crossed the Seine and began walking to the Hôtel Bayonne. As he walked he found himself thinking of Sophia. The last time they had been together had been at the Châtelet theatre on the evening of Stepanova's death. On the following morning when he had arrived at the Sûreté, he had found a note from Sophia waiting for him. She would not be able to see him over the weekend, the note said, for the 'accident' to Stepanova and Karpovna's arrest had thrown the ballet company into confusion. New arrangements would now have to be made for the gala performance on Monday evening and that would mean the whole company and Sophia herself working throughout Sunday.

The tone of the note had been affectionate enough, but Gautier could not help wondering whether he was being rebuked. Once before, when Ranevsky had attacked and assaulted Judge Prudhomme, Sophia had seemed to believe that Gautier should use his influence to smooth things over and protect the ballet company. Now she might be thinking that he should have left Karpovna at liberty at least until after the gala performance of the ballet. If that were what she believed, she was being unreasonable, but unreasonableness itself might be only a symptom of the gradual change in their relationship. Once again he had the feeling that almost imperceptibly they were drifting apart.

Elena Karpovna's room at the Hôtel Bayonne had been searched on the morning after the arrest and nothing had been found to confirm or refute the story she had been telling about Stepanova's death. In accordance with police procedure, a policeman had been left on guard outside the room until the *juge d'instruction* decided that it was no longer necessary. When Gautier arrived at the hotel, he recognised the man and stopped to have a few words with him.

'No problems?'

'None. It has been as quiet as a deaf-mutes' debating society.'

'The hotel manager has not been pestering you?' Gautier

knew that no hotel liked to have a room unoccupied and the management would be pressing for it to be made available.

'No. A man came and tried to persuade me to let him into the room, but I turned him away.'

'A Russian?'

'No. He was French. Told me he only wanted to go inside and fetch a book which he had lent the woman who has been arrested and which he wished to give to an American friend who is leaving for the United States today. Some tale!'

'Then what do you think he really wanted?'

'Who knows? I thought at first he was just one of those ghouls who appear whenever there is a murder, trying to get their hands on souvenirs of the crime, but he didn't seem to be that type.'

'Did you ask him for his name?'

'I did, but he wouldn't give it.'

'What sort of age was he?'

'Late forties, I would think.'

Karpovna's room was not unlike hundreds of other bedrooms in small Paris hotels. The décor was plain, the furniture practical – a brass bedstead, a wardrobe, a dressing table and a wash-stand with enamel jug and bowl. On the dressing table stood a framed photograph of a middle-aged couple, Karpovna's parents no doubt, and in the drawers were lingerie, handkerchiefs, scarves, curlers and hairpins. At the bottom of the wardrobe, underneath a surprisingly modest collection of dresses, skirts and coats, Gautier found a cardboard shoebox.

Opening it, he saw at once that it was a woman's treasure chest, used as a repository for the sentimental mementoes of adolescence and early womanhood: letters, invitations, locks of hair, pressed flowers, ball programmes. He took them out of the box one by one, finding little that appeared to have any connection with Stepanova's death. Neither Ranevsky nor Sanson featured in any of the photographs, although there was one, taken perhaps a year or so ago, of Karpovna herself on stage with a handsome young male dancer. Among the trinkets, Gautier found a brooch in the shape of a love knot encircling the initials E and A. As a piece of jewellery it looked inexpensive, banal in design and devoid of elegance. Gautier supposed it might have been a gift to Karpovna from Sanson, perhaps at an early stage in both their careers. He was curious about their relationship, wondering whether it was true that the love which they had once felt for each other had really cooled into no more than affection.

Among the dozen or so letters in the box was one from the Comte de Tréville, written on notepaper embossed with his family's coat of arms. Gautier read it, conscious that he was intruding on Karpovna's privacy, but feeling no guilt because he sensed that he might be helping her.

I marvel at how, in so brief a span of time, your bewildering beauty, charm and talent have reduced me to such an abject dependence. Only a few hours ago we were together, but now already, like a compulsive drunkard, I yearn for the intoxication of your company.

The separation is made even more intolerable by knowledge that you are unhappy. The monstrous injustice of the way in which you are being treated fills me with fury, but alas, it would seem to be an impotent fury. I have argued and remonstrated with Ranevsky, with Princess Sophia, even with Sanson, but they remain adamant and are not to be swayed. And so the right to dance the leading rôle in the première of the ballet that was created for you, will be taken from you – unless of course we can even now think of a plan to frustrate those who would deprive you of it.

With this letter comes a small gift, a book in which perhaps you may find courage and inspiration.

The Comte's letter continued for another half page with declarations of his love for Karpovna and his name was signed at the end with a fine, bold flourish. Gautier wished that the letter had been dated, for that would have told him for how long the Comte and Karpovna had been emotionally involved. He hunted through the bedroom to see if he could find the volume to which the Comte had referred, but found no books at all in the room. One had to assume then, he decided, that the Comte had come to the hotel that morning to retrieve the letter.

As he waited just inside the entrance of l'Opéra, Gautier watched the audience arrive for the gala performance of the Ballets Dashkova. One could sense their excitement, the feeling that this was to be a very special occasion. The President of the Republic would be there and the presence of the President gave any theatrical event a special social status. At l'Opéra the magnificence of the building added to this lustre. The minor sensation which the death at the Châtelet Theatre of one of the company's dancers had caused was already almost forgotten. Now Parisians were talking of nothing but the gala performance.

Miss Ryan did not keep him waiting long and presently he saw her alight from a fiacre which drew up outside the entrance to the building. When he went to kiss her hand, she seemed relieved.

'You're here! I was afraid to come in until I saw you.'

'This is the time we agreed to meet, is it not?'

'Yes, but I was early so I made the driver go round the square three times in case you had not arrived. I think he thought I was a little mad.'

'Now if the performance had been at the Châtelet, you could have passed the time browsing among the *bouquinistes*.'

'You're laughing at me!' Miss Ryan complained and Gautier saw that she was blushing.

They went into the opera house and up the main staircase, threading their way between the groups of people who, meeting friends on the stairs, stopped to talk. As they entered the main foyer, Miss Ryan stared in astonishment at its painted ceiling, the ten gilded chandeliers and the golden columns along each side, supporting statues symbolising imagination, hope, passion, fantasy, dignity, grace and all the other qualities that an artist must possess.

As they were early she was reluctant to go to Sophia's box and Gautier took her instead to the buffet gallery and ordered champagne.

'You're spoiling me,' she said. 'I'm only a simple country girl and the evening has already gone to my head.'

Gautier could not help thinking that in no way did she resemble any country girl that he had ever met. The evening gown she was wearing looked expensive, a creation of Paquin or Worth perhaps, her deportment and manners suggested a familiarity with the upper echelons of society and he could tell that she was no stranger to champagne.

When they went to the box which was reserved for Sophia on the second tier of loges, they found her waiting for them. Her other guests that evening were yet another Russian émigré couple and Monsieur Labat. Labat, it appeared, as a subscriber to l'Opéra, had his own box, but he had placed it at the disposal of friends for that evening. It was the third time that Gautier had met Labat during the last week and he wondered why Labat's wife had not been with him on any of the occasions.

Sophia greeted Miss Ryan warmly though not effusively. Some women with a title, however obscure it might be, would expect a show of formality when other women were introduced to them but, as always, Sophia's manner was perfectly natural. She had teased Gautier more than once about the Irish girl as a potential rival, but if she believed that to be true, she did not show it. Almost at once the two of them began talking about the ballet. The programme for the evening, it appeared, had been slightly altered.

'We are starting with two very short ballets,' Sophia explained, 'and then there will be an interval before they dance *Le Spectre du Nil*.'

'That must have meant a good deal of reorganisation, I imagine.'

'Yes. We rehearsed throughout Sunday and again this morning.'

'The dancers must be exhausted.'

'They are weary, yes, but they will be fine once the curtain rises. The stimulus of a performance always revives them.'

'Who is dancing the rôle of the Queen in the new ballet?' Gautier asked.

'Missia. There was no one else left who could do it. At one time we thought we would have to cancel the performance or put on another ballet, but Missia learnt the part so quickly. I must say, she has surprised us all. Wait and see.'

When the performance began, Gautier could see at once the changes which the management had been forced to make in the programme because of the absence of the two principal ballerinas. Both of the first two short ballets were little more than solos performed by the two leading male dancers, one by Bourkin and the second by Olenine, supported by the corps de ballet. Although both were charmingly staged and well performed, they were insubstantial pieces, created, one felt, only as items which could be used to fill up an evening's programme.

As the interval approached, Gautier sensed that Sophia was growing nervous. She seemed restless, not paying attention to what was happening on the stage but fidgeting with her programme, her fan and her gloves.

When the second ballet ended and the applause was dying down, she told her guests, 'I must leave you all now.' Then she added self-consciously, 'I am to be presented to the President in his box during the interval.'

'Congratulations, my dear,' Labat said.

'I will go backstage for the second half of the performance in case I am needed there. Who knows how things will go? But when it is over, we will all go and celebrate.' Sophia looked at Miss Ryan. 'You will join us for supper, won't you?'

'I couldn't possibly impose on you.'

'My dear, I insist!'

Miss Ryan looked at Gautier and he could not be sure whether she was hoping that he would find her an excuse for refusing Sophia's invitation, or whether she needed his approval for accepting it. He decided to follow his own inclinations.

'We would all be enchanted if you'd join us,' he said.

The interval that evening seemed longer than was customary and Gautier supposed it must be because there were others who were being presented to the President, Ranevsky no doubt and Sanson and the principal dancers. He was curious to see how Missia Gomolka would perform in what would be her first major dancing rôle and in the exacting circumstances of an important occasion. No one in the Ballets Dashkova had ever been complimentary about her dancing and the suggestion was that she did not yet have the technique needed to be a prima ballerina.

At last the curtain rose on the opening scene of *Le Spectre du Nil* and he quickly realised that, whatever failings Missia might have, lack of confidence was not one of them. Majestic and aloof, she looked the part of the Queen of Egypt. The steps she had to perform did not seem technically too complicated and her miming, Gautier thought, was superb. Though it was scarcely possible, Sanson's stage settings seemed even more magnificent than at the première and the musical score was brilliant, full of an expressive poignancy during the scene in the burial chamber and rising to barbaric splendour in the last act when the Roman proconsul exacted his long-awaited revenge on the conspirators.

When the final curtain fell, there could be no doubting the triumph of the gala performance. Even the President was on his feet applauding. Missia and the other principals had to take repeated curtain calls and Ranevsky came on stage, smiling sardonically, it seemed to Gautier, as the audience called for him.

Finally it was over. The President's party left the opera house first as protocol demanded and the audience, still excited with enthusiasm, began emptying out of the auditorium. Sophia returned, flushed and happy, and she and her guests went down the great staircase to the entrance of the opera house where her Victoria carriage and Labat's automobile were waiting. Gautier travelled with Sophia and Miss Ryan in the carriage, while Labat took the émigré couple with him as they left for Maxim's.

In the carriage Gautier sat between Sophia and Miss Ryan and as they drove down Avenue de l'Opéra he felt Sophia lean against him. He sensed that she was only resting, finding a moment's relaxation between the excitement of the gala performance and the gaiety of the supper party which was to follow. Although her action was in no way provocative, as her thigh pressed against his, Gautier felt a slow stirring of desire. When supper was over they would return to her hotel and he knew that, no matter how tired she might be, she would want to make love. Sheer physical fatigue, he had found, only added an intensity to her need for sex and to her passion.

Miss Ryan was sitting to his left and away from him, deliberately avoiding contact it seemed. Gautier felt a pang of guilt, for she was being excluded. He made a remark to her and reached out to lay a hand on her arm, but she seemed to flinch and move even further away. He glanced at her, but she was not looking at him.

Outside Maxim's in Rue Royale, even though a light drizzle was falling, a small crowd had gathered as it often did to watch diners arrive. One could hear exclamations of admiration from the women among them when they saw the gowns and jewellery that Sophia and Miss Ryan were wearing. Seeing Labat's automobile standing a little further along the street Gautier concluded that Labat and the émigrés must have already arrived and gone into the restaurant.

The doorman standing outside Maxim's came forward holding a large blue and gold umbrella. As Gautier and the two women moved towards him, a man among the onlookers stepped into their path. He held his right hand out in front of him, as though he were offering it to be shaken.

'You do not recognise me then, Gautier,' he said harshly.

Gautier saw then that the man was holding a revolver and that it was pointed at him. Although it was too dark to make out his features, suddenly he knew who the man was. The build, the voice, the accented French all fitted a description that had been filed away in his memory.

'I do,' he replied. 'You're Groeningen.'

'You did not recognise me at the theatre,' Groeningen said accusingly, 'even though I almost knocked you over.'

Gautier shrugged. 'I'm sorry. It's been a long time.'

'Eight years. You took my wife's life and eight years of mine, you and Prudhomme. Now I shall take yours.'

He raised the revolver deliberately. People in the crowd saw it then in the light of the lantern outside the entrance to the restaurant. A woman screamed. The doorman from Maxim's leapt forward, grabbing the revolver. He knocked Groeningen's hand away, but was too late to stop him pulling the trigger. The sound of the shot seemed curiously unreal, no louder than the soft report of a toy pistol. Lunging forward, Gautier grabbed the Dutchman, pinning his arms as the revolver fell from his hand.

Groeningen swore – a string of shrill obscenities as other men in the crowd rushed to help Gautier and the doorman. He struggled wildly but together they overpowered him, knocking him to the ground and holding him there.

'Jean-Paul!' It was Claire Ryan who called to Gautier, her voice strained with shock.

Gautier turned and saw that she was bending over Sophia who had fallen to the ground and lay there, frighteningly still.

19

Princess Sophia Dashkova died two hours later in a hospital run by the Little Sisters of Charity. One of the most brilliant surgeons in France, who lived not far from the hospital, attended her, but there was nothing he could do and she did not regain consciousness.

As he waited in an anteroom of the hospital with Labat, Ranevsky and Miss Ryan, Gautier found himself thinking not of Sophia and whether she might die, for he was already certain that she would. Instead other thoughts, trivial and even banal, crowded into his mind, shutting out emotion. He thought of the Shah of Persia's state visit to Paris and of the precautions that had been taken to protect the royal visitor. Thoughts of Persia reminded him of how he had read that coffee had first been discovered by Arabian shepherds, who had noticed that their sheep became unusually active after eating the beans of the plant. He recalled the handsome livery which the doorman at Maxim's had been wearing that night. People said that after he had retired, the last doorman had bought a château in the Pyrenees from the tips he had accumulated. He thought of Miss Ryan and how she had called him by his Christian name that evening, wondering how she had come to know it. He thought of Missia Gomolka, of her herbal baths and of the leopard which had surprised him in her suite at the Hôtel Meurice. Missia was full of surprises.

When the surgeon came out and told them, as gently as he could, that Sophia was dead, Gautier was aware that the others in the room were looking at him. He did not know what they were expecting of him, a show of emotion, rage perhaps at Groeningen, even tears for Sophia. He could think of nothing he could say that would mean anything.

'What will you do?' Claire Ryan asked him and he could feel that she was holding back her own emotion.

'Come back with me to my home, Inspector,' Labat said.

'You should not be alone. Stay the night with my wife and me.'

'Thank you, monsieur, but no. There is much that I have to do.'

'Surely not tonight?'

'Yes, the sooner these things are arranged the better.'

'Then let me at least drive you wherever you have to go.'

'No, you have been very kind to stay as long as you have. Your family will be worried about you.'

'When will we see you again?' Claire Ryan asked.

'Soon, mademoiselle. We may need to take statements from all of you.'

All three shook him by the hand; three handshakes in the French manner, a substitute for any demonstration of sympathy. Gautier watched as the automobile drove away, Labat insisting that he would drop Miss Ryan off at Parc Monceau and then take Ranevsky to his hotel. They were all silent as they left, shaken and depressed by the sudden horror of Sophia's death.

He found a fiacre to take him back to Rue Royale, but there was nothing that needed to be done there. Groeningen had been taken away, handcuffed and heavily guarded, and two officers from Sûreté headquarters had taken statements from the doorman of Maxim's and other witnesses. Two other policemen from the local commissariat were persuading the small crowd of spectators which still lingered there to disperse.

From Maxim's he set out walking to Sûreté headquarters. He did not take the route he would normally have taken, across Place de la Concorde and along the Seine, for the river, encouraging memories and nostalgia as it often did, would have been alien to his mood. Instead he walked along Rue de Rivoli which stretched in front of him, unswerving and empty, symbolic of the days which he knew lay in front of him.

He passed no one as he walked; no revellers returning from a night's debauch, not even a street girl hoping to prise one last piece of business from a man too weary or too lonely to know better. His footsteps echoed mournfully as he passed the empty buildings of the Palais du Louvre.

Even now, though alone, he did not think of Sophia but of the work he must do. In one violent act outside Maxim's two of the cases he had been investigating had been abruptly brought to a conclusion. The robbery at the Earl of Newry's apartment and the stabbing of Judge Prudhomme required no further action from Gautier. They would be of concern to no one except a handful of clerks who would now prepare the papers that would bring Groeningen to the Palais de Justice and eventually to the guillotine. When he reached the Sûreté, he would sit down and write a report on the two cases which would satisfy Courtrand and the Prefect of Police, if no one else.

That left two cases, the death of the Lebrun baby and the poisoning of Stepanova, still to be resolved. Most people would believe that their resolution was no more than a formality, that the two people known to be responsible for the homicides could be speedily brought to justice. Gautier did not share that view. He felt uneasy. Detection was not, as many might suppose, merely a matter of logic. Intuition and flair had a part to play and so even more had experience. Great chess players had the ability to recognise situations which they had faced before, even when presented in a different form, and know how to deal with them. Intuition told him that in the deaths of the Lebrun baby and Stepanova, he was failing to recognise something, a shape or pattern, perhaps a link between the two crimes, which he should have spotted.

Recognition had not come when he reached Sûreté headquarters. He went to his office and wrote his reports, slowly and precisely, the need for objectivity acting as a welcome screen, blotting out his emotions. When the reports were done, he contacted the duty officer at the Russian embassy, for as Sophia had been married to a Russian prince, she would have Russian nationality. Then he arranged for messages to be sent to the border police that they need no longer be on the alert for Groeningen. It was all work which could have waited until morning, but he was using it to prolong the night and as a postponement.

By the time everything was done it was almost dawn and, leaving the Sûreté, he crossed the Seine and walked to Les Halles, where he could breakfast in one of the cafés which catered for porters who worked at night in the fruit and vegetable markets. There had been a time when he would have felt uncomfortable arriving at the café in evening dress, but not any longer. Now foreign visitors to Paris would go to breakfast in Les Halles, dressed as Gautier was. It had become the fashionable thing to do after an evening spent in expensive restaurants or dubious cabarets. They believed that they were seeing the real Paris and the porters tolerated them, often amusing themselves by exchanging ribald remarks in a French which the visitors would not understand.

Only when he had eaten and was lingering over a pot of coffee, did he allow himself to think of Sophia. He felt a great sadness, not for himself, but for her and because the life which she had so much enjoyed had been so abruptly and so brutally extinguished. She had made life rich for others too, not only for Gautier, and now they were left with only a handful of memories. He felt no anger at Groeningen for firing the shot or at chance which had directed it at Sophia. If anyone were to blame, it was he for not realising sooner the motives behind the murder of Judge Prudhomme and that he would be the next target. Through that failure, he had exposed those around him to danger.

Following that line of thought would, he knew, be sterile, leading at best to remorse, at worst to self-pity, so he disciplined himself to think again of work. Although he found it difficult to believe Elena Karpovna's explanation of how she had come to poison Stepanova, the only step he had taken to test her story had been to search her bedroom at the Hôtel Bayonne. The search had left him dissatisfied, producing nothing of any relevance to Stepanova's death, except perhaps the Comte de Tréville's letter.

He had taken the letter with him when he left the hotel and now he pulled it from his pocket and read it for a second time. The language the Comte had used was unguarded, certainly, but not sufficiently compromising, one would have thought, for him to be afraid that other people might see it. He had made no secret of his passion for Karpovna. The reference in the letter to a book which he had apparently sent her intrigued Gautier. Perhaps after all the Comte's motive for visiting the hotel had been to retrieve the book and not the letter. What might there be in the book that would embarrass him? Gautier did not think that the Comte was the type of man who would send pornographic literature to a lady. And no book had been found in Karpovna's bedroom.

Thinking of books reminded him of Miss Ryan's embarrassment when he had made a flippant remark about her habit of browsing among the stalls of the *bouquinistes*. Suddenly that thought triggered an idea, so tenuous and implausible that he almost dismissed it at once as absurd. But the idea would not be dismissed so easily and so he thought it through, even though he could not see where it might lead him.

When he was a lad, his father used to tell him that while thinking could provoke action, it could never be a substitute for it. Looking at his pocket-watch, he saw that it was now after five in the morning, too early to take most actions, but not too early for a prison visit. In French jails prisoners were not allowed the luxury of leisurely mornings in bed.

The prison in which Jacques Lebrun was being held was situated in one of the less prepossessing of Paris's suburbs. When he reached it and Lebrun was brought to him, Gautier was shocked by the man's appearance. He seemed to have aged by several years, his face was haggard, his eyes bloodshot, his figure bent, shuffling rather than walking. The warder who brought him into a room where they could talk seemed surprised when Gautier shook the prisoner's hand, but one could sense that Lebrun appreciated the gesture.

'I saw Madame Lebrun yesterday afternoon,' Gautier said.

'Where was that, Monsieur l'Inspecteur?'

'On your stall beside the Seine. She was selling books in your absence and with some success.' Lebrun stared at Gautier in disbelief, so he added, 'She is a resourceful woman, your wife.'

'I could not sleep last night, wondering what would become of her.'

'Then don't. Very often in times of crisis people show qualities of courage and resolution which no one imagines they possess.'

They sat facing each other across a table in the small room where prisoners could be interviewed. The warder stayed in the room, as regulations prescribed, but one could see that he was taking no interest in their conversation. The man might well have problems of his own.

'I have come to ask you some questions,' Gautier said. 'They may help to prove your innocence, but I cannot be sure that they will.'

'I shall be happy to answer any questions.'

'You once told me that customers come to your stall looking for books on a particular subject and on occasions they ask you to look out for certain books and, when you could, to buy them on their behalf.'

'That is so, yes.'

'How often does that happen?'

'Not very often. I might get one or two such customers in a month.'

'Would you remember them?'

'In most cases, yes.'

'I have in mind a man who may have come to you looking for a special book not long ago. Within the last two or three weeks perhaps.'

'What kind of books would he have been wishing to purchase?'

'That I don't know, but I can describe the man to you.'

Gautier gave Lebrun as full a description of the Comte de Tréville as he could. Then he added apologetically, 'I am afraid it is a description that would fit a dozen Frenchmen.'

'You have no idea what kind of books he would have been looking for?'

'One on poisons perhaps, or about well-known murder cases in which poisons had been used.'

Lebrun shook his head. 'I have had no such requests recently. In fact now that I think about it, I can recall only two men of about the age you describe who came to me in recent weeks and neither matches the description you give. One is a collector of books on the sixteenth-century poet Pierre de Ronsard.'

'And the other?'

'His subject was not so specialised. He wanted books on Egypt; anything about ancient Egyptians, their life, their habits, their dress, old legends and stories.'

Gautier remembered at once how Alex Sanson had told him that he found inspiration for his ballets in stories of Persia and Egypt. 'Perhaps I know the man. Did he give you his name?'

'No, but I remember thinking that he might be an artist,' Lebrun replied. 'I noticed paint under his fingernails and on his shirt cuffs. He was an untidy fellow; not badly dressed, you understand, but careless with his clothes.'

'Did you sell him any books?'

'Only one which I found in the stock of another *bouquiniste*.'

'Can you remember what it was?'

'Certainly. My business relies on my memory for books. It was a collection of stories which had been translated into French more than a hundred years ago by a scholar named Ravignan. I had understood that they were Egyptian in origin, tales handed down by professional storytellers and dating back to the fifth or sixth centuries.'

'Are you saying they were not Egyptian in origin?'

170

'Apparently not. The man who bought the book was passing my stall a few days later and he stopped to tell me that the stories were not from Egypt but from Arabia.'

'Was he complaining?'

'Not at all. I offered to take the book back, but he wouldn't hear of it. He said he had enjoyed it and asked if I had read it.'

'Had you?'

'Yes, but half-heartedly. I flicked through a few of the stories. They were not to my taste, too childish with their cruel sultans, lovely princesses and handsome princes and at the same time too full of violence.'

'Do you know where I could find a copy of the book?'

'It is a very rare book and there would be few copies to be found, but you would certainly find one in the Bibliothèque Nationale.'

The two of them continued talking for a full half-hour longer, but not about any subject that had any bearing on the murder of Lebrun's baby or Nicola Stepanova's death. Gautier sensed that talking was a relief for Lebrun, allowing him to forget at least for a little while the squalor of prison and the fear of what might be going to happen to him. Gautier did not mind staying with him. It was too early to start work at Sûreté headquarters and he too had something which he wished to forget, however briefly.

When the time came for him to leave, on an impulse he asked Lebrun one more question. 'Did you ever sell any books to an attractive red-headed lady? She must have passed your stall more than once.'

'I think I know the lady you mean. No, she often stopped and picked up the books on my stall, but she never bought one.'

After returning home to change out of his evening clothes, Gautier went to Sûreté headquarters and found a message waiting for him from the police in Le Havre. They knew the man with the hare lip who had called himself Jules. His real name was Jean Tallard. He was a small-time criminal with a reputation for violence, but had never done enough to have served more than two short prison sentences. Within the last few days he had somehow contrived to escape the rather loose watch which the police kept on him and they had only now learnt that he had slipped out of the country, finding enough money to buy a passage on a liner leaving for America. As the Sûreté was looking for him, the police in Le Havre wished to know whether his offence was serious enough to have him arrested in New York and brought back to France.

After reading the telegraph message, Gautier went to find Inspector Lemaire. Lemaire was a good-natured man, dominated by his wife and inclined to neglect his work for that reason. That morning he had arrived at Sûreté headquarters late, which might have earned him a severe reproof from Judge Ducasse but, as he told Gautier, Ducasse had been taken ill, another casualty of the influenza epidemic, and would not be coming to his chambers that day.

'What a stroke of luck!' Lemaire added. 'That man has been giving me a hard time.'

Gautier also thought that Ducasse's indisposition was timely, but for another reason. It would mean that the examination of Lebrun and of witnesses in the case of his murdered baby would be delayed for at least two days, possibly longer. He told Lemaire of the message from the Le Havre police.

'I think you should contact them at once and tell them to have the man Tallard brought back to France,' he concluded.

'But would we be justified in asking for that? We have no real evidence that he was involved in the child's death.'

'The Americans will thank us. He is probably travelling on a forged passport and if they knew he had been in prison, they would not allow him into their country in any case. Immigrants are a sensitive issue in the United States just now.'

Americans, Gautier knew, were at that time becoming increasingly concerned over the number of immigrants entering their country. They particularly resented immigrants from the Catholic, wine-producing regions of Europe who, they felt, were corrupting the country with their loose morals and excessive drinking. America had, after all, been founded by Protestant sects.

'Even if we cannot prove that Tallard was responsible for the death of the Lebruns' child,' Gautier added, 'nothing will be lost. And if we find that he was, even Judge Ducasse will be impressed.'

'I can see your point, old friend.'

When he left Lemaire, Gautier went to ask Judge Lacaze whether the examination of Elena Karpovna could also be adjourned, at least for that day. Time spent listening to the judge questioning Karpovna, the dresser who had seen Stepanova die and other witnesses would be time wasted, for he would hear nothing which he did not already know. Gautier had other plans for that day.

Judge Lacaze listened to what he had to say and then asked him, 'So you believe that by the end of today you will have learnt new facts about this case?'

'I believe it is very likely, yes.'

Lacaze smiled. 'We have trusted your judgement before, Gautier. I can see no reason for not doing so again.'

Leaving the Sûreté, Gautier crossed the river and caught a tram heading towards the Bibliothèque Nationale in Rue Richelieu. For most of a long night and early morning he had deliberately closed his mind to thoughts of Sophia, shutting out the picture of her lying on the ground outside Maxim's, of blood spreading over her evening gown. Travelling by tram would give him the solitude which one could find surrounded by strangers and time for the luxury, at last, of a little private grief.

20

'Where are you taking me?' Karpovna asked Gautier.

'To the Châtelet theatre.'

Karpovna hesitated. She may have been going to ask him why he was taking her to the theatre in a fiacre, but then decided that she did not wish to know the answer. Instead she asked, 'Am I not to appear before Judge Lacaze?'

'Not today.'

'And will I remain in prison until he resumes the examination?'

Gautier would have liked to tell her that before too long she might be released, but it would not have been fair to raise her hopes prematurely. So instead he said, 'I do not have the authority to release you, mademoiselle.'

The effects on Karpovna of two days in the St Lazare prison had been dramatic. All her vitality and self-confidence had vanished and in place of the coquettishness he had come to expect of her, she wore a hunted look. Her appearance too had suffered, her hair was lank and untidy, her clothes crumpled. Gautier remembered seeing Madame Lebrun after she had spent a night in the same prison and thinking how she had refused to allow herself to become demoralised. Karpovna, he supposed, would not have the resilience and courage that a harder and less sheltered life would instil.

'Have you heard from the Comte de Tréville?' he asked her. Friends could make life easier for those in prison by sending in food and small comforts.

'No. Have you?'

'I have not seen him for several days. He was not in the theatre for the première of *Le Spectre du Nil*, was he?'

'Not as far as I know.'

174

'He was at your hotel yesterday, I understand.'

'What did he want?'

'No one knows, but he asked if he might go into your room.'

Karpovna's laugh was short and bitter. 'He probably wanted to take back the letter he wrote me.'

'Or the presents?'

'He never gave me any presents, except for one book. I don't think worse of him for that. He has no money, poor man.'

'What was the book?'

'An anthology of love poems; some of them written so long ago that I could not even understand the French.'

They drove on towards the theatre in silence. Gautier had thought she might have wished to talk about ballet, to find out how the company was managing without its two principal ballerinas, to ask whether *Le Spectre du Nil* had been danced at the gala performance. Instead she seemed crushed and lethargic, not caring what might happen to her.

He decided that somehow he must rouse her from her apathy, arouse some emotion in her, even if it was only indignation. She would have to be more than a passive onlooker, if the plan he had in mind was to succeed.

'Have you no remorse for what you did?' he asked her without warning.

'Remorse? It is a little late for that.'

'How can you be so unconcerned? Did the sight of your friend's horrible death not move you at all?'

Karpovna stared at him in disbelief. 'What are you suggesting? That I took pleasure in what happened? That I wanted her to die?'

'Maybe you did not want her to die, but it did give you the chance to dance the rôle you so coveted.'

'What an odious thing to say!' Karpovna began to grow angry. 'Can you not imagine what I felt when I saw Nicola collapse and when I realised she was dying? The horror I felt, the terror? Even now at night or even when I just close my eyes, I can see her agony. The memory of it will be with me till the end of my life.'

'That may not be for very long, mademoiselle.'

Karpovna looked at him, stunned by the callousness of the remark. Then she began to weep, almost soundlessly, but soon one could see tears trickling down her cheeks and on to the drab, woollen dress she had been given to wear in prison.

Gautier was glad when a few minutes later the fiacre pulled up in front of the Châtelet theatre. He had not enjoyed bullying the girl, but he sensed that now she might be more susceptible to the appeal he intended to make to her.

They went into the auditorium of the theatre, making as little noise as possible and staying at the back, until Gautier could see who was there. As he had expected the ballet company was rehearsing, three principal dancers and the corps de ballet. Olenine was the male dancer and with him were two ballerinas whom Gautier did not recognise and he wondered whether perhaps they had been picked out from the corps de ballet and were being trained to replace Karpovna and Stepanova. He did not recognise the piece they were rehearsing either, but its theme seemed to be a conflict between the forces of good and evil for the soul of the young man. The maître de ballet and Sanson were on stage watching.

Missia was sitting in the auditorium, not far from the stage, with Labat beside her. Seeing Labat, Gautier thought immediately of Sophia and had to fight down a surge of emotion. He had suppressed his grief for one long night without sleep and for most of that day and knew he must not give way to it now. There would be a time for sadness when what he had to do was done.

Taking Karpovna's arm, he led her towards the stage. He had noticed a change in her manner as soon as they went into the auditorium and sensed that she too might be fighting emotion. Perhaps only now was she realising the consequences of what she had done, that her career in the theatre might be finished, that she might never again know the pleasure of dancing and the satisfaction of an audience's acclaim, nor share them with her friends among the dancers.

It was Missia, turning her head, who saw them first as they came down the centre aisle between the rows of seats. At once she jumped up, came towards them and threw her arms around Karpovna.

'Elena, darling!' she cried. 'How wonderful! You're back!'

Labat got up and came to join them. He kissed Karpovna's hand and as he shook Gautier's hand looked at him anxiously. Gautier realised that he was concerned not with Karpovna, but to see how Gautier was facing up to the trauma of Sophia's death.

'How are you, Inspector?'

Missia did not give Gautier time to answer. She had been

staring at Karpovna, at the dark dress she was wearing, at the pallor of her face, the resignation in her expression. 'My darling!' she exclaimed. 'What have they done to you?'

Sanson, who must have heard them talking, stopped the dancers rehearsing and came to the front of the stage. He called out, 'Why are you making so much noise down there? Don't you realise that we are trying to rehearse?'

'Gautier is here,' Labat replied, 'with Mademoiselle Karpovna.'

'What does he want?' Sanson's hesitation was only momentary. 'Does this mean that Karpovna has been released?'

'If you would allow us to come up on to the stage,' Gautier called back, 'I will answer your questions.'

Without waiting for Sanson's reply, he led Karpovna up a flight of steps beside the orchestra pit which led on to the stage. At the same time he beckoned to Missia and Labat that they should follow them. Up on the stage Bourkin, who had been watching the rehearsal from the wings, came forward and he too threw his arms around Karpovna.

'Elena, my little one! How are you? How have they been treating you?'

'Inspector, is this an official visit?' Labat asked Gautier.

'Well, one might say that I am not here for purely social reasons.'

'In that case, as I am sure you will agree, the director of our company should be here.' Labat turned to Sanson. 'Would you be kind enough, Alex, to ask one of the dancers to fetch Boris? I understand he is in the manager's office.'

His tone was that of a man who did not expect that his request would be refused, or even questioned. Gautier wondered whether, now that Sophia was no longer there, Labat had taken over the rôle of principal patron of the ballet company, together with whatever authority that might entail. Sanson looked at Labat, hesitating only briefly, and then told one of the dancers from the corps de ballet to fetch Ranevsky.

'In the meantime,' Labat continued, 'perhaps, Inspector, you would tell us why you have brought Mademoiselle Karpovna here this afternoon.'

'Simply to ask her some questions in the presence of all of you.'

'She is being questioned by a *juge d'instruction*. Isn't that enough?'

'Let me put it another way. Mademoiselle Karpovna has consistently refused to tell us the truth.' Gautier looked at Karpovna but she said nothing. 'Perhaps here in the theatre I can make her understand the rôle she has unwittingly been playing in a drama devised by someone else.'

'What drama?' Missia asked.

'Drama may be too strong a word. Let us say plot then.'

'You're talking in riddles!' Bourkin protested.

'Deliberately,' Sanson said. 'He is doing it deliberately to confuse poor Elena.'

'One question she has not answered – a vital question – is where she obtained the poison that killed Stepanova.'

'I have told you,' Karpovna said quickly. 'I bought it in a pharmacy.'

'It may well have been bought in a pharmacy, but I do not believe that you purchased it.'

Gautier was about to give his reasons for not believing Karpovna's story, when he was interrupted by a loud cry from the auditorium. Ranevsky had come in and was hurrying down the aisle as fast as his short legs would allow and waving his arms. Evidently he had been about to leave the theatre, for he was wearing his broad-brimmed hat and carrying his sword-stick. The sight of Gautier had so shaken him out of his usual pose of aloof disdain that one could not understand what he was shouting. Only when he began climbing the steps to the stage did his anger become articulate.

'This is monstrous! Unbelievable! I won't tolerate it!'

'Tolerate what, monsieur?'

'Is this police persecution? Are you determined to destroy my ballet company? First you threaten me with legal proceedings over some ridiculous fracas, then through your stupidity or negligence, the princess, our patron, is shot and killed. Is there to be no end to this affair? Why have you come here today? Simply to interrupt the rehearsals we so desperately need? Or have you another, more sinister motive?'

'Once I have established who murdered your ballerina, we can bring this whole unfortunate business to an end.'

'Murdered!' Missia exclaimed. 'It was an accident.'

'I believe I can prove to you that it was no accident.'

Everyone on the stage looked at Gautier. He could sense the little frisson of excitement and fear which is always aroused in

178

any group of people suddenly confronted with the reality of a deliberate killing.

'That's preposterous!' Ranevsky said, but without conviction, suddenly nervous of what Gautier was going to prove.

'Mademoiselle Karpovna insists that she did not mean to kill her colleague – rival might be a better description – but only to make her so ill that she would not be able to dance that evening.'

'That is obviously the truth,' Labat said.

'And yet she poured poison into her drink; a deadly poison for which there is no antidote. Would any pharmacist sell her such a poison in error?' Gautier paused, aware now that he had the attention of his audience.

'Then where do you suggest she did get it?' Missia asked.

'Cast your minds back to last week, to the oysters which some of you had for supper one night. The following morning Monsieur Sanson was ill, very ill. Everyone assumed that it must have been a bad oyster that had made him sick.'

'Are you saying that he had been poisoned as well?' Ranevsky asked truculently.

Gautier ignored the question. 'Sanson relieved his suffering by taking a powerful emetic, or so he said.'

'That's true. I did,' Sanson said.

'Very possibly.' Gautier turned to Karpovna. 'When you heard he was ill that morning, you may well have gone to his room in the hotel to see what you could do to help him.'

'That's right, Elena, you did!' Bourkin said. He may have thought he was helping Karpovna. 'I saw you coming out of his room that morning and we talked about him, remember? You told me he had been up all night vomiting.'

'I suggest that in his room you saw the emetic that Sanson said he had taken,' Gautier continued. 'Was it in a medicine bottle on the bedside table? He probably told you how it had helped him; what effect it had had on him. That put the idea into your head. If the emetic had made Sanson vomit, it would do the same to Stepanova. Swallowed shortly before she was due to go on stage to dance in *Le Spectre du Nil* that evening, it would have made her incapable of dancing. Is that not what you thought?'

Once again everyone on the stage was silent, but now they were looking at Karpovna. She did not speak either, but Gautier could see that she was hesitating and he knew that his deduction had been correct. She was on the point of admitting as much, but Missia spoke first.

'If that is true, then it was an accident.'

Her remark and its timing irritated Gautier, but it provoked Sanson into intervening. 'Is that what you did, Elena?' Without waiting for Karpovna to answer, he continued, 'God in heaven! That explains everything! The emetic I took was in a brown bottle, wasn't it? There was almost nothing left after I took it that night, so I threw the bottle away. You must have come to my bedroom and taken another brown bottle which I take with me everywhere. It contains a special liniment which was made up for me by a medical friend who is expert in these matters and which is for external use only. It is highly poisonous, you see.' Sanson paused and looked at Karpovna, accusingly but without anger, a parent looking at a favourite child who has misbehaved. 'That must have been what happened. You did come to my room and take that bottle, didn't you, Elena?'

Karpovna looked first at him and then at Ranevsky. The expression on her face was not one of guilt or remorse, but of misery. Finally she nodded but said nothing.

'Elena, how could you!' Ranevsky's anger began to take on a new dimension. 'After everything that ballet has done for you, that I personally have done for you. What abominable ingratitude!'

'I did not mean to kill Nicola,' she said miserably.

'We accept that, mademoiselle,' Gautier said, 'but someone else did.'

'What are you saying?' Labat asked sharply.

'Did things happen as you have told us?' Gautier asked Karpovna. 'Was it your idea to give Nicola Stepanova an emetic? Or did Alex Sanson suggest it? Was it not really his idea?'

'No!' Karpovna replied quickly; too quickly, it seemed to Gautier.

'Did he not at least hint that you might use the emetic to make Stepanova ill, so ill that she would not be able to dance at the première? Was it he, perhaps, who actually gave you the bottle which you believed contained an emetic?'

'No.'

'This is outrageous!' Missia exclaimed. 'What are you suggesting now?'

'Is there to be no end to this persecution?' Ranevsky complained.

180

'Your loyalty to Sanson, your former lover and close friend, is commendable, mademoiselle,' Gautier told Karpovna, 'but it is misplaced. Reflect for a moment. Who was the person who gained the most from the death of Stepanova? It was Mademoiselle Gomolka, was it not? By getting the chance to dance the leading rôle in the new ballet at a gala performance in front of the President of the Republic, she has won recognition as a ballerina, which was her ambition and one which otherwise might have taken her years to achieve.'

'That's true,' Missia agreed. 'I have been very fortunate.'

'That is not the term I would use. When Sanson said he created the ballet for you, Mademoiselle Karpovna, he was lying. He always intended it as a vehicle for Mademoiselle Gomolka.'

'I don't believe you,' Karpovna said. 'You've made that up.'

'How was it then that she was able to dance the leading rôle competently at last night's gala, even with her limited technique? The rôle of the Queen, with its emphasis on miming and comparatively simple dances, was ideally suited to her. Moreover she had been rehearsing it secretly at her hotel. Sanson had even sketched her dancing the rôle. She showed me the sketch herself but asked me not to tell any of you about it. No, *Le Spectre du Nil* was created for Missia, to launch her on her career as a dancer.'

'Wait a minute!' Ranevsky said. 'Are you saying that Alex tricked Elena into killing Stepanova, so that she would be arrested and then Missia would have to dance at the gala performance?'

Sanson laughed, a short derisive laugh. 'How could anyone entertain such a bizarre and far-fetched idea!'

'This morning in the Bibliothèque Nationale,' Gautier replied, 'I read a book of stories from Arabia; stories not unlike the *One Thousand and One Nights*. Like so many stories from that part of the world they were full of cruelty and violence. One story was of a sultan who had no son, only three daughters. A young prince was in love with the youngest daughter, but he would not be allowed to marry her until her two elder sisters had been married first. That was the custom. So, by pretending to be in love with the second daughter, he persuaded her to poison her elder sister, promising that he would then marry her. He then arranged that her crime should be discovered, she was executed and he married the youngest daughter.' Gautier looked at Sanson. 'That was the book which you bought from a *bouquiniste* by the Seine, was it not?'

Karpovna had been staring at Gautier as he spoke. He saw the disbelief in her eyes turning slowly into doubt; then doubt began turning into horror. When at last she spoke it was to Sanson and her voice was no more than a strangled whisper. 'Alex! How could you?'

Sanson had no answer and he did not look at her. For Ranevsky his manner was an admission that Gautier's accusations were true and he gave a great cry of rage, followed by obscenities.

'You did it to ruin my ballet company!' he shouted. 'To destroy everything I have created!' Grabbing his sword-stick, he drew out the blade and waved it threateningly at Sanson.

'Put that away,' Gautier said firmly. He was growing weary of histrionics. 'It has caused you enough trouble already.'

In retrospect Gautier realised that it was the worst remark he could have made, firing Ranevsky's anger with bravado. Taking up a fencer's on guard position, the Russian lunged at Sanson. One could not tell whether he intended to run the man through, but the sight of a naked blade was enough to dissipate any courage Sanson might have possessed. He backed away, holding his arms in front of him to ward Ranevsky off, tripped over the feet of Olenine who was standing just behind him and fell backwards on to the stage.

Gautier grabbed Ranevsky and, pinning his arms, held him back. Labat and Olenine rushed to help him and between them they managed to wrench the sword-stick away. Sanson got to his feet cautiously, watching them, still frightened.

'You cannot charge me with any crime,' he told Gautier defiantly. 'It was not I who put the poison in Stepanova's drink.'

Gautier decided that he might indulge in a little theatre himself. A staged performance might be the only way of impressing these people. He pulled his watch from his pocket and looked at it.

'Yes,' he agreed, 'proving that it was really you who killed her might be difficult, but at just about this time the ship in which Jean Tallard sailed from Le Havre will be docking in New York. Detectives will be waiting to arrest him and he will be brought back to France. How will you be able to explain, then, why you hired him to kill the *bouquiniste*'s child?'

21

That evening Gautier dined alone in the café in Place Dauphine. The aftermath of two murders – of a ballet dancer and a Mongol child – had been tidied up, the reports written, the statements filed and the first steps taken that would bring the murderers to justice. As always any satisfaction which he felt in solving a crime was dulled by a sense of anti-climax. On this occasion too he was fighting a numbing depression. In retrospect, he realised that subconsciously he had never believed that his relationship with Sophia would be anything more than a passing attachment, bringing a happiness too shallowly rooted ever to be permanent, but the abrupt brutality of its ending had devastated him. Eventually he would find solace in work, but for this evening even that small relief was denied him, for there was no work for him to do.

Immersed in gloom and staring into the glass of cognac with which he was ending his meal, he did not at first notice that someone was standing by his table. Then he looked up and saw that it was Claire Ryan. Concealing his surprise, he stood up, took the hand she held out to him and kissed it.

'Am I disturbing you?' she asked.

'In no way.'

'You seemed so lost in your thoughts.'

'I was, but you do me a service by distracting me from them. May I order something for you?'

'Thank you, I have already dined.' She sat down facing him across the table. 'But I will take a glass of cognac with you, if I may.'

Gautier felt mildly irritated that she should have sought him out that evening. He assumed that she had come to give him sympathy and sympathy was not what he wanted. Once again he reproached himself for being so predictable in his habits. Claire

183

Ryan must have gone to Sûreté headquarters, where they would have told her where she was likely to find him.

She waited until he had ordered the cognac and then asked him, 'Do you suppose that the Dutchman will be sent to the guillotine?'

'Groeningen? Almost certainly. He cannot plead that there were mitigating circumstances in a brutal, premeditated murder.'

'And it was carefully planned, was it not?'

'Very thoroughly. He must have spent weeks studying Judge Prudhomme's habits.'

'And yours.'

'Yes, and mine.'

'When did you realise that it must have been he who shot the judge?'

'When you told me that the supposed antique dealer spoke with a Dutch accent.'

'I wish I had told you sooner.'

Gautier realised what she was implying. Had she told him sooner, he might have been able to track down Groeningen and arrest him, and Sophia would still be alive. Intuition had told her that he felt responsible for what had happened outside Maxim's and she was trying to lessen his guilt, perhaps even to share it. The suggestion was well meant, but he could not shelter behind it. He should have realised from the outset that Groeningen must have a second target, for why else had he stolen two revolvers? The knowledge that, but for his thoughtlessness, Sophia might still be alive would be difficult to live with in the months ahead.

Claire may have sensed what he was thinking. 'I suspect you are too critical of yourself; a perfectionist. A woman would find it difficult to live with you.'

Would Sophia and he ever have lived together? The first question which came to Gautier's mind triggered off another. Why had Claire Ryan come to join him that evening? She had not offered the sympathy he had been dreading and he did not believe her motive had been no more than curiosity. She would not have hunted for him late at night simply to find out whether Groeningen would be executed. He decided to ask her.

'Why did you come to find me this evening?'

She looked at him squarely, as though she had decided to repay frankness with frankness. 'Last night I could see that you wished to be alone. I understand that. Tonight I had the feeling that you might like' – she hesitated over the word – 'company.'

Impetuously, not really caring what her answer would be, he asked, 'For the evening? Or the night?'

Claire blushed, but she did not allow embarrassment to deflect her from her purpose. 'I was thinking of the night.'

Gautier had always thought of her as a striking woman with her red hair and impressive features, striking but not pretty and in no way seductive. Now he saw a difference in her appearance and her manner and realised that she had taken trouble to make herself look more attractive. The yellow dress she was wearing was cut lower than any woman but a *cocotte* would have dared to choose, showing off her throat and shoulders and the fullness of her breasts. She had used cosmetics on her face, but not very expertly, and stray wisps of hair hung down over her temples. Gautier found the thought that she had taken such pains in the hope of pleasing him oddly moving.

She reached across the table and laid her hand on his. 'Am I being too forward?'

He knew then that he did want to be seduced, to spend the night with her, to forget everything else, if only for a few hours. 'Where do you think we should go?' he asked her.

Claire hesitated. 'Could we be really extravagant and stay in an hotel? A really good hotel?' Then she added, 'I have never stayed in an hotel.'

'Then that is where we shall go.'

She did not appear aware that the problem would be to find a luxury hotel that would take them, late at night and without luggage. Gautier could think of only two where the management, whom he had helped out of difficulties in the past, might be accommodating. One was the Hôtel Cheltenham where Sophia had been staying and to which he could not possibly take Claire. The other was the Athénée.

Leaving the café, they found a fiacre on Quai des Orfèvres and drove to the Athénée. There the concierge received them courteously and without questions and took them up himself to a suite on the third floor, which had a view across the Seine of the Eiffel Tower.

When they were alone, Claire said, smiling, 'One can sense that you have brought women here before.'

'Never.'

185

'I would not mind if you had,' she said, but when Gautier went to put his arm around her, she checked him. 'Not yet, Jean-Paul. Let me go next door and undress. Then come and join me.'

As he waited in the drawing-room of the suite, Gautier thought about Claire. She was no longer a girl and she had been educated in a sophisticated milieu, but remained curiously innocent and naïve in many ways. And yet she had sought him out that evening with the intention of seducing or being seduced, calmly and deliberately. He wondered again about her relationship with the Earl of Newry.

When he went into the bedroom she was not waiting in bed, hiding beneath the sheets like a shy bride on her honeymoon, as he thought she would be, but lying naked on the bed. For a few moments he stood looking at her, admiring her body and long, slim limbs. The voluminous clothes which women wore made it impossible for a man to form any impression of what she would be like when she took them off.

'Why don't you undress?' she asked him.

'I shall.'

She lay there as he stripped and he could feel her watching every move he made. It struck him then that she had probably never seen a naked man before. When he began making love to her, she responded eagerly, returning his caresses and giving, from time to time, little cries of pleasure too spontaneous to be feigned. Gautier felt his own inhibitions vanish and he surrendered himself to the demands of her passion.

After the first urgency had spent itself, she propped herself up on one elbow to look at him. 'How was I?' she asked anxiously.

He did not tell her that was a question the man was supposed to ask. 'Wonderful!' he replied, feeling that he was not over-stretching the truth. Then he added, flippantly, 'I am asking myself where you learnt to make love.'

'From books.'

'Books?'

'How else does a virgin learn? I've never been with a man before. Can you imagine that? Twenty-eight and until tonight I have never been to bed with a man. You teased me about my browsing in bookstalls. Do you know what I was reading? Erotic books. Sex has always fascinated me; it has become almost an obsession, but until now I have never experienced it.'

'Why have you never married?'

186

Claire hesitated before answering, but only briefly. 'I am the Earl's daughter – his natural daughter.'

She told Gautier that her mother had been a country girl, living in a village on the Earl of Newry's estate in Ireland. When her mother had been murdered, the Earl had wished to take Claire into his home, acknowledge her as his daughter, but the Countess had refused. Since it was only his American wife's money that had enabled him to maintain his estate, he had not been able to insist. So as a compromise, Claire had been sent first to boarding school and then to finish her education in Switzerland. Afterwards she had worked as a children's governess until the Countess of Newry had died.

'When we came to Paris I became, officially at least, his housekeeper. It was too late for him suddenly to produce a grown-up daughter.'

Gautier had an irresistible urge to tease her, to rouse the Celtic fire he had seen briefly once before. 'Was that the reason,' he asked, 'or would it have spoilt his chances of becoming a member of the Jockey Club?'

'What a despicable suggestion!'

Claire lashed out at him trying, he supposed, to slap his face. He parried the blow by seizing her wrist, then grabbed the other wrist and held her as she struggled, swearing.

'I can see now that you are an earl's daughter.'

He drew her to him and as her anger subsided they made love again. This time there was a subtle change in the part she played. Her hands and her lips were busy, exploring and experimenting, finding answers for the curiosity which had remained unsatisfied for so many years.

When desire and curiosity were assuaged, she lay with her head in the crook of his arm. After a time she said, 'I am told that Alex Sanson is an exceptionally accomplished lover.'

'Who says so?'

'I forget where I heard it,' she replied and then added provocatively, 'Why? Are you jealous?'

'He is not likely to be exercising that particular accomplishment in the near future.'

'Why is that?'

'He has been arrested, accused of complicity in the murder of Nicola Stepanova.'

Claire stared at him incredulously. He realised then that she would not have heard of what had happened at the Châtelet theatre that afternoon. So he told her, explaining how Sanson had engineered Stepanova's death and the arrest of Karpovna.

She listened, appalled. 'How could he have been so ruthless as to kill a girl who had done him no harm, whom he may well have liked? And how could he have been ready to have Karpovna sent to prison? She had been his lover, had she not?'

'He would have gone to any lengths to revenge himself on Ranevsky.'

Greed and revenge, Gautier might have told Claire, were in his experience almost the only motives for premeditated murder and revenge was the most compelling. Had Sanson's plan not been uncovered, he would have left Ranevsky's ballet company to form a rival one with Missia Gomolka.

'Do you think he was Missia's lover?'

Gautier was about to dismiss the suggestion. Surely a woman as elegant and chic as Missia, a woman so fastidious that she had to have a private bathroom and took daily herbal baths, would never choose Sanson, unkempt and careless in his dress, as a lover. Then he reflected that a woman who kept a leopard in her hotel suite was capable of almost any eccentricity.

'Possibly.'

'Why did he arrange for that *bouquiniste*'s child to be killed?'

'Sanson had taken the idea for his plan for the murder from an old, very rare book that Monsieur Lebrun had sold him. Lebrun had read the book and Sanson was afraid that if he heard about Stepanova's death followed by the arrest of Karpovna, he might recognise a similarity to a story in the book. You and I would think the possibility extremely remote, but Sanson is not a man who would leave anything to chance. If Lebrun were in prison, accused of murdering his child, he would not hear of the death of a ballet dancer, or if he did, he would have other, more pressing worries to occupy him.'

'And so he had the baby killed? How could he be so callous?'

'Nothing mattered to him except his plot; devious, secretive and ruthless. Just like the man himself.'

'And like the murder of your judge, carefully, meticulously planned.'

Claire was right. He had been faced not with four crimes to solve, as he had once believed – the death of the Lebruns' baby, the robbery at the Earl of Newry's home, the shooting of Judge Prudhomme and the poisoning of Stepanova – but just two murders, both intricately planned, both for revenge, two murders in parallel. Again he wondered whether, if he had understood that sooner, Sophia's death might have been avoided.

Claire may have intuitively sensed his feeling of guilt, but she put a different construction on it. She asked him, 'Have you ever heard of the English poet Ernest Dowson? He died just a few years ago.'

'No, I am ashamed to say.'

'He wrote a very moving poem, which is the story of a man who has lost the girl he loves. We are not told how. He tries to forget her in a wild life of dissipation, but her memory always returns, inserting itself between his lips and those of other, casual lovers.'

Gautier could think of no comment to make. Claire's remark seemed to imply that she saw herself not as his mistress or even a *petite amie* that night, but merely a partner, casually acquired and, if the inclination took him, lightly discarded. It might be the truth, but by believing it she was denigrating herself and he did not like that.

'It is the final line of every verse of the poem,' she said, 'that I find so poignant.'

'What is that?'

' "I have been faithful to thee, in my fashion." '

Presently Claire fell asleep, lying with her back towards him. Gautier remembered then how he had woken in the Hôtel Cheltenham and seen Sophia lying beside him in an almost identical position. That had been at dawn on a Sunday, not much more than a week previously, and now Sophia was dead. The anguish of her death, of those two hours he had waited in the hospital, knowing she was dying, was still with him, but he had to recognise that a chapter in his life had ended. There had been other chapters before which had closed with a parting, with a woman moving out of his life. They stretched back like milestones on an empty road; Clementine Lyse, the popular singer, Claudine, the unsuccessful artist, Juliette Prévot, the successful writer of salacious novels, Michelle Le Tellier, widow of a journalist, Miss Newbolt, the English ladies' companion, without mentioning his wife Suzanne who was also now dead.

189

Gautier remembered them all, without regrets, with nostalgia and with affection. He would remember Sophia often, perhaps too often. Claire might be right. Perhaps he was faithful, if not to women then to their memory – in his own fashion.